THE FORGOTTEN GIRL

DACO S. AUFFENORDE

INKUBATOR
BOOKS

Published by Inkubator Books
www.inkubatorbooks.com

ISBN (eBook): 978-1-915275-43-1
ISBN (Paperback): 978-1-915275-44-8
ISBN (Hardback): 978-1-915275-45-5

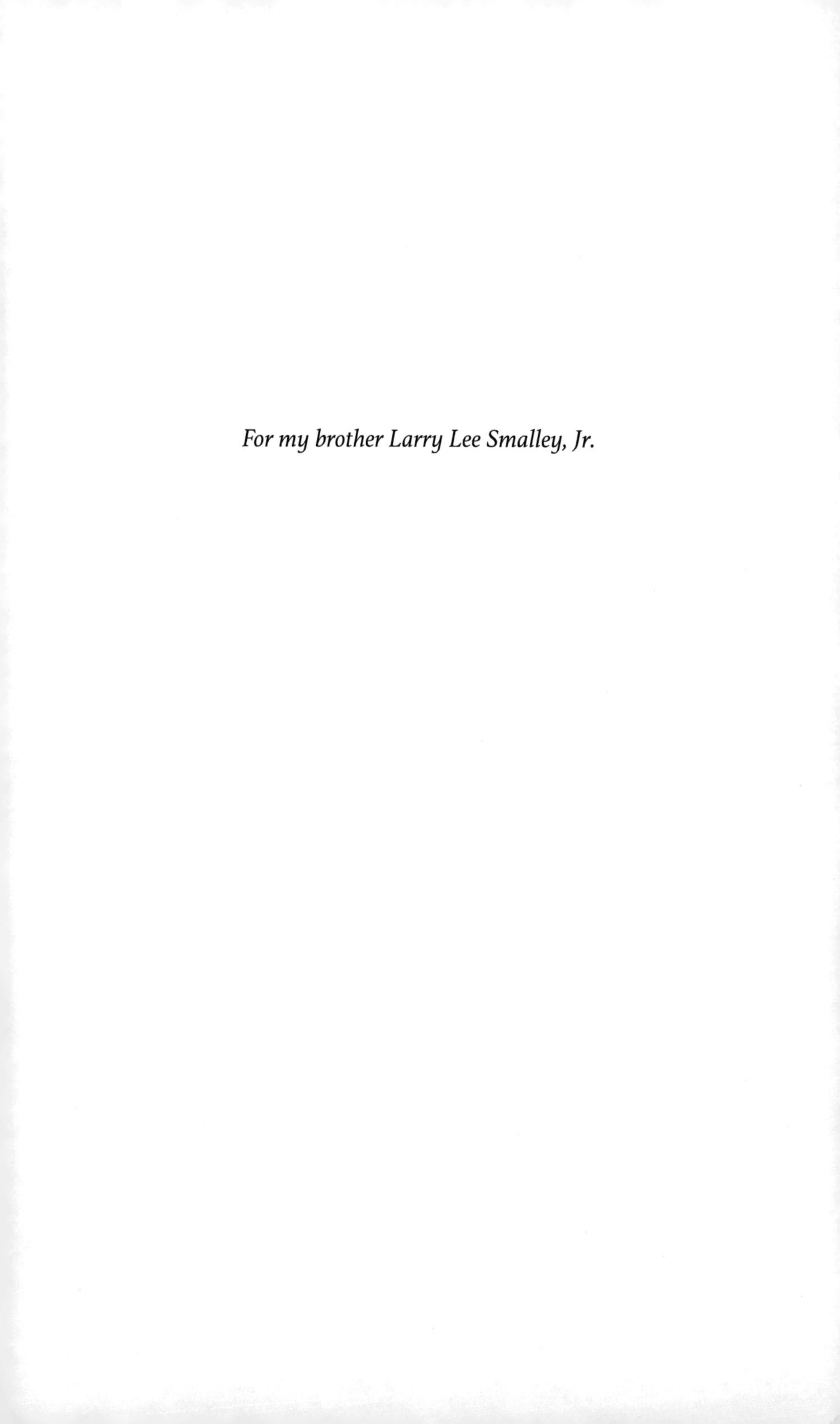

For my brother Larry Lee Smalley, Jr.

1

A sudden flash of light wakes me. I'm lying in a bed in a white-walled prison cell. I try to move an arm, a leg, but I'm paralyzed. *Help!* I cry out, but only a muffled hack passes through my dry, chapped lips.

A trumpet blares; hooves pound across grass; a woman slaps a child. A man says, "Don't get caught."

They caught me.

Something metallic scrapes against the floor. Seconds later, a large man is looming over me—a stranger. I flinch. A heavy weight is pressing against my chest. I kick and flail, trying to free myself.

The man puts a hand on my shoulder. "Don't move."

"Let go," I rasp.

"Stay calm. You're in the hospital."

What?

"You had an accident. Can you tell me your name?"

I stare into the man's eyes.

"Your name?" he repeats.

"Blue?"

A door opens, and a woman dressed in green comes into

view. Before I know it, the heavy weight is gone. I feel so exposed. The woman leans over me and she reaches for my legs, which feel as if they're tied into knots.

The woman gently rubs my arm and says she's a nurse. The bright lights dim. I look down at my body. I'm wearing a hospital gown. My head throbs like someone is hammering inside of it, trying to escape.

"You're all right now," the man says.

"Doctor?" I rasp.

"Detective Matteo DeLuca, NYPD. Homicide division."

My heart skitters in fear.

A gray-haired man with a white coat and complexion to match enters the room. He has a stethoscope around his neck, old-school physician style. He looks to be around seventy. A slew of younger white coats follow.

The nurse greets them, then takes the older doctor aside. They're talking about me. Telling secrets. I've done something wrong. *Did I kill someone?*

The doctor comes over to my bed. He places a bony white hand on the bedrail. "I'm Dr. Whitaker, your neurologist. I understand your name is Blue."

"Why am I here?"

"You suffered a tremendous fall. You're fortunate to be alive, young lady."

I don't remember falling. The people gathered around me glare down as if I'm a sewer rat about to be dissected. I'm so cold; I shiver. "I want to go home," I whisper, holding back the tears.

"Where do you live?" Whitaker asks.

Where do I live? I ... All I know is that my name is Blue.

The nurse leans forward. "Do you remember where you live, honey?"

I look into her kind eyes. "I ... I ... I don't know. I don't know who I am."

The one who says he's a cop steps forward. Any comfort I might have felt vanishes.

Is this some sort of con job? I have to get out of here. Now! I reach for the bedrail, trying to sit up. Then, with all my might, I thrust myself forward and try to escape.

"Nurse!" the doctor shouts. "All of you. Now!"

Feet shuffle and pound the floor. Bodies move in every direction. Arms and hands fly—mine and theirs. I slap at them, claw at them. Can't let them hog-tie me. *Stop!*

They don't stop.

I'm falling. Falling into nowhere, back into that white-walled prison.

2

Detective DeLuca returns to his small piece of real estate at the Midtown North police precinct after the coma patient awoke and had to be sedated. He searches the databases on criminals and victims again—local law enforcement, Homeland Security, FBI, Interpol ... After an hour, he pushes his chair back, wanting to kick the computer to the basement. The doctors say this kind of amnesia is possible, but in his experience, when someone plays the amnesia card, they're typically faking it. And it sure seems to him that she's hiding something, because he can't find anything on her in their system. No fingerprint match. No DNA match. No arrest record of anyone with her name; no record of anyone who matches her profile. Nothing.

"Hey, DeLuca, I hear your girl woke up," Jerry Roudebusch, DeLuca's new partner, calls from across the room. "She proposition you?"

"Stop with the wisecracks, Roudebusch, will you?" DeLuca replies, giving his partner a hard stare. "The woman has real problems. All she can remember is her first name. Blue, she says."

Roudebusch appears at the cubicle opening. "She's singing you the blues is right. I heard that sob story before. Don't tell me you believe her? Ask me, she's protecting her pimp."

DeLuca shrugs. "Not enough evidence to tell either way. Doc said it happens. Not that often, but it does."

"When you see a horse with stripes, you don't call it a giraffe," Roudebusch says. He chuckles. "If it makes you happier, I'll call her a suicidal escort. She looks high-class."

Roudebusch isn't off base in speculating that the woman is a prostitute. That might explain the absence of an identity. Sex workers often leave their lives and identities behind. But it doesn't explain the absence of anyone who knew about her. She would be on someone's radar screen—a madam, another working girl, someone. Suicide attempt? Maybe, but it doesn't make sense that one woman could've gotten that sealed window open, no matter how strong she might be. No, there has to be more to it.

"Maybe *you* ought to take some time to sit with her at the hospital," DeLuca says.

Roudebusch scoffs. "The woman's not going anywhere for a while, and we've got better things to do than babysit. So let forensics do their job for now. It'll iron itself out in no time."

DeLuca shakes his head. "Not everything irons itself out, Jerry. That's why the force employs detectives."

"Oh, by the way, I ran into the inspector grabbing a coffee. He says no go on running the woman's pic in the media."

"How sweet. Can't say I'm surprised though. Unidentified victim in coma who wakes and can't remember her name. I doubt even she has consent to make that call. Maybe her head doc will weigh in."

Roudebusch glances up at wall clock. "I've got to go process in a domestic. Just thought I would see what you knew."

DeLuca grins. "Need any help?"

"Oh, sure. Love some company."

"Yeah, right. Let me get back to work on our girl, Blue."

DeLuca slides his chair close to his computer and expands his search of women named Blue. He can't let this go yet. The woman should've died. She survived that fall for a reason. He will find out that reason.

3

A petite woman with short, dark curly hair that makes her look cute despite her no-nonsense demeanor stands beside my hospital bed. The blazing lights are gone. My arms and legs are no longer restrained, but my wrists and ankles hurt.

"I'm Donna Stallworth," the woman says. "Doctor of psychiatry. Dr. Whitaker thought it might be helpful if we talked about what happened. May I raise your bed? You'll be more comfortable if we can see each other eye to eye."

I hesitate before nodding.

After, she pulls the metal chair over. The legs scrape against the floor. I'm reminded of the police officer who was here when I woke up. Something makes me pull the covers up higher.

"What day is it?" I ask.

"Saturday, June fifth."

"What happened?"

"Two weeks ago, Saturday evening around ten o'clock, you were in an accident. You've been in a coma since then. When you woke up, you had a reactive response and had to be restrained and sedated. It's not unusual for coma patients to experience fear and even anger when first waking up. We kept you sedated until I arrived this evening."

Two weeks?

"What kind of accident?"

"You had a nasty fall, suffered some brain swelling, and lapsed into a coma. It's a way the body heals itself."

I touch my head. No bandages. No cuts. "Why don't I have any broken bones?"

Her lips curl upward into one of those shrink expressions. "It's miraculous that you survived, even more so that you didn't break a single bone."

"Did anyone else get hurt?" Meaning, *Did I hurt someone?*

"Not that we know of."

"Why was there a police detective in my room?"

"It's likely one of the nurses asked him to sit awhile and talk to you. Hearing human voices is comforting and can help bring a person out of a coma."

That's not an answer. Why is she being evasive? I take a deep breath. "I have no memory of my last name, my address, my parents ..."

She smiles reassuringly. "The fact that you remember part of your name is a positive sign."

I struggle to process her words, gripping my blanket. "How can I speak and understand what you're saying, but not remember my past?"

"In medical terms, you appear to be suffering from what we call dissociative amnesia. It's created by the mind as a defense mechanism."

I try not to tremble. "Will my memories come back?"

"There's a good chance they will. But there's no timetable. Could be days, weeks. Sometimes years. You went through a traumatic experience."

"Has anyone been here to see me? Family, friends? I've been missing for two weeks."

"No one has inquired at the hospital or with the police so far." She looks at me with undisguised pity.

"Tell me what really happened. And why a cop was in my room?"

She pauses, looking at me with compassion. "I should warn you that it won't be easy to hear."

My skin feels as if every inch of my flesh is being jabbed with needles. "I need to know. Please tell me."

"You fell from the fourth floor of Le Magnifique Hotel. You're alive because you landed on an awning instead of concrete."

A rush of anxiety spikes through me. "I know that hotel," I say in a shaky voice. "But I don't remember being there or falling out of a window."

"You may never remember that. I know it's hard, but it's best if you try to relax for now and let the past filter in. Stress only interferes with the recovery of memory."

A hospital worker enters the room carrying a dinner tray; I have no appetite.

I look down at my body. How much weight have I lost?

Stallworth stands. "We've made progress today. Tomorrow, we'll begin running a battery of cognitive tests." She picks up her file and starts for the door. "See you bright and early."

"Wait!"

She returns to my bedside, looks down at me, and places a comforting hand on my arm.

"Did I fall or jump?"

"Are you happy to be alive?"

"Did I fall or did I jump?"

Her eyes narrow. "We don't know, Blue."

4

Sunday morning, when the first-shift nurse greets me, I ask her to take me to the bathroom mirror. She warns me not to be hard on myself and helps me out of bed for the first time.

Using a walker, I struggle over to the bathroom and look in the mirror. I recognize that person, but barely. Long, dark chestnut hair. Blue, tired eyes. Strong nose, full lips, jawline with a dimple. Teeth, fine. Complexion, unblemished—better than that. As they say with horses, good bones. A few scratches. It's me. But another version of me. Emaciated. Gaunt. Pale.

Tears form at the corners of my eyes.

"Come on, honey," the nurse says gently. "I told you it'd be hard."

Before I turn away, I reach for my neck. Something is missing. I think I was wearing a necklace. Something dear. Something very expensive.

Over the next few days, I practice walking. The first day, I walk back and forth in the hallway right outside my room. As the week progresses, I walk every couple of hours. My overall strength is improving, faster than the doctors expected. My muscles are always sore. A sign of improvement—so the therapist says. I'm the patient who's piqued the interest of every intern in the hospital, the medical marvel who survived a fall from four stories.

Now, on Thursday, my nurse and I walk down the corridor toward my room. As we approach the nurse's station —one of the joys of my day since, unlike the doctors, the nurses don't ask thousands of questions—I look for the now-familiar faces, the people who don't wonder if I fell or jumped. Thank God. No one has the answers. Not even me. Especially not me.

Detective DeLuca is looking out the window when I enter my room. He turns around and grins shyly, waiting as my nurse pulls back the bed sheets. Giving me a look that clearly says, *get in*, she helps me get settled. I'm tired, so I don't resist, but I refuse to lie down and remain sitting as I wait for DeLuca to speak.

The nurse hooks me back up to the machine that monitors my vitals and says, "Call if you need anything."

Once the door closes, the detective says, "I thought you might like some chocolates. Found them at a French candy store, couple of streets away." He gestures toward a box of chocolates on my bedside table before walking closer and taking the chair beside the bed. The metal chair is now gone, replaced by a padded chair. "The nurse said you had no dietary restrictions."

What the hell? Is this a date? Or some attempt at manipulation?

"Hospital food sucks, though the cheeseburgers around here aren't so bad," he says, glancing at my dinner plate. "Had one last week when they delivered a dinner plate to your room by mistake. I figured what the heck, you're asleep, so why let the food go to waste?"

"I wouldn't know," I murmur, not meeting his eye.

His cheeks momentarily color.

The thought of a hamburger makes my stomach turn. "I'm glad you enjoyed it. I certainly wouldn't have."

"Looks like your memory of beef is there."

"Right now, all I can say is that I know I don't eat red meat. I can't explain why."

"Who can explain anything?" He shrugs. "I would take a rare steak any day of the week. Don't ask me why." He hands me the box.

I smile. "Any caramels? Apparently I prefer caramels over steak."

He returns the smile. His teeth are perfect. Many would pay thousands for a smile like his. I open the box and look at the candies.

"There you go," he says. "Doc says when you start doing more, living again, you'll start remembering more."

I close the box and set it aside. "You're talking to my doctors?"

"Just checking in, seeing if you're okay. If you need anything."

"Aren't there privacy laws against that?"

"I don't mean to get in your business, Blue. Just trying to figure out what happened to you."

We're quiet, awkward. He tugs at his necktie.

"I'm sorry," I say. "I'm just anxious to hear what you've found out so far." I look away and then down at the chocolates. I read the label aloud: "*Jacques Genin.*" Then: "*Merci, mon chocolat préféré.*" The words roll off my tongue. A new door springs wide open. French—the complete language—

falls into place like the wheels of a slot machine winding to a stop. "I speak French," I say.

"Are you French, Blue?"

"Doesn't feel right. But I've been there. Paris. Visited the *Jacques Genin* chocolate shop. It's laid out like a jewelry store —chocolates in cases, clerks in white gloves holding silver tongs. Very upscale." I reflect a long moment. "I was there with an older woman. She was mad at me. Because I ate too many chocolates. I was only a child, doing what children do."

Goosebumps rise on my arms. Whoever that woman was, she was evil. I touch my cheek as if feeling the burn of her slap on my face. Did she hit me?

"Remember who the woman was?" DeLuca asks.

I shake my head. The air conditioner turns on with a whoosh. Did someone really slap me, or am I just recalling a movie, a dream, something that I've read?

DeLuca's eyes dart toward the screen monitoring my vitals. My pulse rate has spiked.

"Are you okay?" he asks.

I release the air in my lungs. I don't remember holding my breath. "I'm fine." I feel a prickle of unease. "How did you know I liked these particular chocolates? Is this some sort of trick? Are you hiding something from me?"

He shifts his weight and tugs at his tie again. "No trick. Lucky guess. Well, not lucky. Who doesn't like chocolates or caramels? Forget it. I was just trying to do something nice. If you don't like them ..."

"I'm just caught off guard here, Detective. One minute, all I know is that my name is Blue. The next minute, I'm speaking French. I'm sorry to be so abrupt. It's not my nature to be cruel. At least, I don't think it is." I look toward the window to clear my head. It's raining outside—a summer shower.

I glance back at him. Dark circles surround his brown

eyes. He looks down at his street-worn shoes. He ought to get rid of them and buy a new pair. *Don't judge him.*

"I don't speak French," he says. "I know a bit of Italian. My mama taught me. I picked up some Spanish growing up in the streets. Some people think I'm a foreigner because of my Bronx accent. You get a Mississippi southerner up here and they can't make out a word I'm saying. They look at me all googly-eyed, as if I'm some sort of specimen in a zoo, here for their amusement. Until they remember I'm a New York cop."

He's funny. I want to laugh but can't. "Let's reset this conversation," I say. "Why did you visit me when I was in a coma? You must've had better things to do."

"It's my job to protect people. We're having a hard time piecing together exactly what happened on the night of your fall. No one has come forward."

"So, no one's filed a missing person's report on me?"

"Sorry, no."

I rake my fingers through my hair. "How pathetic."

"I'm sure you have someone. They just haven't found you. Look, we don't know if you live in the area. Thousands of folks float in and out of this city every day. They come from all over."

"True, but how does this help me?"

"I'll do a search of the name Blue in French-speaking countries and any regions populated with individuals who speak the language, see if anything turns up."

We sit a long moment.

"I feel like a mummy trapped inside a tomb, no lid, no air," I say. "I'm sure it's unfair, but it aggravates me that you don't have answers. You're the cops, you have resources. Just tell me what you know. And by the way, Dr. Stallworth told me about Le Magnifique. The fall. The awning."

"I can't imagine that was easy to hear."

"No." I tuck my arms underneath the covers and wrap

them around my body. "I'm sure your department checked the hotel records. Surveillance cameras. Things like that."

"The internet went down that night, and most of the video surveillance was lost. No backup. But we're still hoping to find something."

"Damn." I paused momentarily. "Sorry."

"I would've said worse. I know how frustrated you are, believe me. Look, we're on it. We've interviewed hotel security. Twice. Same story. The internet went down. Wasn't the first time. We've requested what remains of their videos."

"Did I have a room there?"

"You didn't. But you were in a room registered to a corporation, which turns out to be a shell that leads to a tangled web of nowhere. Techs are on it."

"What about fingerprints? DNA."

"No unexplained prints." Then he half-grins, half-frowns. "DNA in a hotel, that's a little complicated. We've got hotel employees. Your hair. Bunch of dead ends."

I grip my gown. My chest rises and falls on a bag of bones. *Don't lose it. Don't.* The hospital room feels too small. "Does someone want me dead?"

"I wish I had the answers for you. If my take on it means anything, I don't think you jumped."

I'm not safe. Not here. Anywhere.

"No one knows where you are," he says as if reading my mind. "Don't worry, you're safe here."

"I don't feel safe." What the hell did I do for someone to want to push me out of a window?

5

DeLuca pulls into the Le Magnifique hotel turnaround. Jake, the valet who was on duty the night of Blue's fall, heads toward the car.

"Sir, you can't park here," Jake calls out. "You need to pull up to valet services." When DeLuca gets out of the car, the young man holds up his hands. "My apologies, Detective. Park anywhere you like."

"Appreciate it. I won't be long."

"You need me for anything?"

"Not today."

"Learn anything more on the girl?"

"Working on that. You hear anything?"

"No, sir. Detective."

"You have my card. Call me if you do."

DeLuca heads to the security office. A young woman named Cheryl, who looks to be in her early twenties, greets him, and he identifies himself. "I'm here for the recordings from the night when the woman fell. Are they ready yet?"

"Right. I'm sorry, but I can't help you with this. The

employee in charge isn't in today—hasn't been for a few days. I wished you'd called us first."

"Who's in charge here?"

"At the moment, me. But you're looking for Mark Burns, one of the IT guys, I think. I'm not sure what his work schedule is. Maybe check with hotel management?"

"Why don't the two of us walk to the computer room where all the recordings are. We'll take a look ourselves."

"Not my job. I'm not authorized to do that."

"Let's try that again, Cheryl. See this badge? That ought to give me access, don't you think?"

"I'm really sorry, Detective." She pauses and meets his eyes. "If I could work the system, I would be more than happy to help you out."

What the hell is with these people?

DeLuca shifts his weight. "You new here? I haven't seen you around over the last couple weeks."

She exhales hard. "I started a year ago, after I graduated NYU, but I had to take some time off after that horrible accident. When I heard what had happened, I ran outside to see if I could do anything. By then, the authorities were already there. I saw the firefighters get her down and thought she was dead. Nothing like this has ever happened here before. Occasionally people die of heart attacks and that kind of thing, but people falling out of windows ...?" She shakes her head. "This is a five-star hotel. You would think ..."

"Think what?"

"I ... I'm not a prude or anything, but you wouldn't expect management to let a woman like *that* use the hotel. I'm sure that sounds naïve but ..."

"Wait," DeLuca said. "You're familiar with the woman who fell?"

"I don't personally know her. But, yeah, I've seen her here

a couple of times. Never reserved a room. Always meeting someone else."

Hotel records show that Blue fell from a room reserved in the name of a dummy corporation. "Do you know who she met the night of her fall?"

"No idea."

"You think the woman is a prostitute?"

"I don't like that word. I mean, I don't care how people make their living. Life's hard enough. But someone trying to kill an escort puts a black mark on this place. This accident or whatever it was makes me feel vulnerable, you know, as a younger woman? Truth is, I had to see a therapist. This whole fall thing has really bothered me."

"How do you know she's an escort?" Hotel management never told him the bit about a possible high-end prostitute working the place. Why? A cover-up? It makes sense. The woman Cheryl is right—a blot on the hotel's reputation. On the other hand, her assumption doesn't account for a woman frequenting the restaurant for strictly business reasons. She might own a company, or be a sales rep.

"I just assumed. Like I said, she never reserved a room."

"But tons of folks come through here. Why did you notice her in particular? What made her memorable?"

Cheryl's face flushes. "Sorry. I know that must sound strange …" She hesitates, but then says, "That woman is gorgeous, hard to miss."

"Okay. Now, about those recordings …" DeLuca says.

"You could try back later this evening when the shift changes. Have you tried the hotel manager?"

"Next on my list. Thanks for your time. If you think of anything else you want to tell me, here's my card."

DeLuca hands the woman his card and finds the manager on duty, who says they'll need a warrant to allow anyone access to their computer system. Company policy. Privacy laws, the typical. Another stupid obstacle. What a waste of time.

6

I meet with Stallworth daily and continue to build strength. Now that I'm back on regular food, I gain a few pounds. It's Friday morning—again. Almost two full weeks have passed since I first woke from the coma, but I still feel trapped in someone else's body.

A male attendant, Jason, taps on my hospital room door and enters with a wheelchair. He gestures for me to get into the chair. I tell him I'll walk, but he cites those damn hospital rules. I'm not one to follow rules. The hospital feels like a bowling alley to me, and I'm one of the pins. Random people keep stepping up to the line to knock me down.

As soon as I take a seat in the chair, the landline on the nightstand rings. Jason offers to answer, but happy to get out of that chair even for a moment, I hurry to the phone, hoping it's someone I know—a friend, a relative, even a boyfriend. "Hello?"

No one speaks.

"Hello?" I repeat.

Nothing but heavy breathing.

"Who is this?"

No answer.

I grip the receiver.

"Haven't you learned your lesson?" His voice is smooth, and his speech has the cadence of a voiceover actor who grew up in the Midwest or, who knows, maybe the West Coast. He sounds familiar.

"Who is this?"

"You have my property," he says. "Where is it?"

"Excuse me?" I experience mixture of confusion and fear. I hope the caller has the wrong room, but my better judgment tells me he doesn't. I glance at the waiting attendant.

"No more games," the caller says. "Hand over the Cassiopeia, and you won't suffer."

"I swear, I don't know what you're talking about. You have the wrong person. I—"

The line abruptly disconnects. With a shaky hand, I replace the phone on the hook.

"You all right, Blue?" Jason asks.

"I'm not going to therapy today."

"I really think you—"

"I am not going, Jason!" I burst out.

He takes a step back and holds up his hands.

"I need to make a telephone call. Make my apologies to the therapist."

He hesitates but then wheels the empty chair out.

I wait a moment and then follow him to the door, looking down the hallway for anything out of the ordinary. Nothing suspicious.

I dial DeLuca's number. He answers and, in a still-quavering voice, I explain what happened.

"I'm in traffic, not far away," DeLuca says. "I'll get someone up there pronto. Call a nurse or an orderly to stay with you. You'll be fine. Take some deep breaths."

Not long after the call, someone knocks on my door. A

police officer pokes her head inside, waves a badge, and identifies herself as Officer Sanders, NYPD. New York accent, Queens. She waits until I wave her inside.

"I have orders from Detective DeLuca to relocate you. Immediately. For your own protection."

"He told me to stay put."

"Some guy entered the facility on the main floor, got past security. He's armed and dangerous."

"He's after me?"

"Looks that way. DeLuca wants you moved now." The officer pushes a wheelchair to my side. "Let's go."

I get in. She wheels me out of the room and toward a set of back elevators. Soon we're inside. She presses the button labeled "B," and the doors close.

"Why are we going to the basement?" I ask.

"Safest place. Perps heading up to your room, safest place is to go down."

The elevator doors open. The hospital morgue is across the hall. She flips the elevator hold switch and rolls me out and doesn't turn right or left. At the morgue, she pushes the door open.

What?

I'm facing a wall of refrigeration units for the dead. I can't catch my breath. I've come down here for pool therapy before, but I had no idea that the morgue was nearby. No wonder the hospital doesn't make that fact public.

"Why here?" I ask.

"Safest place." Same answer as before. She pushes me inside, and we head left.

The area stinks of disinfectant, formaldehyde, and death. I feel instantly queasy. Half a dozen mortuary trolleys are arranged around the room. The wall opposite the refrigeration units is lined with cabinets, sinks, supply carts, and all kinds of unfamiliar medical devices. I look back and see a window with closed blinds. An office? We pass an examining table containing a body covered with a sheet. How can that be? Bodies aren't left unattended. Ever.

Something is very wrong.

She wheels me toward an exit door—an exit door to the outside world. She can't be taking me out there. If we go outside, surely we'll be exposed, at risk.

Why are we leaving the hospital? DeLuca's not here yet.

When we reach the exit, the woman reaches for the door.

"Wait!" I cry. "This doesn't make sense."

"We've got to get you out of here. DeLuca's waiting."

I twist around and try to look up at the woman, but the glare of the fluorescent lights behind her is bright.

"Turn around," she says in a harsh voice.

She's wearing sunglasses. When did she put those on?

"I want to see your badge again," I say.

A scowl.

She's no cop.

I won't show fear. "I'm not leaving. I'm waiting in here for Detective DeLuca. Take me back to my room."

Ignoring me, she shoves the door open.

There's no sign of DeLuca. I scream, "*Help!*" I push forward to stand. She shoves me back down.

"Quiet," she rasps. "You'll give our position away."

Again, she tries to push the chair outside. I lift my feet and plant them against the wall. The wheelchair jerks to a stop.

She shoves the chair. Hard. It rolls forward. My knees bend. *I can't ...* My feet slide off the wall. With every ounce of strength, I replant my feet and thrust back with legs, arms, and back. My head crashes into her stomach. A hand shoves my head forward.

I scream, "Help!" again and thrust upwards, trying to get out of the chair.

I must get away. Get out of here.

From behind, she grabs the collar of my robe and pulls me back into the chair. I land hard and let out another scream.

She reaches toward the door. A sour odor comes from her armpit. I slap at her, kick, struggle to stand. I can't overpower her. I continue to shriek for help, but my shrieks can't wake the dead.

Her arm wraps around my head and neck. A large hand clamps my mouth shut. She struggles to open the door. I sink my teeth into the fleshy heel of her hand.

She lets go as she screams, "Fucking bitch!"

I scramble out of the chair but crumple to the floor. I use my arms to push my body weight up. I'm too weak to stand. On hands and knees, I scrabble across the cold cement floor to get away. From behind, she yanks my ponytail and pulls. I gasp for air, unable to scream. Feet pound in the distance. Something hard strikes my head.

The world goes black.

7

I open my eyes, expecting to see my captor, but Detective DeLuca and Dr. Stallworth are sitting at my bedside. Both stand and come to the railing.

Stallworth takes my hand. She's warm; I'm cold. "You're safe now. How are you feeling?"

"Groggy." I take my hand back and feel along my head. "Damn, do I have a headache. Hurts like crazy."

"Take your time," she says. "You took a hard knock."

It's all coming back. I look at DeLuca. "That woman ... Officer Sanders ... did you know her? Did you catch her?"

His expression darkens. "We will."

"I don't believe it," I say. "What the hell happened?"

"I got to your room. You were gone. Just. Nurses saw you at the elevator with Sanders. I ran down the hall. The elevator was stopped on the basement floor. I took the stairs, got down there as soon as I could, and found you unconscious. The exit door was open, no one in sight. Whoever it was must've heard me coming. We've got a man down in hospital security looking at the video as we speak. We'll run the perp's profile through the system, see what comes up."

"What about that call?"

"Techs are working on tracing it as we speak. Last report was that the caller used a burner phone. Telephoned outside the hospital, but close by, within a mile's radius."

An image of a clamshell pried open with its meat ready to be consumed flickers through my mind. "Someone found me."

"You're safe now."

"*Bullshit.*"

Stallworth places a hand on my arm and gently squeezes. "Detective DeLuca and the police department will do what they can to ensure your protection. No one saw this coming, not here in the hospital."

"The department is posting an armed, undercover guard outside your door," DeLuca says.

This doesn't make me feel better. "I was supposed to be safe." I pause. "My attendant, Jason. Could he have been in on it?"

"We're questioning the staff," he says. "What did the man on the phone actually say?"

"He said he wants something called the Cassiopeia. He threatened to hurt me. I don't have a damn clue what he's talking about. Believe me, if I did, I would tell you. I called you, and then I got taken."

"Cassiopeia is a constellation in the northern sky," Stallworth says. "Named after a queen in Greek mythology. She was vain, boasted about her unrivaled beauty."

"Mean anything to you?" DeLuca asks me.

"Nothing. I sure don't have a bunch of stars in my pocket. Doesn't make sense."

"I'll check into it," he says.

"What did the caller sound like?"

"Smooth voice, like an announcer or something, but other than that, just a guy."

"Tell me what you remember about Sanders."

"She was tall, close to six foot. Big, well-built, like a body builder."

"Why did you go with her?"

I frown at him. "She said you gave the order to relocate me, Detective. I believed her. She knew your name and mine. It all seemed legit."

"Did Sanders ask you for this Cassiopeia?"

I shake my head.

He's silent for a moment. I don't say it, but we both know that these people must be pros. Coordinated effort. Organized crime, maybe?

"What could they be after?" I asked. "Drugs? Money? Artwork?"

He doesn't answer. "The good news, if you can call it that, is that as long as you have what these people want, you're alive. If they don't know where it is and they think you do, then they need you."

A painful shiver courses from the back of my neck down the length of my legs. "You call that good news? It's terrifying." I try to stifle a yawn, but I can't. Then I yawn a second time.

"Just a few more questions," DeLuca says. "Do—"

"That's enough for tonight, Detective," Stallworth cuts in. "I'm sure Blue will tell you if she remembers anything else." She looks at me. "Get some rest, Blue. You're safe for the immediate future."

Immediate future? I want to laugh. No one's ever safe, not even for a moment.

8

Saturday morning, there's a light tap on the door, and Dr. Whitaker enters.

"How's our patient?" he asks, grinning as he walks toward me. I'm unnerved by his perky expression, which is unlike his typical doctor's demeanor. He doesn't have a chart. That's different too.

"Feeling better physically," I say. "Still don't remember much. And the cops have no leads on the woman who abducted me."

He gives a slow sympathetic shake of the head. "On the bright side, you're almost back to full strength. Way ahead of schedule. I've spoken with Dr. Stallworth, and Social Services is waiting for your discharge papers to be signed so you can be relocated to a women's shelter."

"Pardon me?"

He smiles broadly. "Isn't that wonderful, Blue?"

"I wouldn't call it that. I was sure that by the time I was ready to leave here, I would at least know my last name."

"I'm confident you will in time. Meanwhile, we'll order a

follow-up CT scan and some final bloodwork. If everything looks good, you'll be ready to check out of here."

Really? "I wasn't expecting this," I say. "I'm nowhere near recovered. I can't go anywhere."

"Hospitals are for helping the critically injured and sick. You may not have reached your full cognitive functioning just yet, but you don't fit the criteria to be hospitalized, which is a blessing, Blue, not a curse."

"A blessing that feels like a curse."

"Lying around here isn't going to help. Just the opposite. The sooner you get back into mainstream life, the better. When you're out of the hospital, we'll keep you in physical therapy, and Dr. Stallworth will continue to see you as your cognitive capacity progresses."

On the edge of panic, I wring my hands. "What if I never get my memory back? I can't live in a shelter or some kind of convalescent home like an invalid."

"Try to think of it as only temporary. And if by some chance this is as good as it gets, you'll do what any brave person would do—start over."

I try to suppress tears, but they fall anyway.

"Keep focusing on how lucky you are. Most people who have accidents like yours, well, they end up dead, and if they miraculously survive, they have severe brain damage, complete paralysis, or are left in a vegetative state. I understand you're worried, but we won't be throwing you to the wolves. Plenty of folks are standing by, prepared to help."

"Dr. Whitaker, have you ever heard of the Cassiopeia?"

He looks perplexed. "Constellation, isn't it? As I recall, lots of shooting stars come from that direction in the night sky. Have to check the calendar to determine when. Maybe August. It's interesting that you thought of this. Perhaps you have a background in astronomy. Physics?"

"I feel like I'm good at math. I can't explain why."

"Looks like you have something to investigate. Good luck to you, Blue. I'll see you in a month." He pats my arm.

Though his hand is warm, I shiver.

9

After Whitaker leaves my room, I curl up in bed and hide from the world.

The next thing I know, I wake with a galloping heart rate. My body is moist from sweat. I've been having a recurring dream in which I see a red beacon of light and hear the words *Don't get caught*. Not once have I heard or seen anything that would tell me what or who Cassiopeia is. I peel my hair from my neck and fling the covers aside. I push myself upright, don't use the remote that lifts the bed. I don't need it any longer.

I don't know if I have any clothes or if I had any belongings when they admitted me. I go to the closet and peer inside. Nothing but hangers.

Footsteps pad from behind me. I grip the closet door.

"I didn't mean to startle you," Stallworth says.

I'm grounded again by her voice. "I'm sorry, I'm feeling a little skittish. I guess I haven't fully woken up yet."

"Can I help you find something?"

"Did I have any clothes when I was admitted? I remember I was wearing a necklace."

She pats my arm. "When patients come in alone, things can end up missing."

Alone. That word sends a ripple up the back of my neck.

"Given the fall you had, your clothes might've been cut off and discarded. That happens in emergencies. But it doesn't account for the necklace. Have you asked the detective about it?"

"No, but I will. Just seems like he would've said something."

She gives a noncommittal shrug. We sit, and she sets her briefcase aside.

Then anger bubbles up inside me. "You're sending me to the women's shelter. How could you do that without consulting me first?"

She looks surprised. "I thought you'd be delighted."

"I want to get out of here, but I don't know if I'm ready."

"Understandable. But you're going to a very respectable *and*, might I add, secure facility. Have you had any memories of Cassiopeia yet?"

"None." *Why did she ask that question?* Doesn't she think I would've told her if I had?

"Stay connected with Detective DeLuca. He's here to help you."

I gaze out the window at a cloudless, blue sky. "I feel abandoned. I'm afraid to leave."

"You're clinging to what you know, and that's this hospital. That's not healthy. The authorities are doing what they can."

After we sit a few moments in silence, she says, "I have to ask you some painful questions before you leave. You need to be truthful in your responses."

I know where this is going.

"Are you feeling like you don't want to live?"

"No, I do not feel suicidal. The opposite—I'm afraid because someone has tried to kill me."

"Do you feel homicidal?"

"No, not unless you count my desire to tear the hearts out of the people who threw me out that window—and that woman who tried to kidnap me." I pause. "What do I call myself? I don't have a last name. I can't go around calling myself Blue Doe."

"I encourage you to make one up. DeLuca will secure you an ID card. Just use something you like the sound of. And remember, it's only temporary."

So she says.

Stallworth tells me that I'm leaving for the shelter in the morning. Reaching inside her briefcase, she hands me a blank notebook. "I would like you to keep a journal, so when we meet, we can talk about the memories and thoughts you feel are significant. Give it time and we'll be able to put some meaning to it all. What I'm trying to say, Blue, is that you need to recover your memory through the front door. No tricks or drugs are going to work. We need to find the key."

Key? I can't even find the damn door.

NOT AN HOUR LATER, the nurse enters with a clear plastic bag.

"Look what I found," she said. "I took a peek and I'm sorry to say, your clothes were ruined. But don't you worry, honey, we're going to make sure you're all fixed up before you leave here. Can't have you walking around in the nude." She chuckles lightly, hands me the bag, and leaves as quickly as she entered. Nurses are so underpaid for all the work they do.

I sort through my things. One broken shoe. No heel. My dress, shredded. A purse! Well, a small evening clutch. Gold. Clasp on top. It's mine. I remember it.

I cram the clothing back in the plastic bag and open the purse. It's empty.

Damn!

I check inside a hidden slip pocket someone unfamiliar with this couture evening bag would miss. A girl always needs a place to hide a twenty, or a hundred-dollar bill. There's a slip of paper. A receipt to pick up an order from a shop in the diamond district. No name on the receipt, only a number.

Maybe the Cassiopeia is a jewel. If so, why did I have it? I know the shop, though I don't remember being there—which means nothing. If I'm involved with some special stone, I might be involved in something I shouldn't tell the police about. Not until I know what it is that I've done.

10

That evening, I look down on rush hour six stories below my hospital room and try to remember the fall. All those people down there have lives—the homeless woman panhandling at the corner for a dollar; the young street performer banging out a rhythm on trashcan lids for the generous donor who can spare a five. I touch the window and test the hardness of the glass. Sirens whine in the distance, but I can't see any ambulances or fire trucks or police cars. Scores of taxis jam the streets, blowing their horns.

I again focus on the people. It's a wonder how so many of them dodge gracefully in and out of the way of others, and a wonder that they all know where they're going. How simple to remember which subway to catch and where home is. How unremarkable to have people who know you, care about you.

I'm glad to be leaving. I've got to get to the diamond district. A claim awaits me. I pray to God my name, address, and phone number are on the receipt there. Anything that will help identify me.

I return to the chair and pick up the television remote but then set it aside. I close my eyes and let my mind drift. All is calm, black like sleep.

I'm a child twirling, leaping. I'm happy, laughing. Then I'm an adult, in an unfamiliar room. A hotel?

A voice says, "Hand it over. Now!"

I'm trapped. Standing in front of a window. I can't turn around. Can't move. The room spins like a crimson roulette wheel, then everything is red.

Then white.

"No!" I shout.

A crackling fills my ears. My body jolts forward, and my eyes bolt open. I'm awake, still in the chair. I rub my head hard, as if that will expunge my dream. Blinding red lights flash across my field of vision. I jerk my hands away and fall back in the chair.

A knock on the door startles me again.

"Blue, is everything all right with you?" Detective DeLuca asks.

Did I cry out? Did he hear me cry out?

"Blue, are you in there?"

"I'm here," I say. "Come in."

The door opens. "You didn't answer me when I first spoke," he says, his face concerned. "Mind if I turn on the lights?"

"Please do." When the lights go on, my eyes quickly adjust. "Sorry, I dozed off."

He walks to the empty chair with a stride like that of a trained, confident athlete. I can't help but notice his out-of-date wardrobe. Such a contrast to his demeanor. He doesn't wear a ring. Maybe he's divorced, doesn't care about his appearance. Seems contrary to me. He ought to care about his appearance if he wants another partner.

He holds out a hand. I shake it briefly. Long enough to note how warm yet dry his hands are. When he sits, I feel at ease. Secure. My God. I realize suddenly that I'm attracted to this man.

"What's with the briefcase, Detective?" I ask.

"Call me Matteo."

"So, Matteo, do you have an update?"

"After we got our subpoena for the security videos, our techs were able to recover pieces of the video off their backup server."

"How? I thought the system went down."

"Seems a few of the cameras powered back up after the internet bleep, backed up on the onsite server … I'm not sure of the technical explanation. Computer systems aren't exactly my jam. There were also street monitors working on another operating system, which picked up the fall, but only once you were almost down. I checked with Stallworth, and she says you can watch if you want. Only thing is, she recommends you skip the actual fall. But if you do want to see it, you have the right."

I laugh grimly. "I have no problem skipping that part. For now."

"Yeah, I figured. So listen, if you remember or see or feel something you haven't told me yet, let me know? It may be important even if it might not seem so."

"Sure."

He removes a laptop from the briefcase, opens it, and presses a key. "So, we got lucky. The hotel and the building across the street had PTZ cameras—that stands for pan, tilt, and zoom, we use them for security—which follow a wide range of motion. That's the technical jargon. That tech, I am familiar with."

On the screen, a black-and-white video plays. Fuzzy, but

visible. A black SUV pulls up to the curb near the Le Magnifique Hotel. The bellhop opens the rear passenger-side car door. A woman steps out. *Me.* The camera shot comes in closer than I expected. I'm decked out. Hair styled in a Victorian-roll updo. Black Givenchy dress. Tight where it needs to be. Shoes are Christian Louboutin—though the video is black-and-white, I know from the brand that the soles are red. I'm wearing the necklace. *My necklace that is now missing!* Two doormen open the lobby doors. I walk inside like a leopard sizing up prey, head directly to the guest telephones, and dial a number. I have a brief conversation, walk to the elevator, and take a car up to the fourth floor.

The recording ends.

I sit staring at the black screen.

What in the hell did I just watch?

"That's you, isn't it?" he asks needlessly.

"I don't know what to say. I can tell you the designer brand of the dress and shoes, the style of her hair, that's it. I don't remember doing any of that." Who is that woman who'd walked so determinedly, as if she'd been there and done that very walk a thousand times? That woman who was made up to appear so glamorous that she could've been on a magazine cover—that dress, those shoes, that necklace? My necklace? Is *that* the Cassiopeia? "I need to see the recording again, please. Slower this time."

We watch the tape in slow motion. I stare at my lips as I speak into the phone. I turn away just as I start to speak, as if looking over my shoulder to make sure no one is listening in. I face the wall, and my profile comes into view. I speak and then hang up.

The visit to the hotel had something to do with the Cassiopeia.

"Do you know what you said into the phone?" he asks. "Remember any of the conversation?"

I feel more than a vague sense of guilt, and also the need for self-preservation. "No, I wish I could."

For the first time, I feel like a real criminal. But am I? Is the Cassiopeia code for something? Am I an escort? Am I meeting the Cassiopeia? Maybe I work as a mule for some shady organization and was delivering this Cassiopeia? Did I steal the Cassiopeia from some rich person? A gangster? Too many possibilities, none changing what I feel—that I'm a criminal.

Damn!

The video rolls to the end again.

I want to look at DeLuca. But I can't. I don't know where to start. So I ask, "Am I a prostitute?"

"I don't know, are you?"

Someone taps on the door. A man with a food cart enters the room. "Dinner," he announces.

"Not a good time," DeLuca says. "Please come back."

"But the officer outside the door told me—"

"Come back later!" he barks.

The man leaves. I'm too nauseated to even think about eating.

"Blue?"

I shake my head in disbelief. "Me? A whore?"

"We have no evidence of that. If it makes you feel better, I don't believe you are."

Now I meet his eyes. "No," I say emphatically. "I'm not a whore."

We're quiet for a long, awkward moment.

I clear my throat. "They brought me my clothes. My necklace is missing. The police don't happen to have it, do they?"

"No report of a necklace."

"I need to see the rest of the tape. The fall."

He hesitates. "You sure?"

He plays another file. I'm mortified, but it's not like I'm

watching *myself* fall. I feel nothing. I don't remember any of it. In the last frame, I'm lying unconscious on the awning. I'm not wearing the necklace. I wasn't wearing it when I fell, and it sure wasn't flying through the air. Which means someone took it before I went down.

"So where's the necklace?" And is it the Cassiopeia?

11

Sunday morning, I take a ride with DeLuca in his unmarked Dodge Charger with dark-tinted windows. A typical detective's car.

I feel uncomfortable. Not because of the video. No, what confuses me is the Cassiopeia.

DeLuca looks over at me. He hasn't mentioned any progress in determining what the Cassiopeia is. Is he still in the dark, or is he just keeping me there?

We drive past a group of young people picketing and carrying signs in front of a furrier. Their chants are loud. A homeless man across the street is yelling obscenities at them. Three taxies block the intersection; horns are blowing from all directions. The sidewalks teem with pedestrians.

"It's a madhouse out here," he says. "Gives the city its charm." On cue, a siren blares. He half shrugs and chuckles quietly.

I shouldn't be surprised how loud and chaotic the outside world is compared to my hospital room on the sixth story, but I am. It's a shock. I force a smile. "I appreciate the ride."

His expression darkens almost imperceptibly and then

brightens again, like a fast-moving cloud temporarily blocking the sun. He wants something. He can't possibly know about the receipt I found in my purse. Or does he? No, he would've mentioned it. But there was the box of chocolates that triggered my memory of speaking French. I want to believe DeLuca is playing straight with me, but I'm not prepared to be that trusting just yet.

"Now that you've had a chance to think about that video, is there anything you want to talk about?" he asks.

"No. Could we drive by the hotel?"

"Are you sure?"

I nod.

He drives, and we sit quietly. His radio hisses with codes and orders.

We're approaching the hotel. The place looks familiar, but I remember nothing, feel nothing.

As we get closer, I see the awning. I don't need to ask if it's new; I can see that it is. I count four stories. I imagine falling, remember the video, but I can only visualize someone else falling, not me. Still, I'm light-headed. I glance away and out the side window.

In Central Park, police are on horseback. The sight comforts me—not the cops but the horses. That strikes a chord. A memory? But I'm not sure what of.

DeLuca stops at a red light. "You want to go inside?"

I stare at the hotel. It's a beast I have to slay. Sooner or later. "Yeah, I do."

He pulls into the drop-off and places a placard in his front windshield identifying his car as a police vehicle. The parking valet, whose name tag reads Jake, walks over to greet us.

"How you doin', Detective?" the valet says.

"No complaints, Jake."

So DeLuca has made his presence known around the

hotel. Jake looks at me in recognition. Is it because DeLuca showed him my picture, or did he know me from before?

"We won't be long," DeLuca tells him before Jake can say anything.

"That guy seems to recognize me," I say as we walk toward the hotel doors.

"As he should. I've been showing your picture around. Interviewing employees."

We walk through the lobby. People are everywhere: checking in, milling around, drinking at the bar, and eating in the dining room. I locate the lobby telephones.

Eyes are upon me. Like I'm diseased, a biblical leper. Strangers know me, but I haven't any idea who they are.

"Everyone is staring at me," I say to DeLuca. "Have the employees seen the video too?"

"Don't worry about them."

"Easy for you to say. They're looking at me like I'm a dead woman walking."

"More like a miracle survivor."

"It doesn't feel that way." I stop in front of the phone I used that night. I lift the receiver, bring it to my ear, and listen to the dial tone, hoping the act will spur a memory. Nothing.

I detect a whiff of perfume. It's familiar. Chanel. Number Five. A man and woman approach. I overhear their hushed conversation. "The john, have you seen it?" he asks her in the Queen's English accent.

"Can't you keep such indelicate questions to yourself?" she retorts. "Go ask someone who works here."

That word—*john*—resonates. It's the name of someone I know. The back of my neck tingles.

Don't get caught.

"Someone is watching me," I whisper to DeLuca.

DeLuca squares his shoulders and narrows his eyes. He

turns toward populated spaces, his hand on hip, ready to grab his weapon. "Talk to me. That couple?"

"No, not them. I don't know, it's only a feeling." My mind playing tricks? Is someone named John after me? I've been holding the phone mindlessly all this time. I slam it down in its cradle. The crack garners the attention of the nearby concierge. I raise my hand in apology.

"What about the room?" DeLuca says, still glancing around. "You want to see it?"

"No," I say, suddenly feeling panicked. "Let's get out of here. I can't do this."

He continues to scan the lobby and any entry doors as we make for the exit.

I stop. I can't let fear get in my way. "Wait, DeLuca. I need to see the room."

I see approval in his eyes. We take the elevator to the fourth floor, and DeLuca unlocks the suite. When the door opens, I see crime-scene tape is strung across the door. I duck below it and go in first.

Corner suite. Multiple rooms. It's large and lavish. Decorated in pale yellows and creams from the curtains to the bed fabrics to the furniture to the carpet to the bathroom fixtures and tiles. A set of plush, overstuffed chairs, and a couch and table are arranged like a formal living room. A bedroom sits beyond in another room but is visible. The bed is a four-poster, early American reproduction. Presidential.

"You remember the room?" he asks.

"No." I walk farther inside, studying the details. I stop. Listen. Meet his eyes. "It happened in here? Over there?" I point to one of two windows on the far side of the living area.

"Yes."

I walk to the window. It's a long way down.

I'm light-headed. I hear a man's voice. Arguing. Shouting. Am I making this up? The air conditioner turns on.

"*Cassiopeia*," someone behind me says.

"What?" I ask, stumbling and turning back. "What did you say?"

DeLuca catches my arm. "I didn't say anything."

He didn't? "I thought I heard someone ... Did you hear a man's voice, someone arguing?"

"No. But I heard the door to the room across the hallway close."

I don't question DeLuca more. His face is hard. Concerned.

Now I'm hearing voices? I feel the urge to run.

Don't get caught!

"You remember something?" he asks.

I glance around the room, looking for something more. The smoke detector flashes red. Red. That color means something. Then that word again—*Cassiopeia*.

"Blue?"

"I've seen enough." I hurry from the room. DeLuca follows.

Back in the car, I ask, "Are your windows bulletproof?"

"Yes. Do you remember anything?" he asks again. "See anyone in the lobby?"

"No. Nothing. No one. I just felt overwhelmed." I exhale heavily. "It's a wonder I'm not dead."

He stares hard at me. He doesn't believe me. Doesn't believe I can't remember. For that reason, I make sure not to look away. But, then again, why should he believe me? I don't know what's true myself.

12

DeLuca drives across the Manhattan Bridge into Brooklyn. I recognize the area, but it doesn't feel like home. We pass the Grand Army Plaza, turn onto Prospect Park West, and arrive at our destination—a five-story building near the Bartel-Pritchard Square corner of Prospect Park. I know the place is called New Visions, but there's no sign on the door.

He again uses his privilege as a cop to park in a no-parking zone. He gets my small carry-on bag with a few essentials and outfits the sympathetic and tenderhearted nurses donated. Otherwise, the suitcase would be empty. They must see thousands of indigent people, but I guess my amnesia generated extra-special sympathy. I feel like a stray cat lapping from a dish of milk at the back door of a restaurant.

We get out of the car, and I take several steps and stop, facing the entrance. Happy voices of children come from the park across the street. A mother calls to someone named Rebecca that it's time to go home. The young child responds, "Oh, Mommy, not yet."

The ordinariness of this nearly floors me.

The air smells like newly sprouted grass in a meadow. I remember a woman weaving purple clovers into a chain. She's looking down at me. The sun is shining, so I squint. I can't see her face. But the loving feeling I experience tells me she's my mother. Then she forms a halo and places it on my head. Her soft hands glide across my cheeks. She takes my hand, and we run down a hillside covered in freshly cut green grass. It's time to go home. Thunder booms, and her hand slips from mine. It's raining now. I'm alone. I begin to run, searching for her. Then I trip and feel my body falling through thin air. I feel as if someone has pushed me. Who would've done that? I cry for my mother.

My head hurts now, like I have a hangover. I reach to rub my temples. I step back and bang into something—no, someone. All at once, I'm pushed forward. A grocery bag falls to the sidewalk and splits open, groceries spilling everywhere. A man says something like, "Get out of there now."

I stumble forward but catch myself.

The man looks at me and shouts, "Watch yourself!"

"Who, me?" I ask him.

"What the hell is with you, lady?" the man retorts.

"Hey, watch your mouth, buddy," DeLuca orders sharply.

"Fuck off, bitch," the man says as he stoops down to pick up his groceries.

DeLuca advances on him and flashes his badge. "NYPD. Let me see some ID, pal."

"I'll call you back," the man says, then pulls his wireless earbuds from his ears before facing DeLuca.

"Did you just tell me to fuck off?" DeLuca asks.

"Not unless you're my ex-wife in Candle Emporium with my credit card. No, man, I was on the phone."

"I'm sorry," I say to the man and look at DeLuca. "I backed into the gentleman, Detective."

DeLuca says, "And then instead of catching you, he

shoved you. Which means he's no gentleman. *You're* sorry he shoved you? No way." He gets into the man's face. "That's assault. So either get your ID out now or we'll take this up at the station."

As the man rummages around in his pocket for his ID, he says, "She runs me over and it's the victim's fault. She ought to be thanking me. Another two steps, and she would've fallen off the curb backwards and landed in oncoming traffic."

"I'm fine," I say. "It's nothing, Detective. I ran into the man. It's a misunderstanding." I don't know whether to be flattered by DeLuca's chivalry or alarmed by his Jekyll and Hyde routine. This is New York. People run into each other. I squat down to help gather what the man dropped and together we arrange the things in the bag.

"Thanks," the man says. "I didn't mean to push you. I was startled, and my ex-wife ... sorry."

DeLuca crosses his arms as if he's not done questioning the man.

"Please," I say. "I know you're trying to protect me, Matteo, but I don't need this."

He hesitates, then gestures with his hand for the guy to scram, which the man does immediately.

"Ready to go inside?" he asks, adjusting his tie.

I brush the hair from my face and smooth it down. "Let's do it."

He rings the bell and announces us. Then the buzzer is activated, and a police officer opens the door. She introduces herself as Officer Jackson. Her breath smells like coffee.

"Second floor," Jackson says. "The office is the first door to the left."

We pass through the narrow lobby, beyond the mail slots, and toward a staircase. As I take my first step up, my knees buckle.

"Hey, hang in there," DeLuca says, grabbing my arm and steadying me.

I reach for the banister. "Just nervous," I whisper. "I'll be fine."

With DeLuca still holding my arm, we continue to the second floor. I check in with the woman working at the front desk, who hands me some paperwork to fill out.

As I read, I feel the woman's eyes on me. I look up at her. She makes no effort to divert her stare. She must know about me, wants to study me to see if I'm for real.

I hold the pen in midair and look down at the first set of blanks to fill in.

"Write what you know," DeLuca says.

Which isn't much.

When I finish, the woman assigns me a room and hands over a key. Her demeanor is unchanged—tired and cautious.

"Need help with your bag?" he asks.

"No, thanks, I can manage."

"Go check it out. I'll wait."

"I'll be fine."

He takes a seat anyway.

I head upstairs to my room on the third floor, unlock the door, and go inside. I'm expecting nothing but a small room and a bed, but I've been assigned a small studio apartment situated at the front corner of the building. On one wall sits a small galley kitchen. The corner contains a circular nook surrounded by windows with a 270-degree view and is home to a small table and two chairs. There's a bed and a small bathroom with a shower. Given my outfit in the hotel surveillance video I suspect that I—whoever that is—am used to more opulent quarters, but right now, I am overwhelmed with gratitude for these modest accommodations.

I toss my bag on the couch and look out the kitchen window above the sink. Across the street is a small two-screen movie theater. Out of nowhere a memory surfaces. This movie theater has a whole dinner menu you can order from. I've been there before. How can I know this and not remember my last name?

I return to the office.

DeLuca rises from his chair. "Let's take a walk before I leave. I want to talk about something."

I knew he wanted something. Couldn't he have asked earlier? I have an errand to run.

13

A little league baseball game is going on at the park. Proud parents are cheering and shouting, *Good eye!* and *Run!*

"You like baseball?" DeLuca asks.

I look up and follow his gaze. "I guess it's all right. I don't think I ever played. That or softball."

I follow him to the park. We sit in the stands off to the side. Away from other people.

"Were you a baseball player?" I ask.

"Yeah, as a kid. After that in a recreation league. Always hardball, though." There was pride in the last statement.

"I bet you were amazing." I smile.

He laughs. "The Yankees were a dream. Like every kid growing up on the block, I got some looks from a few colleges and a couple of MLB scouts. Nothing stuck. I was a brawny but speedy centerfielder with some power. The problem was that above the high school level, I couldn't hit a curve ball. My brother, Mackey, was the real ballplayer in the family. At his young age I could tell he was something—or would've been."

"He gave it up?"

"He and my mother died in a fire. Which can happen if you're drunk and leave a cigarette burning."

"I'm sorry."

His brow folds, the lines deep. "He was eight years younger than me. Happened over twenty years ago now. I'd been out playing baseball and went off afterwards with some friends to celebrate our win. Came home late. Too late."

"How horrible." I feel the need to embrace him, but that would be too personal.

He lowers his eyes. "You never get used to it."

"I imagine you've seen your share since, too."

"Enough that I left the church. It's not like I ever went, anyway."

"No father in the picture?"

"My father was a compulsive gambler and, like most of his ilk, an inveterate loser. One day, he left and didn't come back. I learned he skipped out on some goons who were after him for not paying a debt."

"Looks like you dug your way out of it, though?"

"After I decided that filling in potholes, sweating in the sun, and shoveling rocks and dirt wasn't a life for me."

I pat his arm as an offer of sympathy. At least I seem to be a woman who can feel compassion. "I'm sorry about your family."

He watches the young boy running into home. "We don't always get to write our own story. Like you can now."

Write my own story? My own story was erased when someone tried to murder me.

We watch the next batter, a small but wiry ten-year-old, hit a line drive for a double.

I shield my eyes when the sun comes out from behind a cloud. "So why are we here, Detective?"

He swats at a curious bee. The insect flies away and lands

on some white clover. “We haven’t been able to locate the woman who tried to take you at the hospital. She knew how to keep her face away from the cameras. The hotel security employee, Mark Burns, can’t be found either. Hotel management said he’d taken a few days off for vacation. We’ve had another round of interviews with the employees. Any DNA collected matches hotel cleaning staff, no leads there. So that kind of leaves us at a dead end.”

“Seems hard to believe we have nothing.”

An aluminum bat pings, the ball zipping inside third base and down the line. The spectators shout.

“Looks like another double,” he says.

“Matteo,” I say, trying not to let my frustration show, “what’s going on?”

He takes a deep breath. “I haven’t mentioned it yet, but after the failed kidnapping attempt, the inspector had your photo displayed on the internet and TV news to see if anyone would come forward.”

I go cold. “Awesome.”

“We’re getting some pings.”

“Oh my God. You’re only now just mentioning this?”

“So far, all we’re getting are a bunch of kooks and pranksters. You’ve been through a lot. I didn’t want to get your hopes up. But after yesterday and today, seems like you need some hope. I’m interviewing a woman in the morning. Department’s vetting her now.”

“Someone who knows me?”

“Don’t hold your breath. Let’s see what happens.”

14

DeLuca walks me back to the shelter and, before he leaves, hands me his card. I feel as if the cord that has bound us together since I awoke from the coma has started to fray. For the first time in weeks, I'm on my own.

"You need anything or think of anything, call me," he says. He pulls a phone out of his pocket and hands it to me. "This is for you. Anything. I mean it. Night or day. I insist." His phone rings, and he glances down at the screen. "I'll check back in with you tomorrow."

I watch him walk down the stairs and leave—my safety net, albeit a net that might be filled with holes. I return to my room and walk to the nook to stare out at the park.

A man crossing the street catches my eye. I know him by that athletic stride of his—DeLuca.

Why is he going back to the park?

He's carrying a baseball cap that he wasn't wearing earlier and slips it on his head. In his other hand, he's got a mesh bag full of bats and balls. A couple of young boys, around six or seven years old, break free from their moms and charge over to DeLuca just as he reaches the other side of the street. He ruffles their heads. One of the boys actually hugs him. Wait, not a boy, a girl.

I grip the windowsill and lean closer to the glass.

He greets the moms with a broad smile. I see him nodding and conversing. Then he hands one of the kids the bat bag, and they continue on into the park. He didn't just come to this side of town to bring me to the shelter. He also came to coach a bunch of young kids. I have the sudden urge to run back down there and hug him.

I stand at the window and watch DeLuca coach the kids, their moms and dads sitting on lawn chairs.

We sat in that park only minutes ago, and he never mentioned this. I might've stayed to watch. I definitely would've.

15

I leave my room behind, hail a cab, and direct the driver to 47th between Fifth and Sixth. Not the safest move but necessary. I hop out on Fifth and head down the street toward Sixth, checking the numbers on the stores.

Mid-block, I arrive at *Diamonds*, ring the bell, and enter. A long glass counter surrounds the store. In the back is a window, a jeweler's corner with a large magnifying glass and plenty of specialized craft tools.

A short man in his early fifties comes out from the back. He's wearing a name tag: Ashem. I don't recognize him. He gives me his best sales-pitch smile.

Am I a returning client or a new one?

"What can I do for you today?" he asks. His accent is Persian, which means he's not the man who threatened me on the phone. I relax.

I walk to him, pull out the receipt, and hand it to him. "Claim ticket. January first, I believe it reads. Do you have something for me?"

He looks at the paper, then back at me, obviously

confused. "You picked this up a month ago," he says. "It's a receipt, not a claim ticket."

"I've had an accident."

He eyes me skeptically.

"Are you sure I picked it up?" I ask. "You see, I was injured. This will sound unbelievable, but I've lost my memory. If you could just help me to remember what I picked up. The details of this transaction."

"What kind of game are you playing, Ms. Bishop?"

A name. My name!

He frowns. "You wearing a wire?"

"No, no. I'm just looking for help."

"You buy, I sell. That's it. I don't know your business, I don't ask. I'm a reputable business owner here. So don't be bringing the Feds down on me. It's enough they strut down the sidewalk and gawp in the windows. I have nothing to hide. We do a good business together, but not that much to land under someone else's bus. Understand?"

"I'm sorry," I stammer, taken aback. "I really don't mean to upset you."

"You have a nice day." He turns away.

"Please. You're the first real person who knows me. I desperately need your help. Please." I hold my arms out. "Check me out. I'm clean. It's just me." I wait. "I'm trying to figure out what the Cassiopeia is."

He shakes his head vigorously. "You must leave."

"You obviously know what the Cassiopeia is. What is it and how did I get it? Just tell me that and I won't trouble you anymore."

He raises his hands and makes the *stop* sign.

"At least tell me about the transaction. That can't be secret from me."

"John Brownsworth dropped off the merchandise to me, instructions were to give it to you. You made the arrangements. I only buy and sell. Appraise quality. My business is on the up and up."

John Brownsworth. I know that name. I know *him*, whoever he is, and he knows the history of the transaction. I need to find John.

"What is the Cassiopeia?"

"I deal in diamonds, not legends."

"So it's a diamond?"

"Sometimes I sell other precious stones. Like rubies. That's all I'll say about your transaction. I know nothing more. I want no more involvement. So don't include me in any crimes of yours."

"So it's a ruby ... Am I right?"

He bows slightly. "Good day, Ms. Bishop."

He turns to leave again as a young woman, early twenties, walks out of the back room. Her name tag reads Gulshan. She greets Ashem in Farsi, calls him Baba—father.

I've just hit three home runs: my name, the Cassiopeia Ruby, which the dealer won't confirm because he may not know its name, and a contact. "Wait, before I go, any chance you know how I can find John Brownsworth? Please. I need help. Someone is trying to—"

"Hold it right there," he says. "We've never had a personal conversation like this. I don't intend to have one now. Like I told you, I don't want to know your business."

"Baba," Gulshan scolds, and the two have a discussion that I don't understand. She frowns and says nothing more.

Ashem faces me and performs a polite head nod, like a bow. "Very nice doing business with you."

"I'm begging you," I say. "Maybe you read about my accident in the paper, saw my face on the news. Call the authorities, they'll confirm it. Call the hospital. Talk to my doctor."

"You had an accident?" Gulshan asks. "Are you sick, Ms.

Bishop?" Then she says something in Farsi again to her father.

As they stare silently at each other, I say, "My memory is gone. I can't remember things. I need help."

Gulshan says something more to her father.

Ashem lets out a long sigh. "I will probably regret this but hold on. Wait right there." He starts toward the back room.

Gulshan smiles compassionately. "I think he's checking for you."

"I can't thank you enough, Gulshan."

"No worries."

"Another question. Have you ever seen me wearing a necklace? A long chain, circular pendent?"

"Yes." She studies my neckline. "Oh, you're not wearing it. You always have it on."

"I seem to have lost it. I feel like I had a real fondness for it."

"That's awful. I mean, everything that's happened to you is. But I've admired your necklace for a long time. I've told you a million times, but I guess you wouldn't ..."

"I don't remember our conversations. I'm sorry."

"Your father isn't checking on the necklace, is he?"

She shakes her head. "We've never had that."

So the Cassiopeia isn't my necklace.

The buzzer rings.

"Excuse me," she says.

A young couple waits outside, and Gulshan goes to the intercom and has a conversation with them. They're looking for an engagement ring. She asks them to wait, explains that I was just leaving.

A moment later, Ashem comes from the back. "Sag Harbor in the Hamptons. Ask at the yacht club. That is the best I can do."

"I can't thank you enough. If anyone asks—"

"I have not seen you. As usual."

"Always great seeing you, Ms. Bishop," Gulshan says.

I thank them both again and head to the door. As I open it, Ashem says, "You watch your back, Ms. Bishop. You hear?"

I glance over my shoulder. If he saw the news about me, he knows enough. Not hard to connect those dots.

Cassiopeia—a ruby precious enough to kill for.

16

About an hour after I return to my room at the shelter, my phone rings. DeLuca. Did someone tail me and tip him off about my side trip to the jewelers?

I answer and wait.

"There's been a development," he says.

My breathing steadies. He wouldn't sound this upbeat if he'd found out that I committed a crime. He'd be standing in front of me, holding handcuffs. I've got to stop thinking this way.

"That was fast," I say. "What's going on?"

"A couple of our guys just picked up the hotel security manager, Mark Burns. We're about to interview him at the station. Want to come listen in?"

"I thought he checked out."

"Our IT guys found an inconsistency we need explained. I'll pick you up. I'm close by."

Is going down to the precinct a bad idea? A trap? Does DeLuca know that I have—had—the Cassiopeia? Worse, that it's stolen? That I've committed a crime that I've forgotten?

I throw on a sundress and wait for DeLuca to arrive. Not sure how to feel. At least now I have a name: Blue Bishop. But is it my real name, or some cover? Blue feels right. So does Bishop. But something still feels off.

I need to do a little digging of my own to scrounge up the history of this ruby. Figure out how I play into it.

I do know that, as much as I would like to, I can't be open with DeLuca. Not until I figure out my part in all this. Like what I was doing with some jewel called the Cassiopeia. I've got to find John Brownsworth. That means I've got to get to Sag Harbor.

17

Down at the police station, I take a seat behind the two-way mirror. A male officer named Jerry Roudebusch sits beside me. He says he's DeLuca's partner, but I don't like the masculine, dominating vibes he's giving off. Another plainclothes officer, a woman named Detective Jacobson, is also present. I watch as DeLuca walks into the interrogation room and introduces himself to a tall, heavy-set man in his mid-thirties, receding hairline—Mark Burns.

Burns asks if he needs a lawyer. DeLuca says that he doesn't, that he's not a suspect—yet.

"I've already told you guys what happened. I'm happy to help, but I can't tell you anything else."

"Well, let's take a step back and start back at the beginning."

Burns folds his arms, his posture rigid and stubborn. The way he twitches, he gives the impression that he's late for an appointment.

DeLuca goes through the preliminaries, establishes that

the guy was working the night of my fall. "What do you think happened to the security cameras?"

"The internet crashed. It happens all the time. I told you guys that. Just ask the service provider for an explanation."

I look at Jacobson, standing to the side. She scoffs and shakes her head.

DeLuca stares at Burns, who shifts in the metal chair. It's not big enough for his large frame, and he struggles to sit comfortably.

"Let's re-examine that week. Did the system go down at any other time?"

"Sure. Went down that Monday. No, Tuesday for a couple hours. Hey, I'm not there 24-7; it could've gone down both days. It happens several times a month. Most users don't even notice. They just think their logins are taking too long. Or their laptop had a system fart. You'd have to look at the computer log to be sure."

"Seems like it goes down an awful lot for a hotel, don't you think?"

"Not really. Weather can be a factor, number of users sometimes exceeds our server, not often, but it happens, especially on the holidays when we're booked to capacity. And this is the summer, so we're getting a lot of tourists." He shrugs. "Sometimes it just happens. I don't make the rules up. Not the God of the internet. I'm good, but not that good." He half grins.

"What about backup generators, backup onsite servers that keep recordings?"

"Sure, we've got all that. But sometimes when the system goes down, we have to manually reboot monitors that glitch out. Like we did that night. I got to tell you if you haven't heard it before, but technology is far from perfect. You guys have the video. Watch it again."

"How long is the system usually down?"

Burns guffaws. His laugh makes my skin crawl. He's not taking this seriously.

"Seconds to hours," he says. "Worst case, days."

"Could someone have turned it off?"

"Sure."

"Could someone make it appear like the system went down?"

"If they were knowledgeable, I guess they could program something in. Maybe pull the actual plug. If they knew where it was."

"What if the video was deleted?"

"Sure, but it's not easy to do. Leaves a trail."

I fidget in my chair. I wish DeLuca would come down harder on this jerk.

DeLuca must've read my mind. He slides a piece of paper to Burns. "Want to explain this?"

Burns glances at the paper and shrugs a stiff I-don't-know. I hope this is a crack in his armor.

"It's a log from the internet service that shows disruptions in service."

"Yeah, okay. Right."

"Seems the hotel is the only business in the area that went offline. Don't you think that's strange?"

"Like I said, lot of factors go into it," Burns replies like a know-it-all. A long pause. "We all good here? I'm sorry, but I've got a date. Can I go now?"

"Not yet." DeLuca slides another item over. A photograph. Of me. "You ever see this woman before?"

"She's the jumper, right?" Burns pushes the photograph back to DeLuca. "She's one of those high-cost hookers."

Who the hell is this guy? Good thing the cop is sitting next to me; otherwise, I might jump through the glass and try to strangle him.

"What makes you say that?" DeLuca asks.

"Just a feeling."

"You ever see her go to a room with someone?"

"No."

"Don't businesspeople who aren't staying at the hotel ever dine in the restaurant?"

"Sure, they do. Lots of people come in all googly-eyed to gawk at the place, have a drink in the bar. We get a lot of stars ... famous, important folks. It's New York, you know, not the Midwest."

"So what you're telling me is that you've seen her in the hotel before. Is that right?"

Burns muffles a cough, then glances down at the table and shrugs.

"So that's a yes."

"Yes. I've seen her. Not checking in, though. Occasionally she dines in the restaurant."

"With who?"

"A man. And I don't know who he is. That's all I know. I don't know her business."

My stomach drops. Another possibility cut off.

"What's the woman's name, do you recall?" DeLuca asks.

I clutch my hands. This guy better be good for something.

"Sorry, I don't know," Burns says. "I don't work the concierge's desk or open the door. Did you ask them? They keep up with important people, those who come in a lot."

Roudebusch pats my arm and leaves his hand there a little too long. I twist in my chair to show my discomfort. What's his deal?

"What did the man she was with look like?" DeLuca asks.

Burns smirks and looks up at the ceiling. "Tall, thin. Silver-haired. Sixty, I guess."

Brownsworth?

"Do you recall if that man was at the hotel the night the woman went out the window?" DeLuca asks.

"I didn't see her or him in there that night."

"But you remember seeing her there before? Why did you notice her in particular?"

"Hard to miss a woman like that. Don't you think?"

I sigh hard.

"Let's go back to the victim. Did you ever speak to her?"

"Not that I recall."

"You know her name? A woman that's hard to miss like that?"

"Sure don't. I've got a girlfriend. I don't go for—"

"For how long does the hotel keep each video file?"

"We used to store them for ninety days. But corporate decided not to keep paying the tab for that. Those guys are always searching for ways to cut costs." He snorts. "They tried to take away dental last December."

"What about now?"

"Oh, right. Thirty-day cycles."

"Cloud storage is relatively cheap. Seems odd that they would've cut back on something like that."

"It's not like we ever have this kind of trouble, you know? I doubt they've ever given it much thought. But don't ask me, I don't make the rules." He shifts in his chair impatiently. "Anything else I can help you with?"

"When is the last time you saw this woman in the hotel, or anywhere else for that matter?"

"Let's get this straight, the only place I've ever seen the woman is in the hotel dining area. And you can talk to those people in food service. There's a chance they can tell you something. Of course, there's a lot of turnover there. Not like my department. We're all tight."

"When was the last time you saw her, before the night of the fall?"

"It's been a while. I'm thinking the holidays. Around the end of December, maybe."

DeLuca frowns. "That is a while. Mind telling me why you remember that?"

Burns returns another know-it-all smirk. I'm sick of his smugness.

"I'm security," Burns says. "I watch what's going on, who's coming and going. So I like looking at the pretty ones. I'm not a perv, so don't get me wrong. It's just amusement. Job gets kind of boring at times."

Ha!

"Why am I having a hard time believing you?" DeLuca asks. I don't believe Burns either. "December to June is a long time to remember one woman, particularly one you don't know. Pretty or no, eh?"

Burns shifts in his chair, looks around, and then lowers his voice to say, "Me and a few guys, we play a game where we claim certain people. It's kind of a real-life video game. We score a point whenever we spot one of ours. We use real people as game pieces. I guess you could say it's reality real-time play. I admit, it's kind of weird. But everyone in IT is a little off, if you get my drift."

Acid rises in my throat. I look at Roudebusch seated beside me. His steely expression remains unchanged. I glance at Jacobson. Her posture conveys that she wants to pummel Burns too.

DeLuca gives his head one of those disbelieving shakes. "So you *do* know the woman's name."

"No, I traded another player one of my pieces for her and renamed her. We name our pieces. I call her hot chick/old guy. I mean no disrespect. It's just a game. I never would've imagined she would be the jumper."

"You ever see her at the hotel with someone other than the man you mentioned earlier?"

"I really don't remember. The guy during the holidays

could've been the same, probably was. He doesn't count as my player."

How convenient.

"But you called her hot chick/old man," DeLuca says.

"Old *guy*. Lot of old guys come through here. The man could've been someone else. I would say go back and check the video recording on that, but it's already been wiped clean."

"You don't find this game of yours vulgar? Rather disrespectful?"

Burns rakes a hand through his hair. "I can't lose my job, Detective. It's a harmless game. Keeps up morale, keeps everyone in my department watching the guests to make sure they're safe. You know? It's a good thing."

"I'm going to need the name of the others who play your people game."

"Sure."

"Answer me this. Does Cheryl play?"

Another smirk. "No, man. Not her. She's a little wack about shit like that. You know what I mean?"

"No, I don't. Care to explain?"

"The sensitive touchy-feely type. A woman's libber. Might rat us out."

"Write the names of your colleagues down." DeLuca slid him a sheet of paper and a pen.

Burns complied. DeLuca sat silently with his eyes closed while he did so. Undoubtedly to clear his head. I'm sure if I find this game repulsive, so does he.

Burns finishes the list and pushes it back to DeLuca. Then he sits back and folds his arms, tapping his foot.

"Four guys?" DeLuca asks. "That's it?"

"That's it."

"I talked to all these men. No one mentioned your game."

Burns shrugs. "I'm sure they will if you ask."

"Yeah, I plan on doing that."

The air-conditioning switches on. A rush of cold air makes me shiver. All this time, I hadn't realized that I'd worked up a sweat. I move my legs. My skin sticks to the vinyl seat and stings as I pull away.

"How do you think she managed to get the window open? The woman—the jumper, as you call her?" DeLuca asks.

"Windows have been refitted or closed off to prevent jumpers. You'd have to ask maintenance how they did it. The hotel is old; they're constantly doing maintenance. She wouldn't be the first person who wanted to commit suicide, but she would be the first who actually got out the window. But even she didn't die. So go figure. Like I said, ask maintenance, because it's a full-blown mystery to me."

"She strike you as suicidal?"

"I'm no shrink. Don't ask me that. Seriously, I don't know the lady. I'm really sorry about what she went through, but I can't tell you anything else."

DeLuca stares at him.

"Am I being charged with the internet going down?" Burns asks. "Because if that's the case, you may need to charge the provider as well. I gotta be somewhere. My girl is going to chew my ass off for being this late, so can I please leave?" He pushes his chair back and rises. "You know where to find me. How about next time, just call. We could do this on the phone."

"One more question. Where have you been? You haven't been at work the last few days."

"At home. Vacation. Use it or lose it, they say."

"What have you been doing?"

"The regular. Playing video games. Ordering pizzas. Drinking beer. You know."

DeLuca scoffs. "No, actually, I don't." He waves his hand dismissively. "You can go, but we'll be watching you."

"You got to be kidding."

"Not a bit. And I won't be kidding if we charge you with tampering with evidence and attempted murder."

18

DeLuca and I grab a sandwich for dinner before the drive back to the shelter. I'm speechless. I think back to Ashem and Gulshan. Was this older gentleman Burns was talking about John Brownsworth? Did I do something to John? The date on the receipt was January first, New Year's Day, around the time I met up with the older man at the hotel. Maybe it was John that I met that night? Maybe not.

"What's up, Blue?" DeLuca asks.

I look up from staring at the tabletop. I hadn't realized that I'd zoned out. "Has anyone who might know me come forward yet?"

DeLuca shifts in his seat. "No, I'm sorry. Didn't mention it because I knew it would upset you."

I slowly nod. "It's all too surreal."

"I understand this is hard. Let's give it more time."

"Why in God's name would Burns think I'm an escort just because he's seen me in the restaurant at the hotel? That makes no sense. Who comes to a conclusion like that? It's not like he admits to ever seeing me go upstairs with someone. Or did he? And that *game*!"

"The guy is a creep. I'll give you that."

"If you ask me, he's the one who pulled the plug. No other outages in the area. He knows something."

"Do you have any idea who the man Burns described was?"

"If only." I pause. "I think we should get as much of the hotel video as possible, get it right off the cloud and right off their servers, as far back as we can."

"Got that one covered. But, as he said, there's a limit as to how long they maintain the video files."

"Burns is the one who pulled the plug on the system. He admits he's weird, knows who I am, calls me a piece in his game. No. It's more than weird. *He knows more.*"

DeLuca looks at me, chewing his sandwich. I'm glad he doesn't talk with his mouth full.

He finally says, "He's a creep, I agree. But if he's lying, he's a hell of an actor."

I'm struck by the thought that I'm a hell of an actor myself.

19

Monday morning, I wake to the aroma of home-brewed coffee, glance at a bedside clock, and note that it's just seven. No chance I'm rolling back over. I missed dinner last night, so I've only met a handful of the residents, and I'm apprehensive about engaging with the others. I don't want to involve anyone in the mess I'm in. Besides, I don't intend to stay in the city. I've got to get to Sag Harbor.

I dress in a pair of chinos and a pull-over shirt, then walk down the flight of stairs toward the communal dining room, which is on the second floor directly across the hall from the office. My stomach grumbles. No one has mentioned anything about my amnesia since I've arrived, but my instinct is that they all know.

"Good morning," a woman sitting at the end of a long table says when I enter the room. She's a slender redhead, in her early forties. Her eyes are bright, but they also convey weariness, even pain. Something tells me she's a resident, but I don't ask. She smiles a toothy smile, and her gums show. The smile couldn't be more hospitable. "Glad you found us.

Help yourself." She gestures toward the bagels, fruit, and coffee on the counter. The bagels are packaged and look like they could be stale; they're still more than I expected.

I return the smile and take inventory of my surroundings and the people. By the size of the room, it looks as if a wall between what was once a formal dining and kitchen area has been torn down to create a larger kitchen and gathering area. Two long tables span the front half of the area. The kitchen sits back and has a window facing the rear of the building. About twenty-five women, casually dressed in jeans or house dresses, are gathered. Many are seated, some are milling around in the kitchen area where the food is. The place is charming and cozy with its down-home style.

"I love the smell of morning coffee," I say to the smiling woman. "Wild horses couldn't keep me away." Out of nowhere, I detect the odor of horse with a wet coat. I turn away and focus on the scent, the full mélange of sweat, dung, and urine. I realize I was raised on a farm. How do I know this?

I try not to show the turmoil going on inside my head and get in line for breakfast. I introduce myself to a few other women and, when it's my turn, pour myself a cup of coffee. I add an extra splash of cream and, on impulse, also some more sugar. It's a small thing, but I need a crutch, some comfort. I take a sip and savor the sweetness, then turn around to look for a place to sit. There are no unoccupied chairs, and many curious stares.

I walk to a window at the back of the room near the refrigerator and look outside. Last night's storm has passed, but the sky is still filled with clouds. Several women are working in a vegetable garden down below that's located on the right side of the yard. How wonderful a fresh salad or a bowl of freshly picked strawberries would taste. Farm-grown.

There's a flower garden on the other side of the yard and a

grassy area between the gardens with a picnic table. I remember a walk through a garden, I don't know where. The sweet, spicy fragrance of roses comes to mind. I like white roses. Maybe I live near a garden? Or maybe it's the same farm with the horse smells, the farm of my childhood. How strange to be a conscious, thinking adult, but without access to most of my memories. It's like sailing your boat in a swimming pool when you're used to the open ocean.

The redhead comes to stand alongside me. "The women who aren't out looking for a job spend their time working in the garden or cleaning. Therapeutic, they say." She extends a hand. "I'm Ginger Tait. Ginger is my real name. I was born with red hair, to my parents' surprise. I live here and also help out in the office. I've spent most of my adult life in an office, so why stop now?" She grins. "And you are?"

"Blue."

"I don't think I've met anyone by that name before. It's lovely."

I thank her, though I'm wary of her friendliness.

"I'm sure I had that same worried look when I first came here," she says, studying my face. "The truth is, no one in our position knows what to expect."

"Am I that transparent?" I try to smile. There's no chance she'll understand the source of my worry; it's not about meeting these people. My life is a vacuum, my memory gone, and I can't stand it.

"Some of us find living in a shelter a bit trying, while others feel like they've checked into the Ritz Carlton. But it's a temporary home. Can't beat that." She pauses as if reading my mind. "They'll warm up. Give them time."

She's warning me to keep my mouth shut unless, and until, I get initiated into the sorority. I don't intend to participate in a sorority rush.

"A common thread is that we *all* have our troubles, so we

try not to be assholes. Not always so simple, but there aren't a lot of secrets amongst us. I know you fell out of a window."

"How do you know that?"

"I work in the office. People talk."

She pauses, and a silence grows between us. I don't want it to become awkward, so I ask, "Have you been here long, Ginger?"

"Not quite a month. I lived on the Upper West Side for years, lost my underwriting job when the insurance company I worked for was acquired, couldn't find another job, let my health insurance lapse to save money—stupid—and then was diagnosed with breast cancer right after. Burned right through my severance pay and savings."

"I'm sorry."

She smiles. "I'm getting through it. God only knows what would've become of me if I hadn't found this place. A friend got me in here. Most shelters are like dormitories with horrible beds and a cafeteria. Many are dangerous. I plan on giving back when I'm on my feet again."

She touches my forearm. I flinch. She withdraws her hand and smiles. Her smile is disarming, but I'm glad she's no longer touching me.

"Later this week, I have a second interview for a new job," she says, choosing to breeze past the awkward moment. "Just a claims person for auto and homeowner's policies, well below my expertise, but I don't think I've been this excited for a job in my life."

I lift my hand and cross two fingers in support.

Another woman, a stout brunette with tattoos on both arms, enters the kitchen, carrying tomatoes and herbs in a straw basket lined with a kitchen towel. "Anyone for a Monday-night Italian dinner?"

The mood in the room shifts. The women sitting around

a table agree and then begin debating how to make the best marinara sauce.

I go back to looking out the window. When the room goes quiet, I glance over my shoulder. A man has walked in. Some of the women appear a bit in awe of the man's rugged good looks. Or, on second thought, perhaps the badge and police sidearm on his belt have caused their reaction.

A woman asks, "Are you lost, sir? Because I would be very happy to help you find your way." She flashes a flirtatious smile.

He scans the room. "Just looking for—"

I step away from the window. "Detective DeLuca. I take it you're here to speak with me?"

He grins. He's a quiet one. Deep waters. He asks if I have a minute to talk.

One of the women mock-boos DeLuca for choosing me, causing the others to laugh.

We leave the room and go down the stairs. He takes my arm. Unlike with Ginger, I'm not put off by his touch. Such an odd contrast to the way I feel about others. And even though I can't let my guard down, I feel this cloak of protection when he's near, but I remind myself to watch my step. Once outside, he releases my arm.

His sedan is parked on our side of the road. The passenger's side door opens, and a woman gets out.

20

The woman stepping out of DeLuca's vehicle isn't anyone I recognize. She also doesn't seem like a woman I would associate with—but then, what do I really know about who I would spend time with. She's wearing a navy-blue-and-white striped miniskirt with a matching blouse, a Gucci cross-body bag, and a matching pair of stilettos. Way too crass for me. Roudebusch isn't with them. Good.

The woman walks over to us and gives me an enormous hug.

I stand there numbly, my arms at my side.

"Oh my God, honey," she says. "How are you doing? That's the question. Oh, honey, honey, honey."

I pull away from the woman and gape at her.

"Blue, it's Lorraine. Don't you know me? It's true what this guy said. I wondered where you'd gone off to. When I saw your photo, I went to see the cops—excuse me, the police—and I told them I knew you, and I came here right away. And here we are."

I dodge her attempt to embrace me again.

"This is Lorraine Baglietti," DeLuca says. "She came down to the station after she saw your missing-person photo. We've interviewed her, gathered info, vetted her. She checks out a hundred-and-ten percent."

"A statistical impossibility," I blurt out rudely. I find it hard to trust this overly affectionate person, given that I have no memory of knowing her—or anyone. Why would DeLuca bring a stranger anywhere near the shelter?

"Just a figure of speech," he replies. "She checks out completely is my point."

"As what?" I ask.

"Your friend, of course," Lorraine says. "Jeez, you *have* lost your memory. Well, as soon as I saw your gorgeous mug splashed across the television screen, I went to the police. If Gabriella hadn't been watching cartoons on television, I never would've seen you. In fact, she was the one who first noticed you. Said, 'Hey *mammina*, isn't that your friend from the dance school?'"

"Dance school?" I ask. The words trigger the memory of taking dance classes. But that doesn't feel recent. "I dance?"

"Not professionally, but honey, you spin like a top on steroids," she says.

I stand frozen, staring at Lorraine Baglietti. Do I really know her? Why would I choose her for a friend? She's brassy, crass, and dresses over-the-top. I'm sure I'm nothing like this woman. At least, I hope I'm not. I don't think I am. As Stallworth said, personalities don't change that much, not without some organic alteration to the brain. Since waking up from the coma, I've been doing a lot of soul searching. I know I'm not shy. Just conservative. I care about refinement and decorum. Refined and decorous Lorraine is not.

Then again, maybe I'm judging her too harshly. Why wouldn't I have a friend who's so different from me? The old cliché comes to mind: don't look a gift horse in the mouth. Lorraine is a gift.

"Is there someplace private we can talk?" DeLuca asks.

I look toward the shelter. If Lorraine is legit and has plenty to say about who I am, I'm not so sure I'm ready for all those strangers to hear.

"There's a coffee shop down the block," I suggest. "I saw it on the way here. But I don't think Ms. Baglietti is dressed for a walk."

"Are you kidding me?" she says. "I could walk miles in these shoes. And another thing—it's *Lorraine*, like it's always been. Cut the *Ms. Baglietti* crap."

"You two hop in the car. I'll drive," DeLuca says.

"Oh, you guys," she says. "It's a couple of blocks away. I'm fine. If I'm not walking on my toes, my feet get sore. You would think I was the ballerina, not you."

"Nevertheless, I'll drive," DeLuca says firmly.

I sit in front. As soon as Lorraine is settled in the back seat, the car's interior fills with the cloying scent of some perfume that's likely expensive but so over-applied that my nostrils burn.

At the coffee shop, DeLuca orders black coffee for himself, and I get a coffee with cream. Lorraine orders a large mocha with two shots of chocolate and then adds an apple tart from the pastry counter.

We sit at a round table in the corner. Lorraine says, "Just so you know, Blue, Detective DeLuca had me checked out from here to kingdom come. He knows all there is to know about me. Said he wouldn't take me to you until I gave up all my personal information, but I will tell you this, I stopped him when he asked to take my blood pressure." She lets out a hearty laugh.

She still hasn't told me how we know each other.

"The officer here explained your circumstances," she

continues. "I'm so sorry. I can't fathom what you've been through. You're single. You don't have children. You don't have pets—I'll vouch for that, because I never saw you with any pet fur on your clothes. God only knows how cat fur clings to wool coats. I could tell you stories ..." She waves a hand in the air. "So here we are."

I turn to DeLuca for reassurance. He gives me the go-ahead.

"What's my name?" I ask, looking at the woman. Her answer will tell me if she's real.

"You're Blue Bishop," Lorraine answers.

So the jeweler *did* know my name. So does this woman. Blue Bishop is real.

DeLuca reaches inside his shirt pocket and produces an ID. "It's only temporary, but I had it made when Lorraine gave us your name," DeLuca continues. "Without your Social Security number, it's not an official identification card. But it's a start."

"You're going to be fine," Lorraine says, reaching a hand to mine. "Just fine."

I look away, trying to mask my feelings. So much is happening. It's hard to piece it all together. "I don't remember my name," I say. Because I don't. It's familiar. It's the same name the jeweler used to address me. Seems like it could be right. So I accept that it is right, now that two unrelated people have told me the same thing.

"You're in shock," Lorraine says. "Sometimes I wake up in the middle of the night and forget which house I'm staying in —the city apartment, the beach house ... Lord, sometimes I think I'm visiting Rome."

"So, how did we meet?" I ask Lorraine.

"We met at the Masters Dance Studio on West End and 110th," she says.

I'm silent.

"The dance studio people verify that," DeLuca says.

"Do you dance, Lorraine?" I ask.

She erupts with raucous laughter. "Heavens, no. Gabriella is the prima ballerina in our family. Don't you remember? Oh, of course you don't. Give it time, you will. Gaby, my little princess, she got the dancing genes from George. But don't tell him that. He'll think his manhood is being threatened. But no, to answer your question, I'm a dance mom. But not one of those nuts like you see on the tube."

"So I dance?"

"Like I said earlier, you're a real class act on your toes. Dance like a butterfly. Gabriella says she's going to dance like you one day."

I flex a foot, glad it's concealed underneath the table. I flex the other foot and imagine that I'm pirouetting across stage. Then, like floodwaters rolling down a canyon, the language of dance falls into place—the steps, the movement, the music. How can that be? Why didn't I remember this before now? But there it is. I imagine my entire body moving to the music of the La Bayadère, Bacchanale, Novelette.

Of course I dance. I must've taken lessons during my childhood and continued them into adulthood. No better form of exercise. Dance keeps the muscles lean and makes for fast-twitch speed and excellent gait. I didn't play soccer; I danced.

I look over at Lorraine. I don't recall spending any time with this woman. That's what's more bewildering. It's hard to believe we knew one another. I don't trust her yet, despite DeLuca's endorsement. "Tell me more about how we met, Lorraine."

"In the dance studio lobby," she says. "You were watching the little ones through the viewing window, waiting for your adult class. I was standing right beside you, waiting for my little *principessa*. And of course, my husband says that I'm so talkative that I've never met a stranger in my life. I introduced myself. We got to talking, and the next thing you know we're having drinks one Friday night. Blue, you haven't forgotten *all* about me, have you?"

"I'm very sorry, Lorraine."

She waves a hand at me. "That's why I'm here, sister. I'm going to help you. I don't care what it takes. You hear me? That's what friends are for."

"Thank you."

"Nothing to thank me for," Lorraine says. "You'd do the same for me."

"There's more," DeLuca says. He's smiling with those deep, world-weary eyes like he's got another box of chocolates for me. I shouldn't fall for this stuff. I really shouldn't. "We have your address. You live on the Upper West Side of Manhattan, on Broadway."

"My address? My home? How long have you been keeping this from me?"

"Cool your jets, Blue, we just found out. Once we got the name of the dance studio from Lorraine, we called them, and they had your name and address on file."

21

A flood of tears starts flowing down my cheeks. This is exactly the news I've been waiting for.

"I want to go home," I say. "Can I go home?"

"I'll give you a lift," he says. "We'll check it out."

A name, a friend, and now a home. I feel as if I'm beginning to have a purchase on my identity and a place in the world. Soon, the void that's my past will be filled again. And once I'm home, I'll be able to figure out who my family and my other friends are. I hope I'll be safe there.

"I'm ready now," I say. I can leave what little I have behind, except for the case from the jewelers. "I need to get my suitcase."

DeLuca drives us back to the shelter. He and Lorraine wait in the car while I hurry up the stairs and inside the office. Ginger is sitting at the desk subbing for the assistant, who's out on an errand.

I explode with excitement and impulsively turn a pirouette. I can't remember ever being more excited. Of course, I can't remember anything else, either. I don't know Ginger, but I can't help sharing my joy. "Ginger! You'll never believe this."

I tell her about Lorraine, and that someone has finally discovered where I live. That I have a name.

"Wonderful!" she says.

"Seems a woman named Lorraine Baglietti, a friend at my dance studio, recognized my photo. I came to say goodbye and return my room key. The detective and Lorraine are waiting in the car. I have to get my things. I'll bring the key down."

"Right. You just need to sign that you've turned it in. I'll get the paperwork. My gosh, so you're a dancer?" she says in a calm voice. "Who is this friend again?"

"Lorraine Baglietti. A friend from my ballet school. This is so crazy. As soon as Lorraine told me I danced, I flexed my toes and I remembered. The steps, the moves ..."

"Just like that. Remarkable. And you remember this Lorraine?"

"No. Not yet. But she knows things about me she couldn't know unless she was my friend. And that's the best start I've had so far."

"Just be sure you can trust her."

I take a step back. "The authorities checked her out."

Ginger holds up her palms. "Of course. So you're going home. Are you going to be without protection?"

"I'm sure DeLuca will take care of that."

"If not, you can always come back as long as your room is open. Why don't you hold on to your key?"

"No, no. I'm really confident about it all."

She rises from her chair and hugs me. I don't mind the physical contact now. I'm not sure if it's the excitement or what. "I'm very happy for you, Blue."

I'm puzzled. Her tone is measured, no longer as joyous as it was when I first told her the news. Jealous? She doesn't seem the type—or didn't. But, then, I've only just met her.

I step out of the embrace. "I wish you the best of luck. I hope everything works out for you. That you get the job."

"Be careful, Blue."

I rush upstairs and gather my things. On the way down, I hear the phone ring. I glance at Ginger to wave goodbye, and she flags me back inside the office.

"One moment, please," she says. She hits the hold button, and in a voice barely above a whisper, she says, "I think they said it's your doctor."

"Man or woman?"

She appears perplexed. "I couldn't exactly tell. Too much noise in the background. You want me to take a message?"

Another resident enters the office and asks to speak with Ginger.

"I'll take it in the hall." I take the handset, step out of the office, and answer.

"The Cassiopeia, Blue," the man says. He's the same person who called me in the hospital.

My stomach drops. "John?"

"No Johns here. Let's get to the point. Deliver the Cassiopeia. There won't be a next request."

"You're the man who tried to kidnap me."

"You have my money. I want my merchandise."

"I need time to remember what happened. Who I am. I'm not recovered yet."

A long exhale. "So you have memory problems. You better find a way to fix it. Fast."

"But I can't."

"Saturday. Or your mother dies."

My God, I do have a family, and they're at risk. Why is he only mentioning my mother? What about my father? Blood rushes to my head. "Please, help me remember."

"Not over the phone."

"How will I find you?"

"I'll find you. Say nothing to the police."

The line goes dead. I pull the phone away from my ear and stand stupefied. I have a mother who's alive. Again, what about my father? Dead? Divorced? Out of the picture? But is that man telling the truth?

The other resident passes me in the hall and says something to me about Ginger that I can't hear because I can't get the call out of my brain. That man tried to kill me once. He'll really kill my mother if I don't come through.

"Blue, you okay?" Ginger calls from inside the office.

The answer has got to be at my home. I face her.

"Who was that?" Ginger asks. "You look pale."

Maybe I should tell her what just happened, for her and the women's own safety, but instead I say, "Doctor's appointment. They needed to reschedule. I can't stand when they do that. How hard is it to keep one appointment?"

She sits back in her chair. "Yeah, those doctors expect you to wait two hours for them, but they cancel on you in the blink of an eye because they have a last-minute tee time at the club."

DeLuca raps on the door. "Sorry to interrupt, but we should go."

"You take care, Blue," Ginger says. "Keep in touch."

I don't know whether to tell DeLuca about the call. I'm locked in a vise. I have to find John Brownsworth.

22

We move slower than a lazy snail—typical Monday morning traffic. We drive through Brooklyn and Queens, cross the Queensboro Bridge, and navigate across 59th Street along the boundary of Central Park. There's no getting a word in edgewise, because Lorraine fills in every second. I'm glad, because my mind is racing in circles about my mother and the Cassiopeia Ruby and John Brownsworth and who the man is on the other end of the phone.

I'm close, so close to home. To figuring this out.

Lorraine talks about several topics at once—her husband and five children, the latest news regarding a purse snatcher in Midtown getting caught by a couple of street rappers, and the group of New Yorkers who favor an increase in the tax on cigarettes to fatten the city's coffers. She never passes up the opportunity to voice her own opinion. Like how the higher tax won't make much of a difference because people will buy their cigarettes from street vendors who'll be selling them illegally.

"And good for the street vendors!" she says. "I don't want

my kids to smoke—they'll have hell to pay if I ever catch 'em with a cigarette—but taxes are too high already. And I'm for individual freedom. Here's to the bootleggers, if you ask me."

DeLuca glances at Lorraine in his rearview mirror. He's wearing a poker face—not amused, not displeased. What he's thinking?

Several blocks down, he interrupts her and says, "It's on the 2100 block of Broadway. 2124-C between 72nd and 73rd." He glances at me. "Hopefully, you'll recognize it."

So far, nothing about this neighborhood feels like home. How bizarre that I would live in this area, and on busy Broadway. The residences are mostly on the numbered streets. Still, at the moment, I hope a Broadway building has answers for me.

DeLuca slows the car as soon as we pass 72nd Street. It's short for a city block. Just before we reach 73rd, he pulls over to the curb. I look out my side window. We're in front of the Beacon Theatre and Hotel. To the left are the Beacon Hotel and Beacon Bar; to the right is Beacon Wine and Spirits. I search the upper floors. This just can't be right. It's a trick.

"You sure this is the right place?" Lorraine asks.

"I don't get it," he says. "This is the address the dispatcher at the station gave me. Not my typical beat, but I should've known. I'm sorry, Blue. Let me check again." He makes the call, and the address comes back the same.

I twist around toward Lorraine. "Is this really where I live?"

"I don't know," she says. "You never invited me."

"Have I been to your place?"

"You never accepted any of my invitations. But I understand. We're all busy."

And yet, she stepped forward to help me. I can't be upset with her. But this isn't home. This is a hotel.

"I got the feeling you weren't much of a cook, which may

be why you didn't invite me over," she continues. "I mean, look at yourself. I bet you never prepared anything other than celery and carrot sticks. That's the kind of food you ate when we went out, never mind that Dean & DeLuca has those great pastries."

She keeps chattering away. She can't possibly know the hell I'm trapped in.

"Lord, I would have to bribe you to eat half a chocolate," she goes on. I'm glad I don't fall completely apart. "And I could tell by your eyes when you admired all those mouthwatering chocolates that you loved them." She taps Detective DeLuca on the shoulder. "Hey, any relation to Dean & DeLuca, Detective?"

"None," he said, still puzzling over the building.

"And if you came over to my place, you would've had to eat my pasta. I would've insisted you clean your plate, so, there you go."

I just want to go home. Find answers.

"Feel like home?" DeLuca asks, but he damn well knows the answer.

I want to cry, scream, throw something, but none of that will do any good. Did I give the dance studio the wrong address? On purpose? That's insane.

I try to sound confident when I say, "I have absolutely no memory of this place."

"Let's take a look," DeLuca says.

I jerk the car door open.

"I'll go with you," Lorraine says. "And don't worry, hon. There must be some explanation."

Yeah.

I go to the front door and walk through the lobby. It smells dank, dusty, and old. I approach the desk clerk, a man in his fifties.

The man looks at Lorraine first. "Checking in, ma'am?"

"Are you the manager?" she asks.

"Yes, ma'am. Is there a problem?"

"I have a weird question," I say. "Do I live here?"

He gapes at me.

"Answer the lady," Lorraine says. "She's suffering from amnesia. You know, a bump on the noggin that makes you forget who the hell you are?"

I wish she would leave this to me.

The man tightens his jaw and considers me. "You don't live here, ma'am. If you did, I would know. I'm sorry you got hurt, but I've never seen you before in my life."

"How long have you worked here?" Lorraine asks.

"Years. Too long."

"Does the name Blue Bishop mean anything to you?" I ask.

"No, ma'am."

"Check your computer," DeLuca says impatiently. "To see whether there's been a guest by that name."

The manager shakes his head, clearly fed up. "Look, buddy—"

DeLuca shows his badge and glares at the man. The manager raises his eyebrows and hands in submission and checks his computer.

"Sorry, the name doesn't come up," the manager says.

Another dead end.

I thank the manager and walk toward the exit, leaving DeLuca and Lorraine behind. Outside, I stop and turn on my heels.

Lorraine practically runs into me. She moves a lot faster than I could in those heels.

I drop my arms. "This is bullshit. I fucking don't exist. Sure, I have a name, and I speak French, but I have no home. I feel like an American, but am I?"

Lorraine steps forward and, without asking permission,

hugs me. “Don’t worry, honey. We’ll get to the bottom of this. Trust me. We will. Lorraine is here for you.”

I pull back. City sounds fill my ears. DeLuca is now standing beside us.

“This whole thing sucks, DeLuca,” Lorraine says. “What kind of cop are you? NYPD’s finest, my ass.”

I wish she hadn’t said anything. I don’t need her to speak for me.

DeLuca ignores her.

I stare at him. “Now that everything has gone to shit, is there anything at all going in my favor, one single shred of hope? Because I only feel like a victim. Completely vulnerable.” And I can’t lay all my cards on the table. I don’t know who to trust.

DeLuca waits patiently, his expression concerned but also attentive. “I wasn’t going to mention this until I could tell you something definitive, but I do have some positive news. I believe it’s positive, or a good idea. You speak French. So I’ve asked Homeland Security to run your profile through their system.”

“Homeland Security? That’s *positive* news? You think I’m a terrorist, a criminal? Not these people trying to kill me?”

“No, that’s what we would do for anyone. We’ve given them your info—what we have now. Your photo, your name. If you’ve been out of the country, to France, Canada, another French-speaking country, it’ll come up. May take a little time.”

“I don’t have a little time.”

“I understand you’re upset.”

I can’t hold back. I need his help. I’ve got less than a week to find that ruby to save my mother. I hoped the answer would be at my home. But that isn’t happening, and I don’t know when or even if I’ll be able to find John Brownsworth.

“No, I don’t have time,” I snap. “Another phone call came

back there at the shelter, just before I left. Same caller, only this time he threatened my mother's life. I don't even remember her or where she lives."

DeLuca juts his jaw forward. "And you mention this now?"

"I know how this looks. I was going to tell you, but I was in shock. Still reeling from meeting Lorraine. That caller threatened me, said not to tell the police about the conversation. Detective, I'm scared. Confused." I'm talking too much. Time to seem contrite. "I'm sorry, I should've mentioned it right away."

"What did the caller say? Did he mention the Cassiopeia?"

"He did. I don't understand why or how I'm involved in this."

"Did he say what the Cassiopeia is?"

"No." Another lie for the sake of self-preservation.

A truck drives by, catching the sunlight at a right angle, and I'm blinded by the glare. "How can I go back to the shelter? Why go sit in a place like a duck in a pen? And my mother—*who I don't even remember*—is in danger right now."

"The shelter is a safe place," DeLuca says. "And we'll make it even safer. Do what we have to."

"Like you did at the hospital? Don't you understand? I'm not safe anywhere."

"Holy shit," Lorraine says, stepping toward me. "Blue, it's going to be all right."

"Nothing is all right." I look up and beyond the top floor of the hotel-and-theater building. If only I could spring upwards and float away.

Lorraine stares hard at DeLuca. "Well, sir, this is on you. Two people's lives are at risk. I suggest you do something about it. Like figure out where Blue's mother is and see that she's protected. Now!"

Not looking at Lorraine, DeLuca holds up a hand to shut her up. "Blue, you need protection. Real protection. I'll take you back to the shelter. We *can* protect you."

"Right," Lorraine barks. "Doesn't sound like you did such a hot job of it."

DeLuca frowns at Lorraine, his way of telling her to put a lid on it. But there's no shutting this woman up.

"You really ought to be placed in protective custody, Blue," DeLuca says.

"You sending her to prison now?" Lorraine entwines her arm with mine and pulls us around in the opposite direction. "Come on, sister. You can stay with me. I'll be damned if I'm letting you go back to that shelter. And you can be certain my place is safe. I'll help you find your mother."

I don't know where Lorraine lives, but her home will be better than that step backward into the void.

"Not a good idea."

"What the hell, Detective?" Lorraine says. "You inviting Blue to move in with you? Are we calling this personalized police assistance? I've got armed guards at my place. Better than that one cop at the shelter sitting around drinking coffee."

"You're a civilian, Lorraine. How can you protect her?"

"My place is Fort Knox compared to that shelter. We'll catch a cab like real New Yorkers do. Since when did the police get into the Uber business?" She goes to the curb, puts her fingers to her lips, and lets out one of the loudest whistles I've ever heard.

A cab pulls over.

"Get in, hon," Lorraine says to me. "We're going home."

23

The cab driver stops in front of a building on Park Avenue between 89th and 90th. Yet another surprise—Lorraine lives on the tony Upper East Side. Getting away from the shelter and DeLuca gives me a taste of what life before the accident was. At the same time, I'm more afraid than ever.

We get out of the cab and head inside. Two security guards are stationed inside the lobby. I relax.

We ride the elevator up. As we ascend, Lorraine explains her place takes up the top *four* floors.

When the doors open, I get my first glimpse inside her world of luxury. Funny how a simple ride up an elevator gives me hope. I look around the foyer of the apartment and a part of my brain kicks into the number game. A place like this—four floors of a building in this neighborhood—would cost upwards of twenty-five million. I calculate the various monthly mortgage payments at ten percent, twenty percent, fifty percent down, a couple of points above prime. The calculations come so easily. How did I do that?

Lorraine and I walk from the foyer of her apartment and

head inside the adjoining kitchen. A set of double doors that lead to a shallow outside balcony are open. It's not the type of balcony one sits on. Rather, it functions more like a window to let air inside.

"How many times do I have to tell those kids?" Lorraine exclaims.

A group of children come running down a hallway, the younger ones laughing and shrieking.

I glance at Lorraine. She looks aghast. Wonder why.

"Hey, Angelo," Lorraine says to the eldest, a teenager—a young man. "How many times have I told you not to leave those doors in the kitchen open? You want your baby brother to play Superman and jump out?"

She tilts her head to me and says, "Giorgio's thirteen months and walking now. The older kids forget that. The baby's into every little thing."

"I told Angie not to open that door," a younger boy says.

Lorraine rumples the young boy's hair. "All right you, Tobia. Be quiet now. I don't need a tattletale. Facts speak loud and clear."

"Sorry, Ma," Angelo says. "He can't get out. He's in the nursery asleep."

"Don't let me see this again, or you'll be shipped off to the Hamptons until you're sixty. Speaking of which, why are you kids still here? You should've been gone hours ago."

"Dad's not here yet," Angelo says. "I don't think he's—"

"Lord, sorry, don't you guys see I got company? Where's your manners? This is Ms. Blue Bishop. She'll be staying with us for a while."

I smile at them all. This is the first time I've felt any normalcy since my nightmare began.

"I know you," a young girl says, stepping from around the back of Angelo. She hurries to hug her mother, and while clinging to her, she stares up at me.

"Remind me what your name is," I say.

"I'm Gabriella Sophia Baglietti."

"Right, the dance school," I say, smiling. "It's a pleasure to see you, Gabriella."

"I like the way you dance," the girl says. "I've seen you through the window at the dance studio."

"Thank you." How could I forget the face of such a beautiful child? Lorraine and I really must be friends if this innocent child says she's seen me at the ballet school. Seeing a normal family interact is also soothing. But the thought that my mother—whoever and wherever she is—may die is also ever-present in my thoughts.

"Well, they're both beautiful names," I say to the young girl. "Remind me how old you are?"

"I'm eight," she says, a bit annoyed with me. "I'm the *principessa* around here. Isn't that right, *mammina*?"

I hold my hand out to shake hers.

When she touches it, she recoils and clings to her mother. "Your hands are cold."

"Oh, I'm sorry."

Lorraine winks at me. "You be sure you have two daughters, otherwise you'll have one who's spoiled just like our Gaby." The child pulls at her mother's arm and, when Lorraine bends over, Gabriella presses her nose to her mother's. Lorraine melts and plants a big kiss on the girl's cheek.

Then Lorraine introduces me to the rest of her children: Angelo, whom she characterizes as an eighteen-year-old going on thirty-eight; Donato, sixteen going on twelve; and Tobia, fourteen going on twenty-one. When she skips a second introduction for Gabriella, the child nudges her.

"This is Princess Gaby," she says. "And then there's the baby, Giorgio, named after his father, and who is now wailing at the top of his lungs—my future opera singer."

"I'm pleased to meet you all and to see you again, Gaby," I say.

Gabriella curtsies like a prima ballerina, and I return a bow.

"Just where is your father?" Lorraine asks.

"He's gone to the club," Tobia says.

Lorraine releases a frustrated sigh. "Which one?"

"He's golfing in East Hampton," Donato says. "Papa said it was too hot to stay in the city. He'll see us at the house."

"Well, that leaves you as the man around the house, doesn't it?" Lorraine says to Angelo, smoothing the shoulder of the boy's shirt.

"Gaetano is ready to take us to the Hamptons. You coming with us?"

"I'm staying in the city tonight. Have Estella take the baby, too. Next time your papa pulls one of these, you call me. Understand, son?"

The boy herds his siblings into another room.

"Gaetano is one of our drivers," Lorraine says to me. "Estella is the nanny. It's how we live, but don't think I'm not a hands-on mother." She pauses. "Do you remember anything about the Hamptons, Blue?"

"Is there a reason I should?" What I want to say is, *Let's join them*.

"Oh, wow. Sorry. I shouldn't push, DeLuca warned me. But yeah, you told me more than once that East Hampton is one of your favorite places on earth, which I said was funny, because we're there all the time, my family, and we've never bumped into you. Not such a small world. Anyway, you never had much to say about your time there."

"Any idea why?"

"Let's say you're a guarded person. Would only go so far when talking about yourself. You know, you never told me your job." She holds up her hands. "I'm not prying now, mind you."

"I wish I remembered something worth prying about."

"You will, Blue. You will."

"I wouldn't mind getting back out to the Hamptons."

"We have a few things to do in the city. You'll thank me later." She gives me a girlfriend wink. I understand why when, after the children leave, she calls Bergdorf Goodman and asks for a personal shopper. I protest again, but she won't hear of it. "A woman thinks much better when she's dressed well and carrying the right purse," she says. "Gives her a sense of identity and power. Like Supergirl's cape."

We sit a few moments. "DeLuca showed me the video recovered from the night of the fall. When I walked into that hotel, I was wearing a necklace. When I went out the window, I wasn't."

She looks disgusted. "Was the necklace expensive?"

"From what I can tell, yes."

"Think that's what these guys are after?"

"I really don't. But who knows, right?"

"Detective DeLuca can get a close-up on it from that video. If it's nice, especially if it's a designer piece, it'll be easier to check around to see who might've made it or where it came from. There's your first real clue. Want me to send him a text and remind him how to do his job?"

"Actually, yes," I say. "Yes, I do."

24

DeLuca's phone beeps. A message from his partner, Jerry Roudebusch.

"You need to get over here to Mark Burns's place. Now."

Forty minutes later, DeLuca walks into Burns's lobby. The place is old, run-down. No cameras. One mail slot overflows with mail, mostly magazines. He checks the name—Burns. Inside the elevator, he punches the button for the tenth floor.

Yellow crime-scene tape is strung up across the hallway. A dog barks from inside the apartment.

Roudebusch meets him at the door and hands him a pair of plastic shoe covers.

Animal control walks through the door, leading a muzzled black Labrador dog. Roudebusch nods for DeLuca to come inside. Two crime-scene examiners dust the place for fingerprints and collect fibers. A third methodically inventories a suitcase full of clothes.

"Looks like Burns was leaving town," DeLuca says.

"Bingo. Come on, he's in the kitchen."

In the kitchen, Burns's corpse is slumped down to a seated position against a lower cabinet.

A medical examiner who's photographing the body looks up. "The guy OD'd. Probably heroin."

"Brilliant deduction given the fact that he has a hypodermic needle hanging out of the arm," Roudebusch says.

DeLuca gives his partner a disapproving look. "Any preliminary thoughts if it's suicide or accident?"

The examiner looks at the body. "There's a needle hole in his neck to go along with the arm. I doubt the guy would inject himself in both places. If someone else did, they were careless. Best guess is the stick in the arm came second to the neck. We'll know for sure after the autopsy. I doubt the victim could've injected his neck, stayed coherent long enough to inject himself in the arm. But who knows, we see a lot of junk out here."

"Any sign of struggle?" DeLuca asks.

"Bruising on the back, the side of the head."

"Could the bruising have happened when he hit the floor?" Roudebusch asks.

"To the back, possibly. The head not likely." The examiner points to the swelling on the head and then demonstrates the trajectory of how Burns might've fallen or come to rest in his seated position on the floor. "If he hit his head, he wouldn't have been sitting upright. If Burns was attacked, jabbed in the neck with enough heroin, then he would've gone down to the floor easily. He wouldn't have resisted a second poke in the arm. Which looks like the homicide was staged to look like an overdose, given the way the needle was inserted and is hanging."

DeLuca looks back toward the front door. "Doesn't look like forced entry."

"No, it doesn't," Roudebusch says. "Looks like Burns let the killer in, must've known him or her."

"Not well enough," DeLuca said.

"His cell phone is over there, underneath the counter." Roudebusch points across the room. "Looks like it hit the floor and slid."

"The perp must've missed it," De Luca says. "Or it didn't matter if he made the death look like a suicide. Did you talk to any neighbors yet, Jerry?"

"Just about to," Roudebusch says. "Seen enough?"

They knock on several doors. The first occupant to open the door is a young girl, maybe thirteen.

DeLuca identifies himself, holds up his badge, and asks, "Are your parents home?"

The girl tugs at her hair. She gives an insolent shake of the head. "No, they're at work."

"Mind if I ask you a few questions?" DeLuca says.

The girl shrugs.

"Do you know the man who lived over there?" He motions toward Burns's place.

"No."

"Ever see him coming or going? Anyone else who went there?"

"No. But his dog has been barking nonstop over the past few days. That's why we called the police. My mom did."

"I'm going to give you my card," DeLuca says. "Have your mother call me."

DeLuca and Roudebusch knock on the next door.

An older man answers. He didn't know Burns, but he did see him coming and going on occasion. He also heard the dog barking. And he saw an express messenger leaving the guy's apartment. "It was odd. What express messenger goes inside an apartment?"

"Let's check around the area," DeLuca says to his partner after they finish interviewing the older man. "See if anyone noticed someone new in the building. Check the shops around here."

The elevator dings. A maintenance man walks out.

"You notice anything unusual in the building lately?" Roudebusch asks the man. "New people hanging around?"

He shakes his head, starts to walk away, but then stops. "Actually, you know, the basement door around back of the building that leads to the outside was unlocked. Shouldn't have been. I'm sure I locked it last time I was here."

"Looks like our killer left his *message* and just sashayed out the back door," DeLuca says. He glares at Roudebusch. "Looks like there's more to Blue's story than you gave her credit for, Jerry."

25

It's a late Monday afternoon on June 21st, the longest day of the year. It feels like it. The only bright spot is that Lorraine's personal shopper delivered quite the bundle of the latest fashions, not an over-the-top wardrobe like Lorraine wears.

As we're settling down in the kitchen for a snack, her phone rings. She looks at it, holds a finger up to signal that she needs a private moment, and goes into the other room before answering, though not out of earshot. The normally garrulous woman answers in monosyllables—"Yeah, no, fine."

"That was my husband," she says after ending the call. "He always has a gazillion questions about taking care of the little one." She rolls her eyes. "You'd think the baby was our first."

"No worries."

"So, Blue. You're going through a lot, and now with your mother ... this may sound weird, but what if we just act like nothing's wrong? I think it'll help relax you. And maybe, just maybe, you won't be stressed and you'll remember where you mom lives."

It's an odd idea, but it could be a good one.

She talks about her children but also makes it a point to tell me that she earned a bachelor's degree in computer science and that she's a computer operations business consultant. Works on her own schedule. I must look incredulous when she says this, because she shakes her head and says, "You had the same surprised look before. Just like the last time."

"I'm sorry. I didn't mean to. I just assumed you were a stay-at-home mom."

"I'll tell you what I told you last time, Blue. Do not judge a book by its cover. A woman can be pregnant a lot and also have a science degree and a consulting job in the twenty-first century. Because, as you well know, a tight skirt and blouse do not cut off the supply of blood to the brain and can still be a statement of independence."

Lorraine describes her husband, George, as an entrepreneur, devoted to her and the kids, who has one major vice—golf. They were childhood sweethearts from two old Italian New York families. Old-money trust funds and inheritance from both their families. No apologies.

"I'm getting hungry," she says. "How do you like the sound of linguine with white clam sauce? I have a great recipe, but I have to order up some fresh clams. You're not allergic to shellfish, are you?"

Her cell phone rings again. She holds up the phone. Caller ID shows Matteo DeLuca. "He's such a pain in the ass."

"You better answer it."

She answers and puts the phone on speaker.

"No leads on the necklace yet," he says.

"You could've texted that," Lorraine says.

"The call to the shelter came from another burner

phone." He pauses and then says, "I'm calling because I figured you'd like to know I got a call from homicide just a little while ago."

"Doesn't sound promising," I say.

"Mark Burns was found dead in his apartment. He had a dog. If the animal hadn't barked his head off, the guy might not have been discovered for a couple more days."

The floor drops four stories from underneath me. Lorraine gapes at me with wide eyes.

"You said homicide," I say. "He was murdered? What happened?"

"The guy died of an apparent overdose, but who knows? Of course, the medical examiner hasn't conducted an autopsy yet, and toxicology will take some time."

"Doesn't seem right. Yesterday, he was late for a date. Today he's in his apartment doing drugs. He seemed so nerdy; not the type."

"Yeah, well, the guy was a user. A preliminary examination of the body showed older needle marks, indicating use. But he kept a steady job, and there was no history of incarceration or rehab."

"What if he knew something, was involved the night of my fall? If he was paid to turn the monitors off, and then seen talking to the police, those people could've killed him. Nothing else makes sense. Don't you think, Detective?"

Lorraine steps back, folding her arms.

DeLuca says, "He didn't leave a note. That's all I can say for the moment."

"So you don't believe this was an accident?" I ask.

He clears his throat for the second time. "There's no sure way to know yet. But no bullshit, Blue—I don't think so."

26

Tuesday morning, the light streaming into the bedroom is like an alarm clock that won't stop ringing. I yawn and pull the sheet over my head. The blanket of sleep begins to descend again—until the only word echoing in my mind is *murder*.

Time is running out.

Sleep is no longer possible. So I get up and walk into the kitchen to find Lorraine hunched over, working on her laptop. When I enter, she sits up and closes the cover.

"Sorry to disturb you," I say.

She waves a dismissive hand. "Forget it. Work's boring. It's also confidential. Take a seat. I've got pastries and some chocolate-caramel truffles. Your favorite. But you're going to eat them this time." She walks to the counter and fixes me a cup of coffee. "Cream only, as I recall." She sets the cup down in front of me.

I don't ask for sugar like I did at the shelter. I sip the hot liquid, then place the cup on the counter and surround it with my hands. The heat is soothing.

"How'd you sleep?" she asks. "Considering everything."

"Little restless after that call from DeLuca. But the bed is incredible."

"A lumpy bed is great if there's a great guy in it." She winks. "Which is what we'll work on when you're better."

"Did I ever tell you I was seeing someone?"

"No. We always talked more generally, you know? But I didn't get the idea you were seeing anyone."

Which might imply that I had someone special—or no one at all.

"Let's eat," she says. "And don't ever give Gabriella any ideas about skipping breakfast. It's hard enough to get the child to finish a piece of toast."

"Kids eat what they need, or so I hear."

Lorraine snorts. "She's a wisp, that kid. Got to fatten her up some before she withers away. Do you have any brothers or sisters, Blue?"

"I don't remember any siblings." I look out at Central Park. Every window in the entire apartment has a view.

"I was an only child," she says. "Always wanted an older sibling to look up to or a little one to dress up. I think when you don't have a sibling, you want one. Imagine that, an Italian family with only one child. Plenty of cousins, though. Enough of them that I was glad when we went home after parties." She pauses. "Both of my parents have passed away. Mother had breast cancer, father a heart attack. Too young. I miss them every day."

"I'm so sorry."

She shakes her head. "It was a long time ago."

"I remember I had a doll, blue dress with daisies," I say, to change the subject. "But what girl didn't have a doll?"

"If you were like me, you chopped the hair off." Lorraine laughs.

"That strikes a chord. Mine had brown hair, and I'm sure I did just that. Then someone took it away." I frown, recalling the angry woman from my memory of France. My body jerks, and I inadvertently bump my cup, spilling coffee all over the counter. "Oh, God. Sorry."

She waves it off and holds out a napkin.

"I get the feeling I grew up around a lot of children," I say. "Almost like I was thrown into a large group of children."

She howls with laughter. "They call that school, Blue."

I smile, but I'm pretty sure it wasn't. "Tell me about one of our past conversations. Anything. Chances are you'll say something that helps me remember more."

She tells me about a matinee of *Swan Lake* that she invited me to when Gaby got the flu, which I have no recollection of. Apparently, it was memorable. Not in a nice way—the principal ballerina broke her leg. We had dinner after, finished a bottle of wine, and talked about how the older we got, the less we saw our friends. That time changes everything.

What catches my attention is her observation that we're both quick with numbers. She picked that up the first time we split a dinner check. She said we had stuff in common. Apparently, I mentioned a month ago that I was unhappy and was about to make a life change. If it worked out, I would tell her what it was when the time came.

Could that change have involved the Cassiopeia?

I just listen to her talk. I'm caught off guard when she says, "Don't misunderstand, I've got tons of pals and lunchmates. Those friendships only go so far. You know what I mean? But you and me, because I found you after your accident, we now have a *special bond*. So let's focus on you for the time being."

Something isn't right about her generosity. I hope like hell I'm wrong. I consider the odds. I'm in her home, I've met her children, and I have a history with her young daughter. That weighs in favor of Lorraine's credibility but doesn't tip the scales all the way.

Too many permutations, too many uncertainties: the unidentifiable caller, the mysterious would-be kidnapper, my mother's life at stake, Mark Burns dead, John Brownsworth still unknown, Lorraine Baglietti finds me. A thousand more possibilities.

Enemies keep their adversaries close. Until they have what they want. Then they dispose of them. Is that why Burns is dead? Served his purpose, now out of the way?

I'm in a quandary. But I force those doubts aside. I need to get to Sag Harbor. I don't exactly know how to ask. But I also can't hold back. "I would love to get out to the Hamptons, away from the city."

She studies my face. "I would be up for that. Might be safer for you too. If you don't mind though, before I get cramped up in a car, I would like to stretch my legs before we leave, go for my morning walk in the park."

Her leaving could be some kind of setup. I might be paranoid, but I'm not taking the chance. "If you don't mind, I could use a stretch myself," I say. "I'm supposed to keep the blood flowing. My doctors say living life and exercise will help me remember the past."

She frowns. "Think that's a good idea, you going out?"

I made it to the diamond district perfectly fine. I'm not staying here alone. Parks are public places. I can get away or shout for help if I have to.

"There's tons of people around; cops are on horseback. We'll be fine."

27

Lorraine and I head down East 90th Street and enter Central Park at the crosswalk near the Guggenheim Museum. We continue past the Jackie Kennedy Reservoir and walk along the Shuman Running Track.

"Nice morning for a stroll," she says. "Sunny skies and enough breeze to fight off the heat."

I pull the air deep inside my lungs. Just the simple act of getting out of her place reinvigorates me, makes me feel more trusting.

"I've been inside so much I've forgotten what it's like to be outside," I say.

"I love Central Park," she says. "No other city has a park that compares. Has a little of everything."

"I recognize the landmarks."

"Awesome." She smiles. "Who can forget paradise, right?"

We don't speak again until the tennis courts come into view.

"Do you play tennis?" she asks. "We never talked about that."

I swing my arm as if striking a ball. "I don't think so. But who knows, I could get on the court and turn out to be a champion, the way things are going."

"I'm a terror out on the courts," she says.

We share a laugh.

Something metallic squeaks behind us. The sound of gravel crunches and gets louder. I look back. So does Lorraine. Someone is racing toward us on a bicycle.

"Jesus, what an asshole," Lorraine says. "We have the right of way."

She holds her ground, which causes me to do the same.

The cyclist's head is down, but I can see the rider is a man. He's wearing a cycling suit, goggles, a helmet, and gloves. He's not slowing down.

"Watch out!" I holler, both to him and Lorraine.

He closes in on us, not slowing down but speeding up.

I pull Lorraine to the side at the last instant.

"Watch it, asshole!" she shouts. "Like, what the hell?"

The man looks back and, in that brief moment, his front tire collides with a root sticking up from an overgrown sycamore tree. He loses control of the bike but struggles to keep it upright. His handlebars wobble and, a split second later, he's thrown off. The bike slides off the path and into the woods. The man groans and writhes in pain.

"Oh my God, he's hurt," I say and start after him.

"Wait!" Lorraine shouts and follows me.

When we reach the man, he rolls to his knees, pulls out a Glock 20 SF Semi-Auto pistol, and points it at my chest.

28

Through the panic and fear, I wonder: How do I know the make and model of his gun?

I feel myself leaning forward to attack him, but I stop, because if he's any good with that thing he'll kill me.

"We don't want trouble," Lorraine says, shakily. "Take my money and go." She reaches for her fanny pack and pulls out her cash.

The man scrambles to his feet. He's short, stocky. Not tall, not thin. His hair isn't silver. "Don't move a muscle," he says. A southern accent. There's no doubt he'll shoot if we cross him. I can see that from his cold eyes. "Hands above your heads and clasp them together."

I do as he asks, but when Lorraine doesn't move, he brandishes his weapon. I turn my head and glance at her.

"Eyes forward, Blue!" he says.

My blood runs cold. I look at Lorraine. Her eyes are the size of dinner plates. She can't be faking that reaction.

The cyclist motions with the gun toward the woods. "You, Blue. Start walking toward me, slowly." To Lorraine, he says, "Turn around."

"Leave her alone," I say to the gunman. "She has nothing to do with this."

"Turn around and start walking," he says to Lorraine. "Don't look back if you want to live."

She hesitates.

"Please listen to him," I say. "Think of your kids."

He grabs my arm and pulls me into the woods. Lorraine stands there, not moving.

"Go! Now!" the man shouts at Lorraine.

I try to keep an eye on her. She backs off. Then she turns and runs away. I pray she's going to get help.

The cyclist guides me deeper inside the woods, where the trees are dense. I have no choice but to go. A gun barrel is pressed against my back. I struggle to breathe, gulping air.

"Faster," the man growls. The brush is thick. There's no avoiding the branches. With each slap of a twig or limb, my anger intensifies. So does my desperation.

I turn back to the man. "I don't have the Cassiopeia."

He looks at me in momentary surprise, then chortles. His white teeth flash. He shoves me forward, and I stumble. "Keep moving."

More rage builds inside me, now burning white hot. My chest is pounding so hard that my heartbeat is pulsing inside my ears. A branch slaps me in the face and snaps back at me a second time, startling a bird, which screeches and takes evasive action.

And just like that, so do I. I no longer own my body. In one fluid motion, I whirl around, grab the barrel of the gun, and push it away. At the same time, I grab the handle with my free hand—an excellent redirect of the assailant's weapon. No, almost perfect, because the gun falls to the ground.

The goon and I struggle for the weapon. He's far too strong. I scream. Then there's a heavier weight on us.

The man wails in pain.

Someone wraps an arm around his neck and is now clawing at his eyes and cheeks with long, garish-red fingernails. I gasp. Lorraine!

I manage to escape from the man's grasp, put some distance between us, and crawl on my knees for the gun.

The man shoves Lorraine hard to the ground, hollers, "Bitch!" and runs into the woods.

Now, I'm the one holding the weapon, poised to shoot. My body no longer trembles. I grip the gun tight and start to squeeze the trigger.

"Don't, Blue!" Lorraine screams. "There are innocent bystanders in the park."

I lower the gun. I could've fired—would have, but for Lorraine's admonition.

"Let's go," she says.

"Jesus, Lorraine, why did you come back? He could've killed you."

"I'm a New Yorker. No one's going to fuck with a friend of mine."

I don't move, only stand there with the gun in my hand. "Who am I, Lorraine?"

She takes the weapon, using the edge of her T-shirt to keep her fingerprints off it, obviously. She slides the weapon into the fanny pack. She takes my arm and urges me back toward the trail.

Sirens sound in the distance. Lorraine actually had time to call 911?

Two police motorcycle cops appear. Lorraine gives the officers a description of our attacker. I stand stupefied. She doesn't give the gun to the cop. I say nothing.

"We're going after him," an officer says. "A patrol car is waiting at the entrance to the park. Head that way."

On the way, she doesn't speak. She's moving so fast I get

winded. And I thought I was in better shape than this. "Can we slow down?" I gasp.

"How did that guy know your name?"

"Good question. I have no idea."

"This whole thing is fucking crazy."

"I almost got you killed." Then I notice that her pants are torn, and her leg is dribbling blood. "Lorraine, your leg."

She wipes the blood off her pants but never stops moving. "It's nothing. A little scratch, that's all."

Hardly. Nothing today has been a little scratch.

29

Lorraine and I make our way to the waiting patrol car. The officer drives us to the 20th Precinct, where we're greeted by, of all people, Detective Matteo DeLuca and his annoying partner, Jerry Roudebusch.

"Too late and twenty bucks short," Lorraine says. "You two are a couple of Keystone Cops."

"How did you two get here so fast?" I ask DeLuca.

"Early to the station, late to the scene of the crime," Lorraine says.

"Watch your mouth, ma'am," Roudebusch says.

"We were in the area," DeLuca explains. "As soon as the incident was called in, we hightailed it over. The question is, why are you two out walking around, not safe at home?"

"It's broad daylight, Detective," Lorraine says. "Listen, this whole thing with Blue has gotten way out of hand. We almost got killed back there in the park. Like, *murdered*! It's your job to find these people, to protect her and her poor mother, and you two haven't done shit."

Well, that's a relief. Lorraine is back to her old self. The woman I saw in the park was so different—so calm and capable. Does motherhood do this to a woman? It all seems impossible to me. But we never know what someone is capable of until put to the test. And my own actions—unexplainable.

DeLuca shows us to a small conference room, where Lorraine and I recount the events as he takes notes. Roudebusch just sits and stares at us.

When DeLuca sets his pen down, he pushes back his chair, folds his arms, and looks at me. "Do you want to tell me how you were able to disarm your assailant?"

I knew this question was coming. "I wish I could."

"I never saw anyone move like Blue did," Lorraine says.

I look over at her. "You saw it?"

"The good part."

This doesn't make sense. The timing is off. When I took the gun from my assailant, she was nowhere in sight. I look at DeLuca and give a helpless shrug. Now isn't the time to clash with Lorraine. The fact is, I can't explain my behavior—not when I don't understand it myself. Besides, the attack came on so fast.

"Sounds like you had formal training in martial arts," Roudebusch says.

I shrug again. I have no idea.

"The guy knew Blue's name," Lorraine says.

"Same voice as the caller?" DeLuca asks me.

"No. The man on the phone sounded older, and he didn't have much of an accent, I couldn't place him. This one from the park sounded younger, like he might've been from the south, but his accent wasn't strong."

"Perhaps you work in some intelligence role, in security for the private sector?" Roudebusch asks me.

"I don't recall," I reply, frustrated by questions that I don't have the answer to.

"How about a private organization that could make use of

these skills?" Roudebusch asks. "Maybe a foreign government?"

I know what he's implying. That I'm a spy or a criminal. "I'm sure that I don't work for any such organization or another government, but I don't know why. I'm doing my best here. Don't you understand that?"

Roudebusch scoffs.

DeLuca holds up a hand to his partner. "Take it easy, Jerry."

"How about telling us who the hell that cyclist was who came after us," Lorraine says. "Do that and we find these guys. Figure this out."

"If what Lorraine here says is true, someone trained you how to disarm an aggressor," DeLuca says. "This man wasn't simply a purse snatcher."

"No, he wasn't," Lorraine adds. "I thought we were goners, but this girl is like superwoman."

"I'm no superwoman," I say. "I'm a victim and a target of killers."

Roudebusch glares at me. DeLuca looks uncertain. What a change in DeLuca's demeanor since that box of caramels.

"I wish I could be more helpful," I add.

DeLuca doesn't say anything. Neither does his mouthy partner. They both stare at me.

"You want me to make something up?" I snap. "It was a reflex. I don't know how I took that gun. Maybe I took a self-defense course. Maybe my parents, whoever and wherever they are, took me to martial arts as a kid. Maybe I watch too many superhero movies. Who knows? I'm obviously a woman who learned how to protect herself. Probably a *single* woman, based on what we know, which is all the more reason to learn self-defense. But look how much good it did for me the night of the fall. Not much. It doesn't make me a criminal. If it did, you'd have to arrest all the women capable of protecting themselves." I'm too defensive, running at the mouth and unable to stop myself.

Roudebusch leans forward, a snide look on his face. "What are the Feds going to discover about you, I wonder?"

"That someone is trying to kill me," I say. "Wants something that I don't have. Threatened to kill my mother. Did you forget that?"

"Are you a criminal, Blue?" Roudebusch persists.

"You didn't just say that!" Lorraine rasps. "Jesus, I've heard of good-cop/bad-cop, but you guys are too obvious. This is a shit-show."

"Ms. Baglietti, I'm going to ask you to leave if you don't keep quiet," DeLuca says. "Now, let's all take a breath."

"You both will be hearing from my lawyer for police harassment of Blue," Lorraine says.

I raise my arms and pound the table. "Please stop. All of you. Detective Roudebusch, your questions are offensive. And, Detective DeLuca, you're no better. You're both treating me like I'm a criminal when *I'm* the one who was attacked. Lorraine and I are the victims."

DeLuca's eyes widen and he tightens his jaw. Roudebusch crosses his arms and flashes a mean smile. His expression hardens, which sends a current of anger through me. Why isn't DeLuca standing up for me?

I stand and grip the edge of the table. "Am I a suspect for something?"

"No," DeLuca says.

"But you are a person of interest," Roudebusch adds.

"Excuse me, but I'm the victim," I say. "Come up with a better ploy, Detective Roudebusch." Nothing's funny, but I can't restrain the laughter that spills from me. It's harsh and echoes round the room. For a second, I don't recognize my own voice.

Roudebusch looks like he's going to say something, but

he just closes his mouth.

DeLuca's shoulders slump. "All right, Blue, I have a—"

I raise a hand. "Don't tell me you have a job to do, Detective."

"You should seriously consider protective custody," DeLuca says. "That's what innocent victims do when offered that opportunity."

I won't be someone's prisoner. "Am I free to go?"

"I would say you are," Lorraine interjects. "The authorities shouldn't be treating us like we're common criminals."

DeLuca clamps his eyes shut. Is he holding back his ire or playing us? Then he looks up at me. "I can't guarantee your safety out there."

"She knows something," Roudebusch says. "What are you hiding?"

"Let's go, Blue," Lorraine repeats. "I'll look after you." We stand, and she links her arm through mine and turns us toward the door. "I need a Band-Aid."

When DeLuca's chair scrapes against the floor, my skin crawls.

"One more thing, Ms. Bishop," DeLuca says.

I turn back.

"Keep me informed of your whereabouts. Call and report in. Where you are, what you're doing."

"You have no right to give her rules, especially because you haven't kept her out of harm's way," Lorraine says. "My lawyer, who'll be her lawyer soon, will make sure you cops don't overreach. *I'll* keep her safe for now. Let's get out of here."

"I thought you were on my side," I say to DeLuca.

"We're not the enemy here, Blue," DeLuca says. "We're only trying to help you."

How much will these cops want to help me if they find out I'm a criminal?

30

Tuesday midday, Lorraine and I walk away from the 20th Precinct. DeLuca seems to be all over this town, and I can't put a pin in exactly which precinct he normally works out of. I prefer DeLuca when he isn't with his partner, Roudebusch. That man grates on my nerves. Least of my worries. The real question is, why are these two cops pushing to place me in protective custody? Might be the wise choice for most people, but I'm not about to sit behind locked doors. I'm going to Sag Harbor. DeLuca and his partner are turning out to be empty suits. If the police can't do their job, I'll have to.

Lorraine stops at the street corner and whistles. A moment later, a taxi pulls up, and we hop inside. She gives the driver the address of a restaurant in Little Italy called Uncle Gino's.

"Really? You can eat after all that?" I ask. "I've lost whatever appetite I had."

"You never have one, or never give into it. Me, I think better with a full stomach." Then she goes on to lecture me about the top Italian restaurants in New York *and* Rome.

When we arrive at the restaurant, it's like we've been thrown back to a time fifty years ago. Dark red velvet booths and cheesy old-school chandeliers line both sides of the seating area. Tables with linen cloths fill the center and a round table for the special guests sits at the rear. The hostess greets Lorraine by name and shows us to a booth—despite the number of people on the waiting list.

"I recommend the gnocchi," Lorraine says. "But all the entrees are delicious. All the pasta is handmade."

"I'm happy to try the gnocchi." Why not? It's as good a food to stare at as any.

She sits back against the velvet cushion of the bench and glances across the room. I follow her line of sight to a table of men at the circular table. They aren't the type of men who like to be noticed, but they unquestionably notice her. Some of the younger guys leer, but the older guys elbow them and whisper something, and the leering turns to dignified smiles and nods of deference. Then there are waves of the hand that she welcomes.

"I see you're a regular," I say.

She grins, relaxed. "I've been coming here since I was a little girl."

"I hope we weren't followed."

She guffaws. "Honey, anyone who walks in that front door and looks at us sideways, they won't get far. That includes the cops. We're safe. And I'll tell you another thing. Whoever attacked us made a mistake. They pissed off my family."

A waitress who appears to be long past retirement age stops at our table. "Hey, Lorraine."

"Hey, Lucille. Blue, Lucille. A new friend, meet an old friend."

Lucille smiles. "Should I tell your uncle you're here?"

"Yeah, tell him. Me and my friend here will have the Gnocchi Alfredo."

"I'll bring you both some sparkling water."

Lorraine pulls out her phone. "Give me a second, Blue. I need to let George in on the plans."

While she texts, I sit restlessly, still buzzing from everything that's happened so far today. The waitress brings the food and water.

Lorraine puts her phone down. "Kids. Always something. So go on, Blue, taste it. Best frickin' gnocchi in the world. And that includes Italy. Homemade pasta, and Uncle Gino imports his spices from the Old Country."

I take a bite. It's delicious. I nod in approval.

Lorraine beams. "What did I tell you? The taste of family and home."

Without warning, tears stream down my cheeks. I mistrusted Lorraine, maybe still do, but I don't have another friend. And DeLuca is drifting farther away, becoming accusatory. Shouldn't trust him either.

"Aw, honey, I feel the same way when I take a bite of Uncle Gino's gnocchi." Then she understands. "Oh my, have I got a big mouth. Sorry."

I wipe my face with my napkin, laughing through the tears. "I'm sorry."

"I understand how you feel. I had postpartum depression after Angelo. That's bad, but at least I had my memory. In fact, I'll never forget it, I wish I had amnesia on that. Anyway, this isn't about me, it's about you, Blue. I'll say this, if there's a God in the heavens above us, which I believe there is, your mother is being watched over."

A man comes alongside the table and says in a thick Brooklyn-Italian accent, "How's my favorite niece?"

Lorraine laughs. "You say that to all your nieces, Uncle."

The man is short and lean for someone who's around delicious food all the time. He's wearing a chef's jacket and a pair of black slacks; all that's missing is the tall white hat. His cheeks are puffy, almost chipmunk-like, and his smile is welcoming. But there's also an unidentifiable depth to his eyes, a depth that must hide a lot of dark secrets. I've seen eyes like that before, always in bad people. I guess I've been around bad people.

Lorraine sweeps a hand above the table. "When I'm sitting here with a plate of gnocchi, I haven't got a complaint in the world, Uncle Gino."

"No hugs? Not a kiss?"

She hops up and gives him a quick hug and kiss. "Sorry, we've had a day."

When she sits back down, he turns my way. "How you doing, miss? I'm Gino, the owner of this establishment."

"Uncle Gino, this is my friend Blue Bishop," Lorraine says. "Blue, this is Gino Camponeschi, restaurateur extraordinaire."

I grin.

He smiles back, but it's a smile that is also a warning. "Delighted to make your acquaintance, Blue. How's the gnocchi? Made it myself."

"It's the best I've ever had."

He nods in approval as Lorraine says, "Listen, I hate to ask but I need a favor, Uncle Gino." She gives him the short version of what's happened.

He glances at me again. Then to Lorraine, he says, "Anything, sweetheart. But I don't like to hear that you hate to ask. You should ask me whenever you need something."

"I would like to use your guesthouse in South Hampton. It would be best to get Blue out of the city for a while. I can't let her stay at my house now. You know, the kids."

"You need me to talk to some people?"

"We don't know who they are. Yet."

He gives a knowing tip of the head and squeezes

Lorraine's shoulder. "I'll get you the key." He turns and walks to the back of the restaurant.

"I'm happy to stay in a hotel," I say. Although I don't know how I would pay for it if Lorraine doesn't lend me the money.

"Nonsense. Uncle Gino's place is secure. Top-notch. And our summer home is only a few miles away. Gets you where you want to go, will give you time to remember. Especially to remember what the heck that Cassiopeia is. You can thank me later for getting you out of danger. First, we got to do just that."

I'm not out of danger. Neither is my mother. I consider the offer. It's one thing taking favors from Lorraine, who's apparently a friend, but it's quite another taking them from her uncle, a total stranger.

"Stop your worrying, Blue," she says, apparently reading my mind. "The second I feel uncomfortable, I'll tell you."

"Why are you helping me? I know what you said earlier, but I feel like there's something more to it."

"I guess you could say I have a nurturing nature. Don't laugh, but I once took a squirrel Gaby found lying on the ground with a broken leg to the vet, paid the bill, and made house calls on the varmint with Gaby."

"That's sweet."

"With Gaby's consent, the vet released the little bugger inside Central Park." She shakes her head, amused. "Picture that, me making an animal contribution to a park full of squirrels."

"What else? What aren't you saying?"

"Ah. Really?" She turns away, sighs, and then meets my eyes. "Blue, you saved my life."

I gaze at her in disbelief. Another memory lost.

"I can see by the look on your face you don't remember that, either."

Of course I don't remember.

"When we first met, I'd dropped Gabriella off for her dance class, and you'd come out of yours. I didn't know you. We'd said 'Hi' and all, like you do with strangers who you meet over and over again in the same place."

I nod.

"I took off to grab a coffee down the street," she continues. "You left at the same time. We didn't walk together. I got to the crosswalk, not paying much attention because I live in the city and getting around is sort of instinctual."

"So I'm clear, we didn't leave together?"

She shakes her head. "The light changed to walk. I was a couple of steps into the street. A car came speeding out of nowhere. I never heard it or saw it. I walked right into its path. If you hadn't jumped out and pulled me back, I would have been hit."

I gasp. "How could I have forgotten this?"

She shrugs. "I remember people screaming, you grabbing my arm, me looking up at those headlights, us falling back on the sidewalk. It was like nothing I'd ever been through before. You were like some kind of superwoman."

"I'm sure I wasn't superwoman."

"There were plenty of folks on that corner, closer to me than you were. No one else bothered. You were brave."

I'm stupefied. "Why didn't you tell me this earlier?"

"Ah, you know. Didn't want to make it appear like I was paying off a debt. I am, but it's not only that."

"You've gone way beyond nurturing. Any time you want me to leave, I'll understand. You've got more important obligations than looking after me."

"That's why I'll put you up at Uncle Gino's place. You saved my ass; I'm trying to save yours. Call it a mutual bond." She gives me a stern look, an expression I haven't seen before, and says, "Take a good look around you. You *are* safe. You really think Uncle Gino would give me the keys if he didn't know what you did for me?"

There's something comforting, even familiar, about being under the umbrella of powerful people. I realize now, putting any doubt about her aside, that if anyone can help me, it's Lorraine. I have to take a leap of faith.

"I need to do some digging around, see if I can figure out what this Cassiopeia really is."

"If we start at square one and take it forward, we'll figure it out. Don't worry, hon. Lorraine Baglietti can work miracles with a computer."

31

The ride out to the Hamptons that Tuesday afternoon, over long stretches of highway and island vegetation, is a pleasant break from city noise and concrete buildings. Lorraine and I don't talk much, and I enjoy the silence. I would never have imagined she could stay quiet for so long.

By the time we arrive in Southampton, the sun is lower in the sky. The days are slipping away fast. Time is running short. She navigates down Hill Street and out to Captains Neck Lane, and we pass through a secured gate and drive to the end of the road. A mansion with magnificent gardens, surrounded by water on three sides, comes into view. The only way in and out of here is through the gates or by water.

I take a deep breath. "This place is spectacular," I say. I don't ask if Gino is also a trust-fund beneficiary, or if he's someone more nefarious. I would avoid stereotypes even if I hadn't been thrown out a hotel window and if someone hadn't threatened to kill my mother and me.

"This was my aunt Carla's dream house," Lorraine says. "The cancer got her a couple of years ago."

"Oh, I'm sorry."

"Gino has never been the same. He won't come out here except for business, but he can't bring himself to sell it. Even though he's got no kids. I'm an only child, so it was easy to spend tons of time with my aunt and uncle. They could invite only me over without worrying about leaving anyone out. Kept the commotion down, my aunt would say, although she loved my cousins."

"Your uncle looks at you like you're his daughter."

"I have the honor of being the favorite. Don't tell my cousins if you ever meet them, though. They're jealous enough." She laughs loudly.

I make a zipper motion across my lips.

"Listen," Lorraine continues. "While you're at Uncle Gino's place, it'll feel like a vacation. You need one. There are cameras everywhere, so if any trespassers decide to pop in, this place will light up like the Fourth of July. Don't wig out if you see a couple guys pushing wheelbarrows. There's a full-time gardening and maintenance staff. They're very talented in other ways, too." She gives me a meaningful look.

I thank Lorraine for all she's doing for me. We get out of the car and head inside the guesthouse. It's like a mansion in itself, with a fully stocked kitchen, a living area, several bedrooms, a gym, and a wine cellar. Unlike at a typical beach house, the furnishings are traditional, antique reproductions; the color palettes for curtains and the upholstery are mostly deeper shades of red and green, not the beachy, white contemporary style.

Once I'm settled in, we head back outside for a walk around the grounds. The sounds of birds and tree frogs intensify as the day wanes. Lorraine takes me through the rose garden, which is heavenly, and then we cut across the lawn toward the bay.

We stop at the shoreline and stare out at the water. The water lapping against the sand—nature's dance—calms me.

A boat engine roars from across the bay. It appears to be coming our way but then veers out to sea. There's a loud crack in the distance. I tense. But it's only the boat's engine backfiring.

I need to get to Sag Harbor.

"You know, I think if I could get out and drive, it'd help me," I say.

She looks at me askance.

"I'm not sure why. I just need to."

She hesitates. "There's a Porsche in the garage. Keys are in it. If you can wait until the morning, I'll join you."

I can't, and you won't.

"I've got to get going," she says. "Those kids of mine are probably driving George nuts. Giorgio goes to bed early, and if I'm not there to read him his bedtime story, he has a meltdown. Then there's George. He goes into a conniption fit. And there's dinner to think about. Everyone's getting takeout tonight. Do yourself a favor and order out, too. Make sure one of the groundskeepers gets the food."

"I'll do that."

"Another thing, you can connect your phone to the Wi-Fi. The password is Giorgio. I know, not very secure, but easy for me to remember. And if you want to use a computer, there's one in the study. It'll connect to the Wi-Fi automatically. Feel free to use it. Might help jog your memory."

We walk beyond the manor and head to the front driveway. For the first time, Lorraine looks tired. She gets inside her car, shuts the door, and rolls down the window. "Do yourself a favor—watch a comedy, and get some rest," she says.

I nod, try to smile. "I need a laugh."

"I'll call you sometime tomorrow. I've got a full schedule, but I'll try to get down as soon as I can to see how you're doing. Call me if you need anything. Oh …" She reaches for her purse and offers me a credit card. "I know you're in a state, but don't argue, just take it. You can pay me back. But don't go wild, otherwise George will think I've gone wacko." She laughs half-heartedly and starts the car.

I take the card. She reaches into her purse again and hands me a wad of cash. "That's five hundred dollars. For an emergency."

"Oh, Lorraine, it's not necessary. I have the credit card."

"Oh, yeah it is. My mother taught me that a girl should never be without some cash."

She reaches into her bag yet again and hands me a cell phone—the woman is like a magician in a circus act. "A spare. For emergencies. Not traceable."

Half an hour after she leaves, I'm in the car and driving toward Sag Harbor.

32

When I pull into Sag Harbor Yacht Club, the sun is about to set. Plenty of boats are pulling into slips, and others are heading out for a sunset cruise.

I walk to the dock house counter and the woman at the desk greets me.

"Hi," I say. "A friend is expecting me. I don't know which pier his boat is docked at. Can you help me?"

She appears perplexed. As if she's unsure whether she can give me the information.

"He is here, isn't he? John Brownsworth. I'm Blue Bishop."

Her expression eases. "Yes, he was. Let me check the books."

I watch her navigate her computer to the correct screen.

"Okay, right. I thought so," she says.

"I'm sorry?"

"He gave up his slip on the first of May."

My heart sinks. "Where did he go? There's a chance I wrote down the wrong address."

"Can't tell you. Doesn't have a forwarding address in his entry. Sorry."

"How long had he rented a slip here, before he left, do you know?"

"Couple of years." She lowered her voice. "Between you and me, these sailing fanatics move around when they get tired. Follow the crowd. We lost several this season. Gained more. There's always someone with a pending reservation. Is there anything else I can help you with?"

"Could I ask you a favor?"

"Sure, well, it depends."

"Would you do a quick search on your computer, just to see if his name comes up in the area?"

She thinks for a moment. "No problem." She searches. "I'm not getting John Brownsworth. Last address came up as here. How funny."

Maybe not.

"Best of luck," she says. I turn to leave, but she adds, "He used to talk about an Italian place in Southampton that makes a perfect cappuccino. I don't remember the name. Ask around. If you find the restaurant, you might find him or someone who knows him. Good luck."

"Thank you." I open the door and look back at her. "Oh, one more thing. What's your impression of John?"

"Pleasant man. One of those British regal types."

"Not Australian?"

"No. He's from London."

"Married?"

"Yep." She nods. "With kids."

So not a boyfriend—I hope. "Are you sure we're talking about the same man? He's tall, thin, sixtyish, silver hair. Sound right?"

"Yes."

"English?"

A look of suspicion crosses her face. I slip out the door before she regrets helping me.

The man in the park didn't have an English accent. Nor does the caller. I hope this means John and I are on the same side of this business affair with the Cassiopeia, and that finding him will help me neutralize the threat against my mother and me.

Back at the villa, I pull up a list of Italian restaurants in Southampton and start calling. Same answers at every one: "No reservation under the name Brownsworth tonight" and "I can't tell you whether he's been here, that would violate our privacy policy."

Frustrated, I do a search of Bishops in the area. No Blue Bishops, and too many other Bishops to call looking for my mother. I search for a history of Cassiopeia. Plenty on the constellation; nothing on the ruby.

The pre-amnesia me may have been at home with shady deals involving precious gems, vicious criminals, searches for elusive business partners, and threats against herself and her family. The current me is decidedly not.

Frazzled and exhausted, I go to bed.

33

I wake on Wednesday at the crack of dawn. Too early to go anywhere, but I can't get back to sleep. I just lie there in bed with my heart racing and my palms sweating. I can't think.

I throw on a blue sundress and head out of the house to walk it off. I find a grass-and-stone pathway on the estate surrounded by hedges and pass under a trellis bursting with purple flowers and swarming with honeybees collecting nectar and continue along until I come upon a hidden garden filled with white hydrangeas and lilacs in full bloom. I sit down on a bench in front of a small fishpond with a fountain in the middle.

Watching the goldfish swim and occasionally surface to catch a bug, I try to clear my mind, to unblock my imprisoned synapses. I hear the water from the bay lap against the shore, the birds and insects humming around me in the garden, and I relax.

A chickadee lands nearby and hops around on the lower branches of a maple tree. He's soon joined by a nuthatch. Buddies in nature, not territorial. Hummingbirds flit around the white hydrangeas. An image floats through my mind of an apartment decorated in soft whites. My apartment. Large, long windows, and plenty of light.

Then it's gone, and I can't call it back. My life is a book with a thousand holes poked through its pages, the voids slowly being filled with blank putty.

"It'll be a nice day for a swim," a voice behind me says.

I jump up, ready to defend myself.

"I'm sorry to have startled you, miss," a man says. "I'm Manuel, one of the gardeners." He's short and wiry, in his early forties, wearing a straw hat, work shirt, and slacks caked with soil. He's leaning on a rake. Yes, definitely one of the groundskeepers.

I shake off my fear. "Sorry. I didn't hear you. Lorraine did say gardeners would be around the property."

"Easy to get lost in your thoughts out here. The place is my paradise, too." He smiles proudly. "I am lucky to help maintain it. Our hydrangeas took first place in the Home Show last year."

"I can see why."

"It's a beautiful, hot day," he says. "You should take a dip in the pool. Cool off."

My forehead is damp with perspiration; in fact, most of my body is, although the morning air is still cool. I imagine immersing myself in the cool water. "Maybe I will," I say. But I can't. I don't have a bathing suit. Which is an excellent excuse to go to town and find a cappuccino. But Lorraine is coming down this morning, so I need to get away before she arrives.

When I return to the house, however, Lorraine is already sitting at the computer. I try to hide my surprise and disappointment.

After we greet each other, she gestures to the computer and asks, "Find anything on your Cassiopeia?"

"Not yet. I think I know every constellation in the sky, though. There's also a mega-software company called Cassiopeia, and an employment agency, and a handful of smaller businesses, and several book titles, and an art exhibition."

"What's that?" she asks, gesturing toward the journal Dr. Stallworth suggested I keep, which I've been writing in almost every day.

I walk to the desk, close the notebook, and set it aside before she can pick it up. "It's a journal of random thoughts. It's for Dr. Stallworth."

She shrugs, doesn't appear offended.

I pull a chair up beside hers.

"So, how about we focus on Greek history? See if there are any clues to help us figure out what you're looking for." She begins working on the computer again.

While she works, I listen to a gentle clinking of bells—a wind chime somewhere in the garden. The sweet sounds remind me of a jewelry box I had as a child. A dancing ballerina popped up and twirled when the box opened. I recall the jeweled necklace I wore the night of the fall, and I reach for my décolletage. Why hasn't DeLuca learned anything more about the necklace?

Lorraine stops typing. "Okay, so here's my impression from banging around on these keys. We're not going to find anything on the Cassiopeia sifting through the up-and-up internet."

"What do you mean? What should we do instead?"

"Ever hear of TOR? It's a web browser that gets you inside the dark web."

Of course I've heard of the dark web, but I don't admit it. Communications on the dark web are completely secure—the beauty and danger of that platform. People can't see where information is coming from or going to. It's like a hermetically sealed door. Not even the tiniest digital ant can crawl inside without a key. How I know this, but not the name or location of my own mother, is beyond me.

"So let's have a look," I say.

She gives me the once-over and goes back to work. I pace the room. She glances back at me but doesn't say I'm annoying her. I'll leave the room if she does. I can't sit still.

Sometime later, she quits typing and spins around in her chair. She punches several more keys and then removes her fingers from the keyboard as if it's sizzling.

"What?"

"I've got an unusual history here. Might freak you out."

"By all means, lay it out."

"In 1490, Queen Isabella and King Ferdinand of Spain were rumored to have come into possession of a powerful stone—"

"What kind of stone?"

She pauses and eyes me.

Enough with the dramatic pauses, Lorraine.

"A ruby." Another dramatic pause. She studies me.

I sigh inwardly. *The one time I wish she would talk.*

"It was said to have magical powers, a thing of legends." She laughs.

I want to laugh too. Because how far-fetched is that?

She continues, "However, it's not a cursed stone, but a good luck charm. Seems it worked for Izzy and Ferdy. They came into possession of the stone right about the time Columbus 'discovered' America and the monarchs expelled the Muslims and Jews."

"Interesting history."

"That's not all. In 1497, John, Prince of Asturias, Isabella and Ferdinand's only son, was traveling to Portugal for his older sister's wedding. He was bringing the ruby as a wedding gift. Stopping over in the city of Salamanca, the prince died suddenly—of tuberculosis, some said; of sexual over-exertion, said others."

"Odd."

"Yeah, well, a few speculate that he was murdered for the jewel, which disappeared."

"That sounds believable."

"From there, it seems the ruby passed through a lot of different hands. A couple of popes. The Borghese family of Italy had it for a while. The Italians and the Spanish waged a secret war over it. People have been poisoned and executed, la de da."

And someone tried to kill me, *is* trying to kill me, for it.

She continues without stopping for a breath. "In 1610, a commoner stole it from an Italian count. The count was having an affair with the wife of a Venetian Prince. The count's valet deftly stole the jewel from the count while the aristocrats were in bed together. The thief took off north. The jewel was said to have passed through Prussian royalty. Then a peasant girl found the ruby after it fell out of the princess's pocket during a horseback ride."

Now I laugh. "From riches to rags."

"Wait, so the peasant girl, in a stroke of good luck, married a prince and herself became a princess. After that the stone disappeared again, it washed up on the shore at the Cliffs of Dover."

When she finally pauses, I say, "And then it sunk to the bottom of the sea, *Titanic*-style."

"Maybe, but supposedly it surfaced again and here in America in the 1800s, got traded and then lost—no one really knows the details. Then, in the 1970s, it resurfaced. Secret society stuff about it in the 80s. Then nothing—that's all I could find."

"That's crazy. I'm afraid to ask, but is there anything else?" And maybe there was some actual history in this little summation, but there's no way any of this could be more than a fairy tale.

"Anyone who comes into possession seems to have remarkable good luck, and then it slips away from them," she adds. "Almost like the magic genie has granted the wish and moves on."

I stifle the disbelief and try not to scoff. "So why do people think that I have it?"

"A very good question," she says.

Her words stab like a sharp blade. She folds her hands in her lap and sits staring at me. The silent stare of this garrulous woman is unnerving. Why is she cornering me, expecting me to give an explanation that I just don't have?

"I don't know what to tell you, Lorraine."

"Blue, you and I know something ain't right. No one goes around threatening to kill moms for no reason. Or drops a good-looking woman out a hotel window. Or tries to kidnap the same woman when she doesn't die. I don't want to sound mean or doubt you, Blue, but look at yourself."

"What do you mean?"

"You're talented with numbers, so you say. I know that. You were private—secretive, even—about all your affairs, when I knew you before. Except I didn't really know you. Seems like no one does."

I turn away a moment.

"I might just be your only friend, sister. So I'll say this straight. If you got that Cassiopeia Ruby, you're into something real serious."

That's a given.

"I'm sorry to say it, but something real criminal," she says. "Given what you say about your ability with numbers, if you ask me, I think you make deals. Launder money."

"What?"

She raises her hands as if surrendering. "I'm sure you've

guessed about my family history. So, you know, no judgment here."

She's said exactly what I think. What I fear most. "And yet. I have no recollection of laundering money. Be a hell of a lot more helpful if I did."

"Yeah."

"I'm not offended by what you're saying. I've wondered the same thing. But we both know it's also conjecture. There's no proof I'm a criminal."

"That may be true. But that's not all I found. Someone listed the Cassiopeia for sale. And not on the open market."

34

At noon, Lorraine gets a phone call from her kids. Her son, Tobia, the fourteen-year-old who's usually more mature, has taken a fall and wants only his mother. Lorraine flies out at warp speed.

I call DeLuca to ask if he's got any more info on the provenance of my necklace and whether someone has tried to fence it. He doesn't pick up. I leave a message. Half an hour later, I'm driving toward town and, as much as I want to put the top down and gun the accelerator, I refrain. Fast drivers draw attention.

I park off Main Street and walk to a bathing suit store in a small shopping village on Jobs Lane.

A clerk approaches me with a welcoming smile. "Can I help you?"

"Have you worked here long?" I ask.

"Couple years."

"I've had an accident. Memory problems. I wonder, can you tell me if you've ever seen me in here before?"

She looks me over. "Hmm. I'm sorry. We get so many people during the summer months."

I think for a moment, then try again: "Do you keep customer names in your computer? My name is Blue Bishop."

"We try to. Let me check." She taps a few keys and looks up at me. "Actually you were in last year. B. Bishop, if that's you. Big cash purchase. Lapis blue bikini, sandals, cover up."

"Is there an email address for me?"

"Just the name."

I force a smile. "You don't share your customer information, do you?"

"Gosh, no. I would get fired. People out here tend to be very private. Lots of celebs pass through. They sure don't want the paparazzi knocking on their doors or sniffing them out."

"Makes sense. Where's an Italian place in town that makes that perfect cappuccino?"

"A lot of places around here, actually."

"I'm searching for a friend. He goes on about the perfect cappuccino. My memory is the problem."

"You might be thinking of Sant Ambroeus. It's on Main Street. They sell great gelato as well."

I remember driving past the place last night. I peek at the clock on the wall. It's almost one thirty. Most of the lunch crowd will be gone.

"Are you looking for anything else today?" the clerk asks.

"Yes." I set my purse on the counter, go to the rack, and select a one-piece, which I hold up in front of me. Not glamorous, but it'll do.

"There's a matching cover up," she says as a group of five young women and a man come inside the store. The crowd makes me nervous. I skip the cover up and pay for the suit with cash—which leaves no trail. "Can you leave my name off the transaction?"

"No problem."

I exit the shop, toss my bag in the car, and start walking toward the restaurant.

Footsteps beat hard and fast behind me. A rush of fear comes over me, but I turn back to see the girl from the bathing suit shop. "You forgot your phone. It must've fallen out of your bag. The man in the store picked it up at the counter and handed it to me. Thought it belonged to you."

"Thank you. You've been so kind."

She turns and quickly heads back to the store.

As I walk toward Main Street, the phone rings. Lorraine must've discovered that I left the compound. She's like a mother hen.

"Sant Ambroeus, the Italian restaurant on Main Street," a man with an actor's voice says. My body goes cold. I know that voice. "Come now. Alone."

I glance at the phone. It's not mine.

"How will I know you?" I say into the phone, trying to stop my voice from shaking.

"I'll find you."

Now or never.

35

This is my opportunity to negotiate my mother's safety. To explain my situation. To make this man understand that he can have the ruby—when I remember where it is. I know I should call DeLuca. No time. The local police perhaps? No. They'll botch it up. The man will run.

The restaurant is jam-packed. So much for lunch hour calming down. People are milling around, waiting to be seated. It's not just this restaurant that's hopping; the whole town is flooded with people. Tourists and locals in perpetual motion fill the sidewalks, streets, stores, and restaurants. Cars are moving so slowly it's a wonder that people bother to get behind the wheel. Crowds and activity give me a sense of security. Of anonymity. False, probably, but I embrace the feeling anyway.

At the restaurant, I walk pass the alfresco diners out front and make my way inside, dodging patrons and waitstaff. I skip the hostess, don't ask for a table, but go to the standing counter in the middle of the restaurant. There are no tables in this area. People just stand and drink coffees or order pastries to go. I order a double cappuccino and remain at the bar, stealing glances toward the front and back of the restaurant.

I remember this place. The linen curtains, the photographs from Clifford Ross's Hurricane collection.

My drink arrives, and I nearly drop it when I notice a man at a back table watching me. He's older, in his late fifties or early sixties. His hair is a silvery-gray, and he's fit and lean. I know the face, but not the person.

He tilts his head slightly, an invitation to join him.

Not taking my eyes off him, I set my cup down and approach.

"Sit down, won't you, Blue?" the man says when I reach him.

My first impulse is to run, but I force myself to be calm and pull out a chair. I'm still holding the phone from the shop, and I slide it across the table to him.

He looks me over like he owns me. My skin burns.

Be brave.

"I don't recall your name," I say. "Would you mind telling me?" *Did I ever know it?*

"The Cassiopeia Ruby. My property. Where is it?"

"I don't have it. Have a question for you. Why did you push me out a four-story window?"

"Accident."

"That makes no sense."

His eyes remain fixed, indifferent. "Where I come from, a person's word reigns supreme. We had a deal. You were paid. You failed to deliver."

"I don't remember anything."

He opens his phone and shows me a photograph of an older woman who resembles me. A shock runs through me. I know her—my mother. She's wearing my necklace. The one that went missing the night of the fall. I immediately understand the threat this man is making. "You kill her or me, and you'll never get your stone," I say.

He rests his hands on the table and leans forward. "Ah, but if I kill her, I will have the satisfaction of wounding someone who broke her word to me. And if I kill you, I will have the satisfaction of knowing that you won't get the stone, either."

"Why did the deal fall apart? I must've said something."

"Because you're a fraud. You never had the stone."

"I did have it. I picked it up. I don't remember where I put it. I swear to you, the ruby is real. My memories are coming back, but very slowly. I can't control the speed of it, and I wouldn't be sitting here now trying to convince you of this if it wasn't the truth. If it's the money, you can have it back. As soon I figure out what account it's in. I don't remember that either."

He sits back in his chair, folds his arms across his chest, and smirks. "You tried that already. It won't work."

"Why wouldn't you take the money?"

"Because the stone is invaluable to me."

"If what you're saying is true, why did I renege?"

"Greed. Another buyer who made a better offer, maybe?"

I can't respond to that because I don't know. He has all the knowledge. This doesn't feel like something I would do, but on the other hand, none of this feels like something I would do. "It didn't happen that way."

"I'm afraid I don't believe anything you say."

"How can you say that? You found me in the hospital. You must know my condition. You keep threatening me. You follow me. You know exactly what's going on."

"This conversation is over." He takes the napkin from his lap, dabs his mouth, and starts to get out of his chair.

"Wait."

"It's time to take this matter up with my associate. He'll escort you out." Then looks over toward the coffee bar.

I follow his gaze. There's the bright reflection of sunlight off metal. A man in a Panama hat holds a gun judiciously tucked inside his suit jacket, aimed at me.

I glance back at my table companion. He's on his feet, towering above me. I look back at the gunman. I'm cornered. Less than a split second later, glass shatters behind us, a woman screams, and a picture falls from the wall. He must've fired, though I didn't hear the shot.

He could've shot me point blank. This was another warning.

I hunker down beside my chair and take cover beneath the level of the table and away from this man. I search for an exit.

The man beside me reaches down and grabs my arm hard before I can move. He yanks me upward. "You're coming with me. Quietly."

I throw my arm up, dislodge the man's grip, and break free. Crouched down, I start for the side door, looking in the direction where I saw the shooter. He's gone.

A woman is lying on the floor. Broken glass. Did a bullet strike her? I didn't hear a gunshot. Did the shooter use a silencer? The room is panicked. People are rushing to the woman's aid. In the confusion, I've managed to evade the man sitting at the table. I push through the side door of the restaurant and emerge into the alleyway to find alfresco diners. An alley—what a place to die.

36

I reach the sidewalk on Main Street and jaywalk to the other side as fast as I can without drawing attention to myself. I rush toward a group of women walking in the same direction I am and try to blend in.

As soon as I turn the corner, I break from the women and sprint away down the road, gasping for breath. When the Porsche is in sight, I stop. I need to get back to the safety of the compound, but a man is bent down, looking inside the car.

I turn abruptly and duck inside a knickknack store and watch out the front window.

"Can I help you find something?" a salesclerk asks.

"Just looking around," I say breathlessly. "If I need help, I'll let you know."

The clerk smirks and goes away.

Within a couple of minutes, the man standing beside my car starts to walk away but I don't break cover yet. Is he a curious tourist? Doubtful. There are a lot of nice cars in this area, and mine doesn't particularly stand out.

I turn around and, for cover, try to find something I can

buy. I find a floppy hat, a beach towel, and pair of rubber shoes. Perfect. I buy them, throw on the hat, wrap the towel around my shoulders to hide my dress, and slip into the shoes.

I return to the window. The man is gone. Or out of sight.

A group of tourists are crossing the street. I leave the store, blend in with the tourists, and cross the street with them. The Porsche is now on the opposite side of the street. I pretend to window shop, using the reflection in the glass to check around. The man still hasn't returned. I race to the car, get in, and ease out into traffic.

I've gone less than a block when a dark SUV makes a sharp turn at the corner behind me. Fast. The vehicle's license plates are red, not the New York yellow or dark blue. Whoever is driving that car is an out-of-towner.

My stomach flips. I make a sharp turn at the next corner and hit the gas.

I check the mirrors. The SUV is on my tail and gaining speed.

I downshift to build some torque, and then let the Porsche rip. The car does what it's built to do—haul ass. When the road splits between Hill Street and Jobs Lane, I veer left and continue a short distance down Jobs. I cut a sharp left on Pond Lane and drive past Agawam Park at 50 miles per hour, 60, 70, and faster.

The SUV stays with me.

There's a sharp bend in the road ahead. I hit the brakes and take the bend. As soon as the road straightens, ten kids or more dart into the road.

I slam the brakes and honk the horn, but the car can't stop in time. It's skidding. I finesse the steering wheel left, then right, to maintain control. But the car is hurtling toward a teenage girl who stands frozen in the middle of the street. A boy tries to pull her away, and now both kids are at risk.

There's no time to stop. The only option is a pond, a copse of trees, or a ditch.

I brace for impact and do the only sensible thing—steer the car toward the pond. There's a meager strip of land separating road from water. I pray the car doesn't flip. I'm airborne. The front end meets water. The jolt is hard, but the car levels out when the back end hits. The vehicle floats forward for several meters. Water rushes inside.

I tug and twist the seat belt, feeling a sharp pain in my left shoulder and elbow. Ignore it. I tug again, hard. I can't free my arm. I try the door with my other hand. It won't budge. I push harder, but the opposing force is too great. Water rises to my chest.

I fumble with shaking hands for the clasp to unbuckle my seat belt. I bump across the metal and pry at it with my fingers. I can't find the hinge. I try and try. Then a fingernail catches the edge. Finally, the seat belt unclips.

Murky, brown water fills the inside of the car. Only a bubble of air remains.

I turn my head from window to window, but I can't see. The rush of water is deafening. I gasp for air, the sound of my breathing like a shriek. My body trembles. I wait for the inevitable moment when the water forces the rest of the air out. I cry out for help, but who'll hear me?

No, no, no, no ... I can't die like this. Not after I survived that fall. It's not fair. I won't die like this. And, oh God, my mother ...

I twist my body as best I can and plant one solid foot on the door. I push with all that I have. It won't open. The water is up to my neck and creeping higher. I stretch my neck, gulping in air. The car is still sinking. Soon, I'll be completely underwater.

With only inches of air left, I take a breath, curl my body, and shove my weight against the door. The car pounds down hard at the bottom of the pond. The impact reverberates through my body, which rockets upward. My head slams against something hard, and my mind goes blank.

An image of the white-walled room invades my thoughts.

Then something hard strikes the side of the car, jolting my spine.

I must have passed out, but I'm awake again. Miraculously, I'm still holding my breath. I try the door again, using both hands. It opens. I swim up toward the light, reach the top, roll on my back, and float while I catch my breath. Then I turn, swim to shore, and drag myself onto land.

The teenagers run to me, bombarding me with questions.

A police car and ambulance arrive. Two paramedics jog over, carrying a medical kit. The officer speaks to the group of teenagers, their voices atwitter as they all speak at once.

"I'll be fine," I say to the paramedics.

But the EMTs insist on checking my pulse, taking my blood pressure, listening to my chest, and shining a light into my eyes.

Then a dark sedan pulls in behind the police cruiser and parks. A plainclothes officer gets out of the car. He tugs at his tie. Detective DeLuca.

Why is he here?

37

How can I explain all this to DeLuca? How can I reveal that I buy and sell precious rubies people will kill for? That I might actually be a swindler? Or a money launderer, as Lorraine suggested. Would DeLuca even hear me out? I'm certain Roudebusch would send me to a prison cell without hesitation.

Two local cops speak with some of the kids who were present at the time of the crash. DeLuca greets the local cops and then glances toward me. I turn away, embarrassed. I'm glad the EMTs are by my side, happier that I've passed the concussion protocol. When the EMTs are done with me, DeLuca approaches. I expect him to stop, to say something, but he passes me and goes to the pond. He stops by the water and surveys the area. When he turns back, his lips are pressed together in a tight frown.

He speaks to the attending EMT, not to me. "How is she?"

"No signs of fractures, concussion, internal bleeding, cardiac event," the paramedic says. "Vital signs are strong. Heart rate elevated, but not too high, considering. We'll know for sure when she comes in and we perform a full workup."

"I'm fine," I say. "I don't need to go to the hospital. I'm sick of them."

DeLuca kneels. "You should get checked out, Blue. Please."

"I told you, I'm fine. How are the kids? One of the girls froze in the middle of the street. I think I missed hitting her, but ..."

"No one got hurt. But they say you were speeding."

"I may have been going a little fast. Can we talk about this in private?"

He places a gentle hand on my shoulder. His touch is calming. More than calming. It carries a charge. I still can't tell him who I am. I can't admit that I'm dirty. "What do you say you go to the ER and see what the doctors over there have to say?"

Our eyes meet. I don't want to argue with him. The man confuses me. Despite our disagreement after Lorraine and I were attacked in the park, he always seems to have my back. "That's not happening. I need some privacy and dry clothes."

"Okay," he says.

A local police officer comes by and I tell him everything that happened after the incident at Sant Ambroeus. No, I can't describe the man looking in my car, nor did I get a plate number on the SUV. No one pursues the matter. I sign off on the incident report and give the towing company permission to pull the car out of the pond and take it to the dealership. I think of Lorraine. How am I going to explain the car to her?

When the last cop departs, DeLuca asks if he can give me a lift to where I'm staying. It's not an offer, more like a friendly command. He really seems to care about me. But he's a cop, after all, and I'm a criminal.

We walk toward his vehicle; every step is painful. Not physically, but exhaustion hits me like a brick wall. I don't mention it—I know DeLuca is waiting for an excuse to drag me to the ER.

I look at him. His brow is arched. His lips are curled in a grimace. I can't blame him for being upset. I don't know what else to say. When I step off the grassy area and onto the street, I stumble.

He takes my elbow. "You okay?" he asks.

I nod. I wish I could just stop lying to him.

"How in God's name did you find me here?" I ask him.

"You called me, remember?"

I wait for a better explanation as he opens the passenger's side door. "Where's your partner?"

"I don't spend my free time with him. I also heard a report of the incident over the radio and had a hunch it was you after a description of the driver was given."

I hesitate before getting into the car. "I'm drenched with pond water. I don't want to ruin your seats."

"Just sit on the towel the medic gave you."

"It's wet, too."

He waves a hand. "Get in. It's only water. It'll dry."

He gets in but doesn't start the car. "Where were you before the accident?"

"A bathing suit store, then Sant Ambroeus restaurant."

"Why did you leave the compound?"

"To buy a bathing suit."

"Why did you go to the restaurant?"

"For coffee. And I was thinking about grabbing some lunch."

"You're taking huge risks, considering the attacks on you."

"I was attacked in the hospital, got a call while I was in the shelter. So-called secure places. Doesn't seem to matter where I go. And my memory seems to improve when I'm around people. Stallworth said that would happen."

A little muscle moves in his jaw. The small corner he's got

me in is getting smaller. I have to tell him something. "Did you hear about ... what do you cops call it ... the *incident* at the Sant Ambroeus restaurant?"

"Yeah, I heard the EMTs were called over there as well."

"I was there. Someone was shot."

"No. An elderly lady who had an episode of angina and managed to cut her shoulder on the edge of the table when she fell."

I'm reluctant to tell him what occurred at the restaurant.

"What made you ask if someone was shot?" DeLuca asks, staring hard at me.

"A man was pointing a gun at me."

DeLuca looks at me for a moment longer, shakes his head, and looks toward the pond. Then he starts the car. "You need to be in a safe place. Even if you simply imagined you saw someone with a gun—and it's conceivable that you imagined it given all you've been through—you still need to be in a safe place. I think you should go back to your friend's place, pack up, and we'll put you in protective custody."

My body tightens. "You think I'm making things up?"

"Blue, I'm prepared to have the district attorney go to court to declare you incompetent because of your amnesia. You're putting yourself and others in harm's way now. It's not rational."

"I'm completely rational. Without a memory."

"Do you know how ridiculous that sounds?"

I do, but I can't go to some virtual prison. The only place I'll find the ruby and save my mother is in the real world.

I break eye contact with DeLuca. I can't tell him what that man in the restaurant said to me today. Or what I remembered. DeLuca doesn't trust me; his partner certainly doesn't trust me. And the fact is, now I don't trust DeLuca. Not after he's threatened to lock me up.

38

DeLuca drives toward town, not the compound.

"Where are we going?" I ask.

"Can you manage a stop in those wet clothes?"

"Stop where?"

"Back to the restaurant. I want to talk to some of the staff. You can wait in the car. I'll keep the heater running."

"I'll come in with you. As a wise man once said to me, it's only water."

I'm surprised the place isn't crawling with the authorities. Was I wrong? Could it be there wasn't a man with a gun? No, I'm sure I saw a weapon. But the police wouldn't lie about a woman having an angina attack. I guess it's feasible she saw the weapon and suffered the attack. I'll insist that DeLuca follow up, find out what brought her episode on. If I can prove that someone fired a gun, then DeLuca won't think I've lost my mind and then, I hope he'll stop trying to force me into protective custody.

We go inside the restaurant and walk toward the back. DeLuca seems to already know where the incident occurred. The dining room is cleaned up, and the back area cordoned off. A new picture hangs on the wall above where the elderly lady had been sitting.

There's got to be a bullet hole in the wall behind the picture, but there are no other holes in the wall or any damaged drywall nearby. I step forward, remove the picture, and set it aside. No bullet hole.

DeLuca leans in to take a look. He holds his hand out for the hook and, when I give it to him, he replaces it in the wall. Then he rehangs the picture. He doesn't mock me. He doesn't say anything.

A waiter walks to us, and says, "Can I help you? The dining room is closed."

DeLuca pulls out his badge.

The waiter studies us and zeros in on me. "You were at one of my tables. Weren't you? With some guy. You both left without paying the check."

"I was in here, but you weren't my waiter. I ordered a cappuccino at the bar, not lunch."

"Are you going to pay the check?" the waiter asks.

"What?"

"They'll dock my salary."

"I paid for my cappuccino."

The waiter places his hand on his hips. "Fine. Anything else I can help you with?"

DeLuca gives me a hard stare. "What guy were you with?"

"I thought I saw someone I knew," I say. "I was mistaken."

"She was sitting across from him, talking to him," the waiter says. "Right before the old lady had her stroke."

DeLuca looks at him. "You didn't see anything else unusual, did you?"

"Only the woman who had the stroke. Her arm got cut up a little. The sight of blood. Scary. The ambulance came and took her. We called the hospital. Her daughter said she'll be fine. This isn't about the lady, I hope? She's not blaming the mussels, is she?"

DeLuca shrugs, conveying a *beats me.*

"We had four plates sent back, including hers. Lunch is the worst time, so rushed, and everyone's uptight. Now dinner, I'll take that shift any day."

"Food poisoning isn't within my jurisdiction," DeLuca says. "Your local police had a look around the place?"

"No police came. Only the paramedics."

"Who replaced the picture on the wall?"

"You're looking at him."

"Did you inspect the wall where the picture fell off?"

"For what exactly? There wasn't anything to see. I popped the hook back in and put up a new picture."

"Did you find a bullet in the wall? Anywhere else in here?"

The waiter scoffs. "Now, if that were the case, don't you think we would've called the police? Believe me, no one fired a gun in here."

"What did the man sitting at the table look like? The one who didn't pay the check."

"Like almost every other rich guy who comes in here," the waiter says. "Middle aged, tall, thin, silver haired. Dressed well. We get a lot of tourists. This guy was nice, until he stiffed me. Even the well-dressed customers pull tricks like that."

"You ever see him before today?"

"I don't recall the man, but, Officer, like I said, tons of people traipse in and out of here. If he hadn't stiffed me, I wouldn't remember a thing about him by the time evening shift rolls around."

"And you say my friend here was sitting at his table?" DeLuca asks him again, not looking at me.

"Yup."

Back in the car, we ride in silence to the estate. When he drives onto the property, I point him toward the guesthouse. "You can't keep secrets from me," he says. "Not if you want my help. So I'm going to ask you again. Do you know that man who was at the restaurant?"

"I thought I recognized him, so I walked over to his table. I thought I saw another man threatening me with a gun. I didn't stick around. I headed back to my car, and that's when I saw another man looking inside it. As soon as he left, I got into the car and took off. Then the SUV came barreling down the road in my direction. I got spooked."

"Okay. Let me get this straight. You go over to the man at the table. What did you talk about?"

"I asked him if he knew me."

"Did you sit?"

"Briefly."

"Did he say he recognized you?"

"He laughed," I lie. "He acted like he thought I was playing some flirty game."

DeLuca rakes a hand through his hair, makes a fist, and props it on the steering wheel in front of him. He's not buying a word of it.

"Before anything else happened, I saw the other man with the gun. Or so I believed. Listen, if the guy at the table knows me, I would love to find out who he is. Also, the man with the gun."

"That's all?"

"That's all."

The front door of the guesthouse opens, and Lorraine walks out, holding her baby.

I grit my teeth. Her coming and going as she pleases feels like an invasion of my privacy. But she has every right to be here, and I don't belong here at all. I don't belong anywhere.

39

The authorities must've contacted her about the vehicle. Oddly, she doesn't seem upset. On the contrary, she is as always buoyant.

"Oh my God, I'm so glad to see you!" she says to me as DeLuca and I meet her in the doorway. She gives me a hug that nearly cracks my ribs. "Oh, honey, are you sure you're all right?"

"I'm fine, but I'm so sorry about the car," I say. "How's Tobia?"

She waves a hand dismissively. "Nothing but a scrape. I'm just glad you're safe. You're lucky—maybe Blue's an Irish girl who speaks French. Gino was selling the car anyway. My aunt drove it, so sad memories. Don't give it another thought, really. The insurance will cover it."

"No, Lorraine, I couldn't—"

She smiles. "You did my uncle a favor." She glances at DeLuca and smirks.

The baby reaches to touch my mouth. I offer my hand, and he squeezes my fingers.

"I need a shower," I say. "Can you give me a minute?"

I hurry to my room, hoping that DeLuca will leave. Increasingly, I get the feeling I'm a person who often hides behind untruths. Right now, doing that to someone who genuinely seems to care about my well-being makes me ashamed.

When I'm done showering and dressing, I go to the office. The French doors are closed, and Lorraine and DeLuca are visible through the glass, standing face to face, talking with animated expressions. I can't make out their conversation, which is punctuated by the infant's shrieks. The discussion is so intense that Lorraine is ignoring her baby's wails; she doesn't even pick him up.

The truth is crystallizing in the voice of that crying baby: *I can't trust either one of them.*

I strain to make out what they're saying. When the baby slaps his hands on the glass door, DeLuca and Lorraine stop talking mid-sentence. DeLuca turns and sees me, walks to the door, and opens it. Lorraine picks up the toddler.

"Come on in, Blue," she says. "We were talking about Gino's Porsche. DeLuca says it can be repaired, but I don't think so. Not after sinking to the bottom of that pond. *Plus*, he says I was irresponsible for letting you have the keys to the damn car. Right. Out in here in the Hamptons. I told the detective we're perfectly safe out here. End of story."

Yes, sure—a New York City police detective is deeply concerned about the salvageability of a mafia don's expensive car. I could understand how he would be upset at Lorraine and me for my venture out on my own. But I had no choice. I need answers.

I sit down in a cane-back chair, as uncomfortable as it is expensive. I shift my body, trying to relax. The air in the room feels several degrees too cold, and my skin prickles with goosebumps.

"So what brought you out to the Hamptons, Detective

DeLuca?" Lorraine asks. The baby squirms, and she lets him down. He begins running around, playing with toys he gets from his carry bag.

"Blue said she wanted to talk," DeLuca says.

"I didn't say to jump in the car and get out here," I reply. "I was reporting in, just as you asked me to. Did you find out anything about the necklace I mentioned in my message?"

"Not yet."

"You came a long way to tell us nothing," Lorraine says. "What *do* you know?"

"The department sorted through video from the hotel, trying to identify the driver who took you there on the night of the incident. We found him. Some ordinary guy, originally from Turkey, with three kids. He remembered you."

Lorraine snickers. "*Duh*. He's a man."

"He said you didn't talk much. The only substantive thing was you asked him where he was from. When he told you, you spoke to him in Turkish. Said you only spoke a few words." He looks at me. "Ring any bells? Do you speak Turkish?"

I speak Turkish? "No memory of that," I say, feeling my cheeks heat. How can I be cold and hot at the same moment?

"The credit card you had on file with the ride-share company also leads to that phony address we went to, on Broadway."

"So, what do you think that makes me, Detective?" I ask.

"No matter what you did or might do, a person is innocent until proven guilty in this country," he says.

Interesting that he added *in this country*.

"So says the Constitution," Lorraine says. "I wish the cops would follow the letter of the law more often. Of course she's not a suspect. She's a girl in a world where there's no damn privacy anymore." She shakes her head.

DeLuca tugs on his necktie. "You know, in this day and

age, no honest person can hide their identity. I've never run across an ordinary citizen who could do that. Somehow, Blue, you've managed the impossible—unless, as I think we all suspect, you're not an ordinary citizen."

"What the hell is that supposed to mean?" Lorraine scoffs.

"I have amnesia, Detective. I'm doing the best I can to remember who I am. Do you think making accusations is going to jog my memory?"

"You remember so little, and no one has any real information on you. Are you sure you didn't recognize the man in the restaurant today?"

I don't reply. *Don't get caught.* Words of advice to a criminal.

The baby throws some toys on top of the desk and bangs the surface.

I look at the desk; my journal is lying on it in plain sight. Bad idea to write down my thoughts. I have to find John Brownsworth.

The baby begins reaching for his board book. Lorraine picks him up to distract him, hands him a toy truck.

"I'm staying over in Southampton tonight," DeLuca says. "I'll be by tomorrow to give you a ride back into the city. You have an appointment with Dr. Stallworth."

Stallworth—another person who's had my blind trust. Well, from now on, my eyes will be wide open.

40

When everyone leaves the guesthouse, I return to the computer and search for John Brownsworth. There are too many. I narrow the possibilities down to the area and come across a business address for J. Brownsworth. I call the number and get Jennifer Brownsworth, a realtor. The only John she knows was her late grandfather, who died twenty-one years ago.

I sit back and fold my arms. I think about the apartment in the city and pull up a 3D street map of Manhattan. I scroll through streets one by one and scan the buildings near parks, looking for any detail that fits. Nothing stands out, although I still feel that my residence is there in the city. Can't explain it. It just has to be.

I put the street search on hold and check out marinas in and around the Hamptons to see if I can find John Brownsworth. Nothing turns up.

I do another search on Lorraine's uncle. There are reports about a sordid history, but it doesn't look like he's served jail time.

After several hours of staring into the monitor, my eyes

are strained, so I take a break and find an online radio station that plays classical music. I walk to the window and stare outside, pondering what my childhood must've been like.

The air conditioning switches on, and a rush of icy air meets my exposed flesh. I'm again on that hillside and running through the grass. Out of breath, I roll to the ground. Soft hands touch my cheeks, hands so gentle—my mother's hands. I'm certain of that now. My family was having a picnic that day. I remember the afghan blanket we sat on. I can hear my father telling me that his grandmother made it, using all the colors of the rainbow. I can't see him, but I know his voice. Why can't I see beyond the colors of the afghan? Then I remember my mother saying that a rainbow brings luck. This must've been the happiest day of my life. I want to step back to those earlier days. I want to be carefree.

The wind chimes sway and clank. I shudder as I recall mud-caked windows. I am a young child. Dressed in a leotard and tights. I am inside the car. It is going off the side of the road. An old woman screams.

Why am I remembering this when I need to be remembering where my mother lives? And where I live?

I return to the computer and search for obituaries of Bishops. Again, too many. I need to make a note of the memory and to broaden the search for my mother. It's likely if I'm Catholic that I was christened. A church might have records of that. I reach for the pen I keep lying to the side of the computer, and my journal.

The journal is not there. I search on and around the desk. I don't remember moving it. I was going to, but everything happened so fast. The air catches in my throat. Did DeLuca take it? Would that be legal? DeLuca never has seemed dirty, but who knows?

I search the kitchen, bedroom, and everywhere else I've been inside the house. I can't find the journal. I flop down on the couch and cover my head. The book contains lines and lines of my fragmented memories, bizarre thoughts, and perhaps incriminating statements. Nothing I want to share.

I close my eyes.

Then the front door opens and closes with a bang.

"Blue, I'm back," Lorraine calls out.

I sit up and try to focus.

"Did I wake you?" she asks.

I glance at the clock. It's nearly eight thirty and almost dark outside. "I must've dozed off."

She switches on the light and comes over to me. "I would've been back sooner, but I got caught up with a rush project from work. Are you all right?"

"Yeah, considering I drove a car into a pond today."

She hands me a paper bag. She's holding my wet purse in her other hand. "I brought you some lasagna. Made it myself. And your purse. The mechanics are honest, I'll give you that. They could've kept the bag and claimed nothing was in the car."

"Did you check the contents?"

She frowns. "What kind of friend do you think I am?"

I open the paper bag. Along with the lasagna, my journal is in there, damp with something other than water. Something sticky.

41

Damn it—Lorraine must've shoved my journal into the baby's bag with his toys when she left. How else would she have it? Inadvertently, or intentionally?

"Cash, credit card, phone. All good," I say. "What's my journal doing in here?"

"Sorry about that. It got mixed up with the baby's things. That rascal Giorgio, he grabbed it, was about to tear it to shreds, so I snatched it away and, without thinking, put it in my bag with his things. I had some backup bottles in there. One of them broke open. I'm sorry."

"No, don't worry about it," I say, trying to keep my tone light. "It's just full of garbage anyway."

If I didn't completely doubt Lorraine earlier when she was speaking to DeLuca, I do now. What are she and DeLuca keeping from me, and why did she take my journal? I have to tread lightly. Can't let her know that I suspect her of theft and that she's gaslighting me now to cover her tracks.

I have to get out of here. I'll head out first thing in the morning with DeLuca. If Lorraine would steal my secrets, she would turn me in. Worse, blackmail me. She may be after the Cassiopeia Ruby.

"I take it the bathing suit I bought earlier is history?" I ask.

She looks askance, then grins. "I seriously doubt your bathing suit would fit any one of those mechanics." She laughs. "It wasn't in the car."

Must've floated out.

We go to the kitchen table, and I gorge myself. I'm starting to realize I eat when I'm nervous. Lorraine chatters on about her children learning to ride horses.

"What type of horses?" I ask.

"Thoroughbreds."

"Racing or show?"

"Oh, not racing, not us. Not yet, anyway. Who knows, with my brood? Because of my family connections, I guess you assumed we invested in racing."

I force a nonchalant shrug. I hear again in my head what I heard when I woke from the coma—a trumpet playing and hooves pounding across grass. A memory: I've ridden horses. And not just casually. I feel that horses have played a large role in my life.

As I eat, Lorraine is unusually quiet. The only sound in the room is the hum of the refrigerator's motor.

Once I've consumed every morsel of Lorraine's wonderful lasagna, I say, "I'll have to run ten miles for three days solid to work off this meal. But it was so worth it."

"Yeah, you told me you were a runner. I said running is what you do when someone's chasing you. Which really happened in that park, yeah?" She laughs. "Here's what I've been thinking. Tell me if you think I got it right. Somehow you came into this Cassiopeia stone. Who knows, it might even be a fake. Doesn't matter. You made a deal, then pulled back and kept someone else's dough. Didn't deliver the goods. Works every time to tick someone off, so he found you and came after you. You probably thought you could get away with it."

My stomach drops. *What is her angle?* "So you *do* think I'm a criminal?"

"Here's what I think," Lorraine says. "You're a good person. A lot of good people are close to criminals, even love them." She gives me a you-know-what-I-mean look, obviously referring to her relationship with her uncle Gino. "Sometimes people just take a left turn. Get in above their head ... oh, sorry, dumb figure of speech. I may talk a lot, but bad taste isn't my style."

"I'm not that kind of person."

"Just so you know, you never struck me that way either. It was just a thought. Here's another. DeLuca is ambitious. Sees you as his ticket to a promotion, if he can use you to catch a bigger fish. Happens all the time. Ask my uncle."

"Where's that leave me?"

"Hmm," she says, nodding knowingly. "A little word comes into play. One that Uncle Gino hates. *Immunity*."

I gape at her. "So, you really *do* think I'm a criminal?"

"Of course not, honey. I'm playing this whole scenario out based on what you've said. But tell me the truth. Are you sure you're not involved in something illegit? And I'm not judging you. You must've gathered that by now. Listen, I think we should find that ruby. I know people who can keep it safe. Keep *you* safe."

There it is, in plain words: she wants the ruby. What else could this be about? She's basically saying she will stop at nothing to get it. I trusted her, thought she was a friend. Not a chance. Once *she* has the ruby, I'm a goner.

When I don't respond, she sighs. "Honey, you must be tired."

"Oh, by the way, I did a computer search. Nothing's ever been proven about Gino."

Lorraine laughs. "Nothing to prove. He's a very successful restaurateur. That's it. Speaking of restaurants, why did you go to Sant Ambroeus today? It's one of my favorite spots. Don't tell Uncle Gino if you see him again. He gets his feelings hurt. Can't see why. The clientele out here is quite different. Doesn't matter to my uncle. He calls all restaurants like this 'bogus Italian,' doesn't like the upscale BS."

"I had lunch with a man there once. Can't remember when that was."

She winks. "A *man* man? Like a guy? A date?"

"I don't think so. My recollection was that he was quite a bit older than me."

"Like that matters." She laughs aloud, and then says, "The point is, we find him and *bingo*—we know who you are."

"If it were only that easy."

42

After Lorraine leaves, it takes me an hour to calm down. I head toward the bed. Another long, tiring day. Morning can't come soon enough. Just as I'm closing my eyes, a green motion sensor flashes. Someone is inside the guesthouse.

The alarm didn't sound. How did they get in without the alarm sounding? How did they breach security at all? Lorraine? Can't be. She would've called out. Knocked. Wouldn't be here in the middle of the night.

I want to scream, but I don't—it's too dangerous. *Run*. Run where? If I get out of bed, I'll be seen. But I can't just lie here, or they'll take me—to that man. To be tortured until I remember, and then killed. Or killed if they conclude I'll never remember.

Outside my room, the floor creaks.

I cringe but chance it. I slide from the bed, crawl to my bathroom, where there's a landline. Inside, I stand, push the door to, and engage the lock. I fumble around in the dark without turning on the light until I find the phone attached to the wall near the commode. The phone is dead.

Someone cut off service.

The window. I unlock the latch. Push upward. No alarm. I push the window up. Before I can get a leg up, something yanks the back of my nightgown.

I scream. Shout for help. Struggle to free myself. Twisting, thrashing, slapping, and kicking. Connecting with air, walls, and counters. Something rubbery and hard.

A silhouette of my attacker flashes across the mirror. A man. A big man.

Screaming, I try to kick my leg back, aiming for his groin, but I hit the wall instead—it hurts like hell; I yelp in pain. He lifts me off my feet and then drags me through the dark, into the bedroom, and toward the bed. I struggle, and he slaps my face. Oh, God. Am I about to be raped?

A moment later, my attacker releases me. I fall to the bed and kick my legs furiously. Why did he release me?

The room goes eerily quiet. The room is dark. I can make out shapes but not faces.

"Don't move," a man says, and first I think he's talking to me, but then I realize that there are two men here, and that cordial gardener, the one who loves flowers, is talking.

"Keep calm and let's talk this over," a man says in a thick southern drawl. He must be my attacker. "I can pay y'all."

"Shut your mouth," the gardener says in a tone so threatening that my attacker starts breathing heavily.

"Are you okay, miss?" the gardener says.

"Yeah, I'm fine." I'm in a daze and my foot is throbbing.

More footsteps, and then more men. How many? Don't know. It's too dark to see.

The gardener, my rescuer, says something in Spanish to the others. In English, one of his colleagues says, "Move, asshole. Nice and slow."

My assailant starts to move and then attacks the other men. Curses and shouts fill the room, and I scramble off the other side of the bed as I hear flesh meet flesh, groans and grunts. Someone grabs me, then I'm free, and I hear someone else drop to the floor. I manage to run out of the room. What happened? Are my rescuers down, or is it the attacker? I start toward the back door, unsure whether outside is safer than inside, but willing to take the chance.

A whoosh, then gunfire, *pop-pop-pop*.

A light comes on as I open the door to get out.

"Ms. Blue," a man shouts. "Wait. You're safe in here."

The word *safe* rattles around in my mind. No way.

I don't stop. I'm through the door. I race across the cement patio. I can't trust anyone. As I step into the grass, not knowing where I'll go other than to hide until I can get out of here, I run full force into the chest of a man. He surrounds me with his arms. I struggle. My strength melts. I'm a dead woman. Or soon will be.

43

I'm limp in my captor's arms. My ears are ringing.

"It's over," a man repeats. "The bad guy is dead."

Recognition. The gardener. I'm so dizzy, I can't stand. My body is jelly.

The next thing I know, I'm lying in bed. When I realize I'm not dreaming, I startle and take in my surroundings. This isn't the room I was sleeping in.

"It's all right," a familiar voice says. "You're in the guesthouse."

I scramble to a seated position and stare into the face of Matteo DeLuca.

"God, what happened?"

He comes to sit beside me on the bed. Uninvited, but I don't mind. His presence gives me comfort. I feel protected. "A man attacked you."

I almost roll my eyes. "I got that part. Who?"

"We'll know very soon."

"What happened? How did he get in here?"

"Apparently, he got onto the property from the bay. Came over on an inflatable dingy, left in the water. Suited up and swam to land. Seems he knew how to avoid the rocks close to shore. Got past the tripwires. You have the gardeners to thank for rescuing you. The night man caught him soon after he entered the house."

I hold my head in my hands, trying to process it all. "Where's Lorraine? Does she know what happened?"

"She's down at the station, speaking with the local police. I said I would cover the situation here."

His phone rings, and he picks up, still sitting beside me. He says "right" and "gotcha" and "okay" and "under control" and hangs up. "We have the man's identity," he says to me. "Derrick Nelson. Career criminal, originally from Louisiana."

I hug my stomach. I feel the blood drain from my face.

"He won't be bothering you again. He's dead. We're pretty sure he's the guy who killed Burns, the IT guy from the hotel."

But his associates are alive. "Do you have his picture?"

He opens his phone. "Fair warning, it's not a pretty picture."

"Show me." He pulls up a photograph of a dead man shot in the chest. I recognize him instantly. He's wearing a scuba suit—the rubbery material I touched in the bathroom. There's blood on his face, but I know it's him. "He's the man from the park."

"Did he say anything to you?"

"Not a word." I talk DeLuca through what happened.

He takes down the details on his phone, and by the time he's finished typing, I'm shaking but doing my best to hide it.

DeLuca looks up but doesn't say anything. Instead, he takes me into his arms.

I place my head against the crook of his arm and chest. "I saw you coaching those kids."

He pulls back and looks at me, a question on his face.

"Back in the city, I saw you that day after we talked in the park. You went back to coach those little kids. I wish I could've stayed and watched."

He smiles. "You know, kids sports can be boring if you're not a coach or parent. I love the sport. They never have enough coaches." With pride, he adds, "And some of the coaches don't know baseball that well."

"DeLuca, it's bewildering to me how bad your suits are, but if some woman someday can overlook that, you'll make her very happy. Don't know why you haven't already."

He looks away.

I wish I hadn't opened my big mouth. "Sorry. None of my business."

He says nothing, his face still turned away.

"I shouldn't have said that." I reach out and touch his hand. "I'm sorry."

He clears his throat. "So, back to the present. Here's your choice. I'll stay here with you tonight, sleep on the couch, or we head for the city now."

The change of subject throws me a little, but I meet his eyes steadily. "I'm not going into protective custody." He gazes back at me. He's here taking care of me. I do appreciate that.

I have a strong desire to touch him. We're here alone.

"Stay with me," I say.

"I would like that."

My lips meet his. Two minutes later, he's lying beside me on the bed. Two minutes later, I'm lost in him.

44

Early the following morning, DeLuca and I agree to forget the previous night ever happened, an agreement I can't keep. He's back to being all business. I'm not sure how I feel. A cop and a criminal—laughable—except it's really not.

I dress in a pair of beige slacks and a button-down blouse, then grab my sunglasses and check the contents of my purse. I leave my clothes and suitcase behind—I don't need them. I follow DeLuca to his car, and we drive away.

"I want you to know I went back to the restaurant," he says. "The only thing I got from the staff were recaps of the older woman having the heart episode."

"Did you check to see if the restaurant had a video security system?"

"I did, and they don't."

I breathe a quiet sigh of relief. God only knows DeLuca would completely lose faith in me if he were able to view the conversation I had yesterday.

As we drive, I watch the passing vehicles to kill the time. "I read somewhere that life is like a quilt. We search for those pieces that are missing; those pieces that we need to complete the quilt. The parts that we've already pieced together aren't as important, even get forgotten."

Our eyes meet. One of his brows is raised.

"Once we have something, we take it for granted, and in a way, it becomes meaningless."

He turns back to the road. "That's heavy, Blue."

I lean against the door and yawn. I'm tired. DeLuca is quiet, concentrating on the road. Doing his job. Was he doing his job a few hours ago when we were together? Was I only doing my job, because I can't stop thinking that someday I might be able to use our romantic encounter to my advantage? *What kind of person am I?*

"Are you allowed to listen to FM radio?" I ask. "Not the police radio, the real radio. I'm feeling a little tired."

He tunes the FM radio to a classical music station. We're quiet for the rest of the trip.

In the city, he pulls the car to a stop in front of Stallworth's office building and reaches his hand toward mine. Just before he touches me, he stops himself from making physical contact. Which means that last night meant something to him, that if he was playing me, he felt something that got in the way. "I'll walk you in," he says. "Wait for you."

"I don't understand how you can spend so much time with me. Don't you have other work to do?"

"I take my work with me wherever I go. Also helps that I get a few days off every week."

So he's spending off time with me. To protect me. Not sure how I feel about that.

He lifts a questioning shoulder. "Ready?" he asks.

"Walk me in. Fine. But don't wait in the lobby. People will get the wrong idea."

"Okay. Then I'll walk around the block for a hot dog while you see the doc. Can I bring you one back?"

I wrinkle my nose. "You know what Lorraine says about my eating habits. But if you can find a celery vendor ..."

"I'll be waiting."

He gets me inside the building. When the elevator opens, I place a hand on his chest to stop him coming along. "I've got this."

He looks hurt, but I can't help that. He turns and disappears into the New York throng. Soon, I'll disappoint him even more. After my session with Stallworth, I'm going where he can't. I have people to talk to, and people don't talk when cops are around.

45

Floor-to-ceiling windows in Stallworth's office provide a view of the courtyard below and the tops of skyscrapers beyond. She knows about the auto accident. DeLuca must've called her. I tell her about last night's attack. I leave out the part about sleeping with him.

We talk about memories and how to regain them. She asks me the same questions. Am I suicidal? Am I homicidal? I tell the truth and also lie.

"So let's get to the neurological test," Stallworth says.

"I'm fine."

But my protests don't prevent her from doing her job.

We start with a simple motor test. Menial. I insert pegs into a pegboard using one hand then the other. Then a memory test. I repeat words and sentences. For cognition, she hands me two photographs. I explain the difference between a dog and a cat and a few more things. The last test is verbal. She points to places around the room, and I name the items. All goes well until she points to an old, faded photograph of herself standing beside a horse. I never would've imagined this petite, no-nonsense woman as a rider. I want to believe the photo is just a coincidence. Lots of people ride. Is this a set up? How could it be?

"Is that you on the horse?" I ask.

"I was sixteen. Took the silver in dressage. You know what that is?"

"Sure."

She tilts her head, clearly prodding me for more of an explanation.

"Right," I say. "It's the highest expression of horse training, where the horse and rider perform a series of predetermined movements. From memory."

She's playing me. Toying with my memory. Why? Would she really gaslight me?

"Blue? You look as if you've seen a ghost."

I shiver. Can't hide the reaction. "Why is that picture in here?"

Her eyes gloss over a moment. Her simple smile is wistful. "Proud moment. That medal was such an accomplishment. I broke my leg a month after that, never returned to the sport."

I believe her. I want to believe her. "I'm sorry," I mumbled. "That must've been terribly hard on you."

"Thanks. But I was entering college that fall, so I moved on to other things." She sits up straight and folds her hands in her lap. "None of this explains the reaction I'm seeing in you, Blue."

"I think I grew up around horses too. Don't know any details. So the seeming coincidence between us just threw me."

"I understand. Let's focus on the important aspect. Recalling something like this from your past is a good sign. It means the rest will come."

But how soon?

She checks the clock on the back wall. "We have to stop now. Please make an appointment with my receptionist for next week. Also, considering everything you're going through, I want to prescribe you a mood elevator."

A mood elevator? No chance. I want to keep my wits about me, and I can't trust Stallworth entirely. I decline the medication, thank her, and leave.

I take the elevator, this time not to the lobby but to the second floor, then use the stairwell to exit into the back alleyway. To avoid DeLuca, who I'm sure kept his promise to wait for me, I hurry down the side street, find an open back door to a nearby building, and go inside. Then I emerge through the front entrance on the avenue around the block from where DeLuca is parked.

It's morning rush hour, so the sidewalks are teeming with people, and the streets are bumper-to-bumper. The noise and commotion hit me like a twenty-ton hydraulic jack. I am terrified. And thrilled.

I glance down the street in both directions, then head toward a subway station not far away. About halfway down the block, I sense that someone is tracking my movements. Justified or not, I ring the buzzer of a boutique with Asian-inspired silks and duck inside. As I walk toward the rear of the store, I keep an eye on the front window.

"May I help you?" the clerk asks, keeping in step with me.

"Just looking," I say cheerfully. I wander through the racks while studying everyone who walks past the store. After several minutes, nothing appears suspicious. But I still can't shake the feeling that someone is following me. I leave the store and head down the sidewalk as fast as I can. I meander through the crowd and then go inside another clothing shop several stores down—modern, hip, geared toward the youthful customer. No buzzer required, but a bell rings when I walk through the door. I'm greeted by a clerk, a tall woman who could be an Olympic javelin thrower or a runway model or both.

I head toward the back of the store. She follows.

A few moments later, I see a dark, curly-haired man in a black suit peering into the shop window. His eyes are big and dark, and he has arched eyebrows and a long nose. His jaw is a tight V. My gut says tells me he's not buying a gift for his wife or girlfriend.

Part of me wants to walk up to the guy and ask him to tell me who I am and why he and his buddies want to harm me. Instead, I squat between the clothing racks.

"I need your help to get out of here unseen," I say to the clerk, who's standing nearby.

She looks surprised when she sees me crouched on the floor.

"That man outside the front door is my ex-boyfriend. He's after me. I have a restraining order against him, but he's still stalking me. Please, I'm desperate. Help me." The whole time I'm saying this to her, from the floor, I'm half-wondering if I've lost my mind and he's just some harmless guy window shopping. Nevertheless, I reach inside my purse and offer her three twenties.

She refuses the money at once. "No. I hate men who hurt women. How can I help?"

"Is there a back door here?"

She shakes her head. "If he comes in, I'll have to get him to the back and distract him. You go out the front." She directs me to an overfilled rack of clothes. "Hide behind them."

Just as I comply, the man enters the store.

She moves toward him, beaming.

"I'm looking for my wife," he says. "She came in here a few minutes ago. Dark hair? Wearing blue jeans and a white blouse?"

Okay, so I'm not completely crazy.

"Oh yes, she's in the dressing room trying on a skirt," the clerk says. "Come with me, sir."

As she guides the man to the rear of the shop, I make for the door in a crouched position.

Another customer opens the door and sets off the bell.

"One moment, sir," the clerk says.

I go hands down, praying my pursuer doesn't see me. I stay low, but to keep my cover, I swivel around so I can keep watch underneath the racks, while also pretending to adjust one of my shoes. I count to five, giving the man plenty of time to check out the door and turn back around.

"Hey, there," the clerk calls to the new customer. "Please let me know if I can help you."

"Thank you," a woman replies. Not another assailant —thank God.

As the door starts to close, I toss my purse between it and the door frame. Bullseye. The purse prevents the door from closing and setting off the bell.

The clerk speaks to the man loud enough for me to know that they're now in the back of the store.

That's my cue. I crawl to the door, pull it open, make my exit, and duck walk until I disappear inside a crowd of people. When I'm several yards down from the shop, I stand and walk in pace with the others around me. I tuck my hair underneath the back of my shirt, toss a vendor a twenty, and grab a ball cap. I love New York. Everyone moves like the wind.

I continue down the sidewalk and toward the entrance to the subway, not looking back, though I know the man must've exited the shop by now.

It occurs to me that he's probably not working alone, and I realize it's too risky to try for the subway station. I need to walk until I can hail a taxi unseen.

A small church with a courtyard in front is located at the

end of the block. There's a break between the buildings creating an alleyway. When I reach it, I juke left and sprint. At the end, I make a sharp right down another alley behind the church. I glance back. No one.

Relieved for the moment, I stop and lean against the back wall, breathing heavily.

But then I hear two pairs of leather soles pounding heavily against concrete.

I should've stayed with DeLuca.

46

I'll never make it to the end of the alleyway and out to the road, but there's a back door to the church. I try the handle, and miraculously, the door opens. Once I'm inside, I bolt the door and lean against the wall again.

A truck engine roars outside—garbage day.

I remain planted against the wall, frozen, except for my heart, which is pounding like a drum. The truck continues to approach down the alleyway. The two sets of footsteps—male, going by the heavy impact—continue to pound hard on the concrete.

A man shouts something unintelligible. Another man answers but doesn't stop running. Someone tries the door.

The urge to flee is overwhelming, but if I do, they'll hear me.

The pursuer shouts to his accomplice that the door is locked. He tries jerking the handle more vigorously, but he finally gives up and leaves as the truck's brakes squeal and the truck comes to a stop.

I inhale and hold my breath as I tiptoe into the dimly lit sanctuary of the church.

The room isn't gigantic, but it has an angelic feel I associate with religious spaces. The apse, set inside a semicircular recess, has a light blue-and-white-painted dome above it. The walls are inlaid with columns framing six large paintings, with the centerpiece a statue of the Virgin Mary.

I walk down the side aisle, passing the rows of pews. Maybe it's the relief of momentary safety, but I feel an overwhelming awareness, as if I was raised in a religious household and understand the ceremony and symbolism. The hair on my arms rises, and I face the pulpit. Underneath the statue of Mary, a bright light is shining.

"I remember," I whisper. Not *this* Catholic church, but *a* Catholic church, somewhere. I struggle to pull the memory forward. I'm wearing a white dress and going to mass with my parents. I'm Catholic—or was.

In my memory, we enter through one of three arched gothic-style doors. Inside, a blue-lined pathway leads to an altar that is surrounded by statues of saints set along the walls. Above, a glass dome is illuminated in a royal heavenly blue light. The interior structure is all ornately carved wood, from the upper arches and walkways to the pews. I remember the church is La Chapelle Notre-Dame de Lourdes de Montréal. What if my birth records are there? That would make me Canadian.

"May I help you?" a man asks, startling me. I turn to see a priest approaching.

"I was appreciating the peacefulness of the church," I say. "I just love small churches. I sometimes become overwhelmed in cathedrals, forget I'm on earth. That must sound odd."

The priest smiles. "I understand. God's spirit feels closer to me here, too. Vigil Mass begins at five o'clock. Please join us."

"Thank you, but it's been too long."

The priest folds his hands in front of him. "It's never too late to return. God be with you. Stay and pray if you like."

"I'll come back." I turn away from him.

He accompanies me as I walk toward the front entrance.

When I reach the doors, I stop. "You might want to keep your doors locked."

"God's doors are always open."

I reach for the door handle but hesitate. "I think I'll light a candle before I leave. For my parents."

"Very well."

I walk to a stack of candles, place a twenty-dollar bill in the donation box, select two candles, and light them. I place them in the sand and stare into their light, then close my eyes. Am I praying or stalling for time? No. I'm praying. For my mother, my father too, if he's alive and also in danger.

When I open my eyes, the priest is standing beside me. His presence is comforting.

"You look as though you have something on your mind," he says.

"Father, I've lost myself."

I expect him to ask what I mean, but he says only, "When we feel that way, we should start by looking where we remember last knowing ourselves."

"Like what you do when you try to find a lost house key?"

He smiles. "Not quite a celestial description, but well put."

I take a seat in a back pew and stare up at the statue of Mary. Tears stream down my cheeks, and my stomach feels hollowed out. I know with certainty that my confusion about who I am did not start when I fell from that window, and it's not just about being unable to remember the facts of my life either. I want to drop to my knees, but I don't know how to ask for forgiveness. It seems I've lost not only my identity, but also my faith.

I think of the priest's words—start by looking where we

remember last knowing ourselves. I can't remember that, either. Yet, that's exactly what I'm going to do.

47

When I finally leave the church, it seems the men are gone. I hurry to the road and hail a cab on the corner. One pulls over right away, and I get into the back and slump down in the seat.

"Keep driving," I tell the driver. "I've got to find the address." He doesn't blink an eye. We travel two-and-a half blocks before I manage to sit up and give him the location of the Beacon Hotel.

The drive takes ten minutes. I hand the driver a twenty, get out, and walk inside the hotel lobby. At the desk, the same manager we saw before is finishing up with a guest. As I wait, he keeps eyeing me—subtle but definitive. He recognizes me.

When the guest leaves, the manager signals me over with a you're-next-in-line look, and I walk forward. "Blue Bishop, you remember me, don't you?"

He looks around nervously and says in a low voice, "This wasn't the arrangement."

I talk fast, quietly, and emphatically, keeping watch. "I'm sure it wasn't. The problem is I really did have an accident, and now I'm suffering from amnesia, so I need your help. What were the arrangements? Do I have a room here?"

He considers this. "No, you don't have a specific room. You have a safety deposit box. You pay, but I don't know you, never seen you before in my life. No exceptions. Ever. You come late at night. Give notice ahead of time."

"Deposit box?"

"Vestige of the old days," he says, his voice still low. "You don't keep a particular room. I give you one when you come in and request one—which, I might add, is extremely rare, except this is the third appearance you've made recently. What's the problem with the cops? That detective came back. Twice."

I feel a rush of anxiety. DeLuca's probably searching for me now. "The cop's only trying to help. You haven't said anything?"

He looks at me, disgusted. "We have an arrangement. But I can't be a part of any crime, understand?"

"You aren't. I need to see the box." I take a breath. "Thing is, I don't have a key."

"Well, that's a problem."

"We've got to break the lock."

"No can do."

"So get a locksmith in here," I say with growing frustration.

"Too many eyes. Not part of your instructions."

"Well, I'm here now, changing my instructions."

He shakes his head, an emphatic *no*. No exceptions.

"Here's the deal," I say. "Someone is threatening my mother. I've got to figure out who my mother is and where she lives."

He looks at me, incredulous.

"Yeah, that's right. I don't remember my own mother. If I don't get to her soon, I won't have a mother. Please."

He stares at me long and hard. "If this comes back on me, I'm turning it back on you. Understand?"

"Of course."

He beckons me to come back. We go behind the desk and inside a private room near the vault. "Stay here." He goes inside the vault and returns with the box five minutes later. "It's unlocked. Make this quick."

I don't ask how he opened it. Don't want or need to know.

He goes to the door, closes it, and tells me he'll stand watch. To tap on the desk three times when I'm ready.

I open the lid of the security box. Inside is a black velvet case and an envelope. I open the envelope and find a key. Then I open the case and there it is—the Cassiopeia Ruby. Breathtaking. Exquisite. Pear-shaped. Pigeon-blood red. Flawless. I have to hold it. To feel its weight.

I listen to make sure no one is about to open the door and take the stone out of the case. The ruby fits in the palm of my hand. Its feeling of luxury is indescribable. I hold the stone to the light. Red beams reflect off its faceted surface.

Beacons.

Of course.

The red beacon. Memories that surfaced from the moment I woke from the coma. The flashes of red lights in my dreams.

Outside, I hear the manager cough, a *get-moving* signal.

I tuck the ruby back inside the box, then take the key from the envelope, study it, and stuff it inside my purse. I can't risk taking the ruby. Not yet. Not until I understand what's going on. I close the lid, and it locks. The Cassiopeia Ruby is safe here—well, as safe as it can be. I obviously trusted the manager before, and the jewel is still here, and I don't know of a safer place. No one would ever suspect that it's here. Not unless someone spotted me coming in.

I slide a pair of sunglasses on, then tuck my hair under

my shirt again and pull my collar up. I knock three times. The manager appears, and I watch him put the box away.

Next and final stop coming up.

48

With me in the ballet school elevator are four young girls dressed in leotards and tights. I pray for the sake of these children that I wasn't followed here.

When the doors open, I step into a lobby filled with adults and children. The room is lined with chairs for waiting moms and dads. Several studios have windows for parents to watch classes; others have shades pulled to deter onlookers. I follow the sign to the office, which is swarming with more giggly girls. The woman in charge looks up at me, then smiles in recognition. Her name tag reads Mandy. I don't remember her, but I wave and smile anyway.

"We missed you, Blue," Mandy says. "Are you okay? The police came by, said something about an accident. Is everything ...?"

"I fell and hit my head," I say. "I'm on the road to recovery. Not quite there yet. I wonder if you have a minute."

"It'll have to be quick," she replies, glancing around the room. "I'm processing in some new students—Moms who insist that I let their children in now, even though the registration deadline is long past."

I shoot her a look of sympathy before asking, "Did the police mention that I lost a lot of my memory?"

Her hand flies to her mouth. "Oh my God, no."

"This is going to sound crazy," I say, lowering my voice, "but I'm trying to find out where I live. Apparently, the address I gave you was either old or inaccurate, for some reason."

A young girl chases another around Mandy, screaming and laughing, holding Mandy's skirt. Mandy places her hands on her hips. "Your class has started, girls. Miss Pointer will be upset if you're late."

Together the girls charge out of the office, their feet in pink leather slippers pattering against the floors—a sound I know well.

"Is the ballet teacher really named *Pointer*?" I ask.

Mandy laughs. "Wow, you really have lost your memory. Yes, the teacher's name is an amusing subject of conversation, especially with the newbie parents."

A loud bang comes from somewhere down the hall, making me jump.

I struggle to control my breathing. Was I followed? I scan the office, searching for anything to use as a weapon. I spy a metal rod of some kind. I lean outside the door and search both directions. There are no apparent thugs. But people like that don't come in one size.

"Blue," Mandy says. "Are you okay?"

"I don't know. That bang."

"Oh, that's studio one, down the hall. The door lost its springs, slams like crazy if one of the girls pushes it too hard. I suspect our culprit is one of those two little lovelies who just skipped out of here."

I swallow, feeling stupid. "I'm sorry. I'm still not recovered. Loud noises alarm me."

"You poor thing." She gives me a concerned look. "Okay, so I gave the police your paperwork. That's all I know about your address."

Piano music begins playing in the background from one of the studios. "Maybe there's a credit card receipt?"

"I'm afraid you always paid in cash."

I deflate. "Who were my friends? Do you happen to know?" I ask, trying a new tack. "Did I ever speak with anyone on a regular basis? Someone who could tell me something more?"

"That's something I can't tell you. You weren't what I would call the gregarious type. You've always been so mild-mannered. Shy, if I had to put a label on it."

"Or aloof, maybe?"

She gives me an embarrassed frown. "You kept to yourself, came and went."

"What classes did I take?"

She glances at the ceiling and thinks for a moment. "Thursday evening and Saturday morning classes, if that's any help."

"Did I ever leave with someone? Arrive with anyone?"

"Not that I remember."

"What about Lorraine Baglietti? I was friends with her. Her daughter Gabriella remembers me, too."

"I didn't know the two of you were friends. But there are lots of people passing through here every day."

"Who was my instructor?"

"Lloyd Prosser."

"I'm sorry, I don't ... Is he here?"

She points to an older gentleman in black tights and a white T-shirt. He appears to be in his mid-seventies. "If you hurry, you can catch him before he shuts the door."

I thank her and rush over to Prosser.

"Blue!" He beams. "It's wonderful to see you. We heard you were in an accident." He looks me over. "You're not dressed. Not joining us today?"

"Oh, I ..."

"If not, I look forward to seeing you soon. Remember, wait too long and you'll lose the muscles." He waves a hand through the air with a flourish, as though on stage.

"I've suffered a fall. I have memory problems. Severe. So forgive me for sounding strange or asking weird questions." I reach out and take his hands in mine for a moment. "Could you tell me who my friends were here?"

He sighs and slides a hand across the silver strings of his sparse hair. "I have no answer to that. Adults come, dance, and leave. Polite conversation—hello, how are you—that's all I ever hear. Every class has a different makeup of students. It's not like the old days, where students were required to attend a prescribed set of classes. People mix it up these days. Such a hodgepodge. You'll have to talk to Mandy. Will you be rejoining us at a later date then?"

"I don't know. I'm feeling a little like Dorothy from *The Wizard of Oz*. I've got to find my way home first."

"Well, my dear Dorothy, you look remarkably well, considering everything you've told me. So when you've settled your affairs, I would love to see you back. There aren't many who dance like you."

"Do you remember where I danced as a child? Did I ever tell you?"

"Canada's National Ballet School and Le Grand Paris." He pauses. "I'm not sure why you didn't dance professionally." He turns toward his studio door. "I have to run now, my dear. Do join us again and feel better."

"Wait, please." When he stops and looks back with raised

eyebrows, I ask, "Did you ever mention those other ballet schools to anyone else?"

"You mean the cops?"

I give an encouraging nod.

"Hardly." He steps toward me and whispers. "When I was young, I was in the Christopher Street Liberation Day March in 1970. I was present during the police raid at the Stonewall Inn a year earlier. I can't count how many times the authorities turned water hoses and dogs on us. You might say I developed an aversion to cops. But no one spoke to me. Had they … it would not have mattered. My lips are sealed." He makes the zipped-lips gesture with a thumb and forefinger.

I thank him. Our short exchange has given me two leads. I could be Canadian or French. If I could convince either or both ballet schools to give me information, I might have my first solid clue to my life.

I look through the window into the studio. I don't remember a single person in there, and no one pays attention to me. I watch the warm-up, hoping for some glimmer of recognition. Nothing. Resigned, I give up and head toward the elevator. I'll grab a coffee. Think. Figure out what the key unlocks. Find a computer.

49

I punch the elevator down button to leave the dance school. Before the elevator comes, someone touches my arm. I turn, surprised by the physical contact. It's a woman I don't recognize. Of course I don't.

"Blue?" a woman asks. "We heard you had some kind of accident. Are you okay?"

"Yes. I'm sorry, but a head injury has erased most of my memory. I'm trying, but I don't remember you."

"I'm Amy, Daniela's mother. Please forgive me, but I overheard part of your conversation with Mandy just a minute ago. I was in the office, dropping off a payment."

"Are we friends?" I ask tentatively.

"No, not really. Daniela and Gabriella are friends in class, though. But that's not what I want to say. Look, I think I can help you."

I smile, trying not to get my hopes up.

"You and I get off at the same subway stop," she continues. "I don't usually pay much attention to where others are going, but one evening our class ran over. We were on the same number 6 train, heading downtown, and we both got off at

59th. I was walking behind you—not stalking you, I just happen to live in the neighborhood—and I saw you let yourself into an apartment building on 64th Street between Lex and Park."

My heart starts to race. "Do you remember which building?"

"It wasn't far from the corner. It's the four-story building, Renaissance style, light-colored stone. Only one on the block like it. I don't mean to be nosy or get in your business," she says hurriedly. "I just remember the building because it's quite lovely. Lavish. I wasn't surprised you lived there. Seems to fit your style." She blushes slightly. "I've watched your dance class through the window a few times."

I hug her.

She startles but laughs lightly. "Wow, you've changed."

I'm sure she didn't mean to damn me with that faint praise. I thank her, then say, "Gaby's mother, Lorraine, recognized my picture on the news. She's taken me in."

Her face wakes with astonishment. "Really?"

"You look surprised."

"Yeah, it is kind of surprising. I'm sorry. What I mean is that it's quite generous of her to lend a hand."

"Why? We're close friends, aren't we?"

She tilts her head. "Do you remember it that way?"

"No, but Lorraine says we are. What do you know about her?"

"Gaby's mom never said much more than hello to me. Once I tried to arrange a play date for the girls, since they get on so well in class, and Lorraine blew me off. She acted standoffish."

"I thought *I* was standoffish," I say.

"You seemed shy, an introvert. Lorraine is just plain rude. She's always on the phone or her laptop during the kids' class."

That's not the Lorraine I know. The Lorraine I know would be pals with every mom in the room. Make her presence known as a supermom. More proof that she isn't who she claims to be. But who is?

"Lorraine and you didn't hang out at all, as far as I remember," Amy adds.

"May I ask a favor?" When she nods, I lower my voice to a whisper. "Would you please not mention our conversation to anyone? I don't mean to frighten you, but I want you to know my fall was no accident. Someone is trying to harm me. I don't want anyone else to get hurt."

Her eyes blink rapidly, and then she nods. Before I can say anything else, she clams up and hurries away.

And I change my plans.

50

In the lobby downstairs, I peer outside the window. It's after three p.m., and 80th Street is teeming with people. I glance around to check that someone isn't waiting for me.

A cab pulls to the curb near the school entrance. A passenger gets out and I dash outside, grab the door to the cab, slide in, and stay low in the seat.

"Drive until I give you the address, please."

"Which direction?" the driver asks.

"Anywhere, you choose."

He flips on the meter. Three blocks down, I tell him to head to 64th Street between Lexington and Park.

The driver frequently glances at me in the rearview mirror. He doesn't trust me. I get it—I don't trust me either.

When he turns on Lexington, the arteries in my neck are pulsing hard.

"Take it slow," I say. "I have to figure out which building."

He glances at me in the mirror again and looks at me as if I'm nuts, but he slows to a snail's pace anyway, ignoring the vehicles behind us, which honk their horns.

"Up there, on the right," I say. "See the light sandstone building? Pull to the curb across the street, please."

He drives forward and parks.

The four-story building is in the Renaissance Revival style, just as Amy said. I study the place from the bottom floor to the top. Long windows fill the upper floor, allowing in plenty of daylight. This has to be my home. I don't fully recognize the building, but the long, tall windows tell me this is home. I want to race from the taxi, bang on the front door to get inside, and search every floor.

Wait. What if those thugs are waiting for me inside? Do I chance it?

Of course I do. I have no other choice.

I pay the driver and get out. He pulls away, and I'm just about to step off the curb when someone grips my arm.

I gasp, yank my arm, and try to run.

"Blue, stop." It's DeLuca.

"What the fuck, Matteo?" I shout.

"Why'd you run?" he shouts back.

"The real question is, how did you find me?"

"What the hell are you doing? I'm trying to help you, and you're throwing it back in my face."

I stare at him.

"Why did you try to ditch me?" he asks.

I shut my eyes for a moment, trying to calm down. "Just how long have you been following me? Because I could've used some help ..." I stop without saying more about the earlier events, and instead say, "... finding this place."

He clamps his lips together hard, clearly displeased. "Mandy at the ballet school called. I asked her to call me if you ever came in. She said you were jumpy. Seemed paranoid, like someone was following you. Then another mother spoke to her after you had a chat."

He's a cop, and because I'm very likely a criminal, he

should be the last person I should trust. But I do trust him—or is it that I'm attracted to him, or just need to use him for a bit longer? "Okay, DeLuca, so someone remembered me. The mother of one of the ballet kids, she also knows Lorraine. Just what is your business with Lorraine?"

"She's your friend."

"You know what I think? I think Lorraine is after this Cassiopeia, whatever the hell that is. Maybe she works with her uncle. Maybe you do, too. You two knew each other before I came into the picture."

"You're being paranoid."

"Everything checked out with Lorraine, and you haven't denied what I said."

He raises his hands. "Look, if you feel that way, I'm happy to step away from your case. Roudebusch can take it from here. Would that do it for you? Just say the word and I'm gone."

I stare at him. Is he bluffing? Am I close to the truth? I break eye contact. Let him figure out my answer.

"Let's hit the replay button," he says. "I told you from day one, Lorraine checked out. But if you're not comfortable there, don't go back."

"I won't. Glad we agree."

"Yeah, let's agree on something else and cut the bullshit. We both know that the Cassiopeia is a valuable ruby."

"I don't know what—"

"I asked you to please cut the bullshit, or I will arrest you."

I scoff. "On what charge?"

"I'll think of something. You'll be in custody long enough for me to figure this out."

"Okay. So yeah, I remembered what the Cassiopeia is. How did you know?"

"I'm a police detective, so it's my job to figure out stuff like that."

"You're obviously not going to tell me. So much for cutting the bullshit."

"It's not rocket science. It went on the black market, and someone thinks you have it." He waits a beat. "Do you?"

"I don't believe you."

"Answer me, Blue!"

"I don't have it," I say, which is technically true if you add a silent "*on me*" to the end of my sentence. Have I always lied with such ease?

He puts his hands in his back pockets and looks up at the sky for long moment. "What are we doing here?"

"I think I live across the street."

"Then let's go find out."

51

I tap on the electronic directory. First floor, Sue Bramsen—the landlord, I now remember. Second floor, L. Grant. Third, Lin Su Chan. Fourth floor, no name. I hit the buzzer for Sue and look into the camera.

"Blue?" Sue asks.

"Hey, Sue. I don't have my key, can you let me in?"

The buzzer sounds, and we head inside toward the elevator. Sue's door opens. She's an elderly woman, in her eighties, with a cane. She flags me over.

"You okay, honey?" she asks, when I reach her. "I haven't seen you in a while. I don't like to pry, but who's the fella over there?"

"It's all fine. He's a friend."

"Where have you been?"

"I'll tell you all about it later. I had an accident and was hospitalized."

Her face creases with worry. "You should've called me."

"I'm sorry, it's a little more complicated than that. I was in a coma for a couple weeks."

She looks aghast.

"Has anyone been around here?" I ask. "To my apartment, looking for me?"

"No, honey. So sorry to hear about your accident." She pats my arm. "You look thin, thinner than you were, and you were already a bean pole. Hospitals really ought to hire people who know how to cook, not starve a person to death by offering them garbage for meals. I'll bring you some dinner. Would the fella like some, too?"

"Oh, that's okay," I say. "I wouldn't want to put you out."

Childish screaming comes from her apartment down the hall. "It's no trouble," she insists. More screaming, something crashes to the floor. She throws up her hands. "My God, I love those grandkids, but sometimes they're like a fried egg under my armpit. They'll tear the place to shreds if I don't get back in there." She winks. "Here's your key. Be sure I get it back, or we won't have a backup."

I thank her, and DeLuca and I take the elevator to the fourth floor. When the doors open, I see the entrance to the apartment. We step off the elevator, and I'm overwhelmed, speechless. I stop in the foyer, facing an alcove with a French-style hand-carved console table. A black antique marble clock with a gold façade—French, too—is sitting in the center. It's an eleven-day clock. The pendulum is no longer swinging. A glass sculpture sits to one side of the clock, and several books sit between bookends on the other. Above the table is a magnificent gilded mirror. I look into the mirror, and I feel like Alice peering into the looking glass.

"Place look familiar?" DeLuca asks.

"The clock is French antique. I don't remember buying it. But it's mine." It's the opposite of *déjà vu.* I feel as if I'm seeing all this for the first time, and yet also know I'm not, because I know what these things are. The feeling is *jamais vu.*

I turn back toward the elevator and look at the wall. Just

as I thought. I have a security system, but it's not armed. I recall the code.

I look down the hallway toward the back of the building. "Kitchen, dining room, guest bedroom." I look in the other direction. "Master bedroom, living room."

I walk toward the living room. Expansive windows overlook the street below. The color scheme is a soft winter white, the sofa a nubuck suede, and the gold metal tables have glass tops. A Louis XVI sideboard lines the wall. A vineyard tapestry hangs above it. Long silk curtains drape from the ceiling to the floor at the edges of the windows. I know where the switch is that opens and closes the curtains—the far-left side, near the fireplace.

A painting hangs above a mantel.

"Salvador Dalí," I say, responding to a question DeLuca hasn't asked. I walk to the painting and study the canvas. Oil. Dalí's signature. Not a reproduction. Recently discovered. I'm baffled at how I know this. Seagulls, leopards, a woman carrying a crucifix, a man on a pedestal, a castle. Similar to another one of his works. The painting represents coming to a new land.

DeLuca doesn't say it, but his expression reveals that he knows that the painting is worth a fortune. He doesn't appear envious; he's only lost in wonderment. Or perhaps he thinks it's stolen?

Then he says, "I knew there was something about you."

I don't reply. The price of the painting has registered in my mind, as though it was long ago filed away in a cerebral ledger, and I'm too distracted to give his words much thought.

"How are you feeling?" he asks.

"Eerie," I manage to say. "I wonder if I recently moved in here. It feels like home but also feels new, a bit foreign. Every item seems like it's in its place. Like a model home that no one lives in."

"That doesn't feel right to you?"

"No, it's normal for me. I like order. But still." What I don't say is that I also apparently like beautiful material things. I'm acquisitive and possibly shallow, it seems.

We cross the foyer and walk down a hallway to the back of the apartment, where we find the kitchen. White marble countertops, white cabinets. An island extends the length of the room. The cabinets are glass-paneled, and the dishes inside are stacked in perfect order. I open several cabinets and drawers. I recognize the items. But doesn't every kitchen have forks and spoons? A coffee pot, mixer, baking sheets, and the like? The items are only familiar, yet they have no real significance. There's a sunroom off the kitchen with a few plump stuffed chairs facing the windows.

"I thought it would all fall into place, like the way I remembered speaking French or dancing," I say.

He walks to the sunroom. "No computer in here. No landline, which doesn't surprise me." He rests his hand on a cabinet pull. "Do you mind?"

"Go ahead."

He opens it, and a few more. There's nothing except kitchen supplies. "You like books," he says, and we both scan the collection on the built-in shelf. Cookbooks and literary novels, the classics.

We walk through the dining room, a guest bedroom and its adjoining bathroom. Nothing. We enter my room. Here, everything feels especially familiar. I run my hand across the white silky fabric of the bedspread. My hand tingles from its luxurious feel. I remember the painting above my bed. It's a landscape of rolling hills and meadows. I've been there. It's Canada, but I can't remember exactly where.

I look around on the night tables and the dresser for photographs. None. "I haven't seen one photograph. Everyone keeps photos of their loved ones. Who the hell was

I, DeLuca? Why was I so lonely?" I wish I could retract those questions. It makes me sound too vulnerable, and I really don't know what his game is. I probably wouldn't have blurted them out if he'd been slightly less handsome.

"Everything is electronic these days. You might have pictures on your phone? Stored in the cloud. If you could access it." He leaves out the part about me not having a computer anywhere around, which is unusual. He pauses as if not sure he should say more, but he does when I give him a look. "Unless you were keeping your identity under wraps."

Of course I was; I'm a criminal. I wrap my arms around my torso—all ribs. I realize I haven't eaten since early that morning. But food will have to wait.

I open the drawer of the bedside table and I'm greeted by a Smith & Wesson M&P Compact pistol and a box of shells. Which I know how to use. I also know some tricks for disarming another person.

We enter my bathroom. Like the rest of the apartment, everything is in its precise place. Or, at least, doesn't feel out of place. I walk through the room, run a finger along the countertop, and hold it up. "Awful lot of dust."

"That's a good thing. It's something I've noticed in every room we've been in."

I look down at the floor. No footprints.

I enter my walk-in closet and then silently gasp, feeling as if a powerful sorceress has magically waved her hand.

I'm home. I remember.

52

I recognize everything in my closet. I open a drawer. Socks. I open the drawer and voilà, a mound of folded socks. I open another to reveal panties, bras, T-shirts, gym clothes, ballet tights. Okay, this is it; now I'm home. Grounded. I have a feeling there's something in this closet that will fill out the picture, but I don't know what. I've either got to get rid of DeLuca or distract him so I can sort through my things in private.

The intercom buzzes, and I head back to the foyer to answer the door.

"It's Sue. Listen, I've been collecting your mail. I'm bringing it up now. I don't like to leave things lying around." Soon after, the elevator doors open, and Sue appears with a thick stack of mail under her left arm and her cane in her right hand. I invite her inside, but she only holds out the mail.

"You shouldn't have gone to the trouble," I say and thank her.

"Can't stand the mess. I'm afraid those kids ripped up your Nordstrom's catalog. I'm sure you'll get another one tomorrow, though. A stack comes every day. The mailman, mailperson, or whatever you call those people these days, I told them to quit bringing them, but they don't listen." She grins wryly.

I smile back. "I always toss the junk out anyway." *Did I?*

"My mother use to take coffee and donuts to the troops back in the forties during the war. They called her a Donut Dollie. Stuck until her dying day. She quite liked it. Now they would call her Baked Goods Delivery Service Personnel. Or something." She winked at DeLuca and did a little dance alternating her shoulders.

DeLuca grins.

"Oh, well," she says. "I've taken up enough of your time."

"Thank you for looking out for me, Sue."

She looks me up and down. "I've got a lemon chicken ready to come out of the oven. I know you said no thanks on the food, but you look a little pale. I'll have one of the grand-kids bring up a plate for you both." She retreats back into the elevator. "Okay, I'm leaving. I got to get back downstairs. My granddaughter, Victoria, is having a conniption fit over some dating show. Hollering and screaming over every little thing. Imagine dating twenty men at once." She shakes her head in disbelief. "One was enough for me."

We say our goodbyes and, not five minutes later, one of Sue's cute granddaughters delivers dinner. DeLuca joins me in the kitchen at the bar.

I practically gulp the food down as I sort through my mail. Junk, more junk. Magazine flyers. Why aren't there any bank statements, insurance premiums, or a doctor's bill? The addressee on the envelopes also read *Mr.* B. Bishop. There's nothing addressed to *Blue* Bishop or even *Ms.* Bishop. Maybe that's not all that unusual for a single female living alone? No, I think. Plenty of single women live on their own and get their mail delivered in their own name.

Maybe I'll find my identity in the garbage, but all I find is an empty plastic bag.

After we eat at my antique kitchen table, I clear the plates and wash the dishes. DeLuca appears at my side with a dish towel and begins drying.

"Okay, this is weird," I say.

"What?"

"I'm not your wife," I say with too much force. "You don't have to dry the dishes. Go sit down!"

He steps back. His face looks like he's a kid who lost his puppy. I don't know if I want to slap him or mash my lips against his.

He recovers and says, jauntily, "Okay, this is me going and sitting down."

"Sorry. That was ... Hey, look. I enjoy your company. Really. But, uh, don't you have things to do? Like figure out where my mother is? Track down those people who've tried five times now to abduct me?"

"Five?"

"Uh, four ... maybe three. Listen, I'm not thinking straight. What are we—what are you really doing here?"

"You shouldn't be alone."

"So you're inviting yourself to spend the night?" I would love him to spend the night, but it can't happen. He's a cop. "I appreciate the offer, but I need some time to myself."

"You're awfully confident."

"I have to become confident to heal. I need to take a bath, have a moment alone. I'll remember more—hopefully, where my mother lives."

"Okay, fine. I'm parked right across the street. I'll be in my car. Flash the lights twice if you need anything."

"Seriously? You're being a babysitter?"

"Nope. A concerned detective on a stakeout."

Something bangs into the kitchen window. I jump,

thrown off kilter. Any confidence I'd been feeling is stripped from me.

"Just a bird," he says.

"Okay, all right," I say. My voice still quavering. "Sleep on the couch. I'm also going to send you to the store to pick up a few things. But this is not a two-night sleepover. Also, my mother's just out there somewhere like a sitting duck. What exactly is your plan?"

"Tomorrow morning, first thing, we're going to the station. I've arranged for you to meet with an artist. Seems the man in the restaurant back in the Hamptons paid for a coffee at the counter when he was waiting for a table, used a credit card."

"He was that careless to use a card, knowing it could be traced?"

"More complicated than that. He used a prepaid card. But we traced where it was purchased, and the guy used a credit card for that—the store didn't take cash. The owner's a germaphobe. The good news is that we were able to trace the company. Found his name. Shane Culbertson. A businessman based in Denver. We ran the name through the system. Feds say he has ties to that assassin who came after you. We don't know what that means, but we want to get a description from you, see if the man you met up with that day is Culbertson."

"And you're just telling me this now?"

His phone rings. "I've got to take this call."

Saved by the bell.

I leave the kitchen but stay in earshot. Another one of those calls with terse responses—*yes, no, that's right, got it*.

I retreat to my bedroom to search through my drawers while he's occupied. I retrieve the 22 from the bedside table. It's loaded. Good. I put it back. A moment later, I hear DeLuca arguing loudly. I step back into the hallway to listen, but the call finishes before I can catch anything of substance. I walk back to the kitchen. His face shows anger, but he's doing his best to suppress it. I never took him for having a temper like this—well, except for that time with the guy outside the shelter. Still waters.

I walk to him. "So? Everything all right? Any news?"

"I'm sorry, nothing to do with your situation. It's another case. A homicide. I have to go deal with it. I won't be long."

"Don't worry about me," I say, trying to sound nonchalant. "I'll be fine. And despite Sue Bramsen's old lady demeanor, no one will get past the door without her noticing."

He looks at me, and his expression eases but only slightly.

"I also have a gun in my bedside table. I know how to use it. In case you forgot. And don't ask; I don't know how I know."

He takes some time to process this information before saying, "I'll come back."

"You don't need to."

He hesitates. There's hurt in his eyes. My mind returns to the day I saw him walking back to the park to coach those little kids. Our talk last night. The way we fit together ... No. Another time. Another life.

"I would like to come back," he says eventually. And I know he means as a man, not as a cop.

I pause a long moment, searching for my answer. "Not so sure that's a good idea. Someone needs to keep their wits about them."

He lumbers off to the elevator.

53

Once DeLuca's gone, I hurry back to my closet. Something is in here that I need to find. I'm sure of it. I just don't know what, or where. I can't be sure DeLuca won't return. No, I'm sure he will. The only question is whether he'll knock on the door or sleep on the street in his parked car. So I may not have much time. I've got to figure out what I'm mixed up in before he has a chance to come back.

I rifle through many empty purses. I sort through my hanging clothes, searching inside the pockets, while also hoping an outfit will trigger a memory. Nothing. I open cabinets, drawers, shoeboxes. I recognize these things as my own, but how I acquired them still remains a blank.

A mannequin is dressed in a red gown. A padded hanger hangs on a wall hook nearby. An open Christian Louboutin shoebox sits empty on my vanity seat. I must've been deciding on my outfit the last night I was here.

I exhale hard and glance up and around at the many shelves and cabinets. My eyes stop on an upper shelf enclosed behind a glass window. I open it and find a riding helmet and a crop. I touch the hat. Memories of riding horses hit me in a massive wave. Stables. Mucking stalls. Grooming and feeding horses, walking them in the early morning and again at night. The thick horse smell.

I know I was raised on a horse farm. That's why I recalled hooves pounding when I woke from the coma, and why I remembered so much about horses when Lorraine and I talked in the kitchen.

I open a side drawer to my vanity and take out some folded scarves. Hidden beneath them is an old wooden music box, hand-painted in Bohemian floral patterns. The once brightly colored paint has eroded and is now cracked and peeling. I gently take the box in my hands and admire it before opening the lid. As soon as the top is upright, a ballerina pops up and begins twirling around on a spring. At the same time, the encasement is activated, and a small drum layered with pins begins to rotate. The set of protruding pins plucks the tuned teeth of a steel comb, clinking out a melody. It's a lullaby, but not one I've heard played in a long while.

At the bottom of the box is a tiny handle that opens an inner compartment. Inside, I find a small envelope, unsealed. In the envelope is a washed-out photograph of a man and woman, who I recognize as my parents, standing arm in arm. In the photo, they are far younger than I am now. The edge of the paper has a date penciled in, 1983—likely before I was born. I turn the photograph over and find faded pencil marks. Annette and Jean Claude. 14 Rue du Clermont, Québec City.

I feel as if I've dissolved and rematerialized in a different dimension. I take a step back and use the wall to brace myself. I steady myself and examine the box again. There's a label, the name of a shop, and the designation Québec City. Of course. I lived with my parents in Canada. That's why I speak English and French.

So much is returning, and all at once. I'm overwhelmed with so many mixed emotions—the dominant one is joy. I hold the photograph to my chest. More than anything, I want to go home, to Canada. I only pray I'm not chasing ghosts. But all I have is a photograph and a city. I grab my phone and begin to search for their address in Canada and the States, using their first names and my last. Nothing.

There's got to be more in here.

Where would I hide something?

I've searched through my belongings. Nothing. I glance up at my riding helmet.

I close my eyes, and my body sways. I will myself back to my riding days. I think of the music box and hum lyrics I've made up. Words come to me: *In the barn, in the barn. Under the rafters, behind the stalls. In the barn, in the barn, bury the coins, not in the mud, snug in the walls. In the barn, in the barn …*

I recall being inside a barn, the horses snorting and whinnying. Racehorses. I drift back to a day I was playing in the barn. I have several precious gold coins that I've placed in a match box, and I need a secret hiding place. Someone is coming, so I slide the box between the wood slats at the back of a stall.

My eyes pop open and I pivot around toward the cabinets.

That's it!

I haven't checked behind these cabinets! But they're attached to the wall, so is that even possible? I zero in on a set of long cabinet doors. I open them and find four drawers below and four open shelves above that hold sweaters and shirts. I shove the clothing to the floor. When the cabinet is empty, I stand on a chair in front of the cabinet and run my hands across the back paneling, applying pressure. The grooves and corners are tight except for the bottom shelf. I hop off the chair and press on the center of the back wall and then the corners.

The wood creaks. There's a gap.

I imagine I'm holding reins of a galloping horse, speeding to the finish line. I move my hands to the edges and push. The gap around the panel widens. I continue to push and tug downward, and then, like magic, the panel gives way and slides away.

I gasp at what I see.

54

I stare into the built-in compartment behind the cabinet. A locked metal box. I find my purse, grab the key I found in the safety deposit box, and try the lock. It opens! Money, papers. Passports—not one but three. And a small bundle.

I gather the items in my arms, kick the articles of clothing out of the way, and plop down to the floor. I drop the papers in front of me, the items scattering. I take deep breaths and pick up the passports and fan them out like playing cards—Canadian and French and American. The name inside the American passport reads Bleue L'Évêque. No middle name.

The photograph is of me, but I'm a blonde. I'm thirty-two years old, born April 11. Or, at least, Bleue L'Évêque was. I study the photograph. My eyes are dark, not blue. I read my personal information; sure enough, the eye color is listed as brown. The pages are blank. No stamps from other countries. The passport is unused. A fake? I check the date of issue—eleven months ago.

I'm stunned as I look through the other passports. The

French passport reveals that I'm Bleue L'Evêque, too. The blonde version.

I open the Canadian passport last and study the picture. I appear three to five years younger in this photo than I was in the others. More importantly, the image is the real me. My hair is dark, my eyes are blue, but my name is still Bleue L'Évêque. I thumb through the pages—Monaco, France, Luxembourg, Holland, Italy, Spain ... I can't believe my eyes. Whatever fun, carefree life I've been living has also taken place in Europe.

My hands drop to my lap. Blue Bishop is a variation of my real name. In French, *Bleue* is, of course, the feminine spelling for the adjective *blue*. And *l'évêque* is "the bishop". I've renamed myself Blue Bishop. I'm Blue Bishop without any official papers. I see a bundle and open it to find a blonde wig and a small flat box. Inside is a pair of dark brown contacts. My God, I use an alias—Blue Bishop—in America. More proof I'm hiding.

I set the passports aside and count the bundles of currencies—one hundred thousand in American dollars, money that can be used anywhere in the world and converted without question. The same in Euros, and in Canadian dollars. I set the money aside and pick up the credit cards. The cards are in Bleue's name, not Blue Bishop.

I search for my parents again on my phone, using the new last name. Nothing.

Calm down. Think. I can work this out.

I thumb through the credit cards again to be sure. A business card is stuck on the back of one of them, attached via the gluey gel that adheres a credit card to the cardboard it arrives on. I gently pull the card loose and flip it over and see only three faded words: *Marché aux Fleurs*. Flower market. The name *Alfie* is penciled in above the printed words.

I reach for my phone and do a quick search for a business

named Marché aux Fleurs. Nothing comes up in the New York and surrounding areas. I try using Alfie in the search. Nothing. I expand my search to florists in the Province of Montreal and get a thousand hits.

There's only one thing I can do now—go to Canada and begin asking questions. I have a photograph of my parents and an address to begin my search. I studied ballet at the National Ballet School in Toronto, so I can search there as well. I have a business card that may very well lead me to John Brownsworth.

I place the cash in a large purse, along with my passports and the credit cards. I begin to clean up the mess, but just as I'm pushing the piece of wood back in place, a journal flops down from the secret compartment. I open it and begin to read.

There are dates, names, and numbers in this journal—but also a portal to the past. I remember much, not all of it. Not enough. Since this nightmare began, numbers have made sense to me.

"My God," I say out loud.

I do launder money for criminals. No surprise, just solid proof. Which makes me a criminal. No doubt about that now. I come across the number to my bank account in the Grand Caymans. Banking there, well, that's no mistake.

Out of nowhere, I see my father in my mind's eye. He is lifting a bale of hay, so physically strong. He sniffs. Looks at me strangely. Drops the hay bale. Falls face forward to the dirt floor of the barn. I run to him and roll him over. He manages to gasp, "Take care of your mother. Stop, and if you don't stop, don't get caught." My invincible father, dead from a massive heart attack. He was only fifty years old.

So he knew. He knew the road I was venturing down. And then he was dead. He took care of himself, but the stress—a bad time for horse breeders, especially small mom-and-pop breeders like my parents. And then the bad decision to invest in Sullivan's Silk, a stallion with a great track record but questionable bloodlines. He was an anomaly, as it turned out; his offspring were not. Failures at the track. My parents hemorrhaging money, lying awake at night, and in the daytime walking around like zombies. The overwhelming stress.

I started cleaning cash to save the stables—I had good intentions. But I continued because I liked what the benefits brought me.

My history of money laundering surfaces like carbonation racing to the top of my brain. The bubbles pop and another memory bursts full on. I illegally used my family's horse-breeding business to get us out of trouble. I betrayed my sweet, honest mother. She, unlike my father, knows nothing about this. Like many trips to hell, my journey started with good intentions. The horse-breeding business, and particularly my family's business, had hit a recession. The Sport of Kings had lost popularity. Many of my parents' business ventures hadn't panned out.

So, taking advantage of my business degree and my acquaintance with the shady characters who inevitably hang out where gambling exists, I worked some deals for the mayor of a city in Halifax—open up a "horseman's account", rapidly sell and resell horses, and take a hefty commission. That's all I remember about the mayor. I can't even visualize his face. Like so many of the other criminals that I aided and abetted, he has become a ledger entry. Forgetting faces—a way to salve my guilty conscience.

So, yes, I saved my family's stables and more, always intending to stop when we had enough to keep going. I didn't stop. I moved often to keep a low profile. I liked the fancy dresses, the real estate I bought and sold in the world's richest cities, the travel, and the exciting, meaningless hookups. Liked it until I couldn't stand it anymore, couldn't stand myself.

The memories flow into me. I can't control which memories come and which don't. I now know how I got into the money-cleaning business, but I still don't know who John Brownsworth is, or who's pursuing me and why.

Strange to discover that I am someone whose whole life has been organized around greed.

55

I flip through the pages of the journal and little by little, all of the transactions begin to come back to me.

I stop when I come across John Brownsworth's name. A transfer to an account in Grand Cayman in the amount of one hundred fifty million. One hundred thirty-five million transferred to Brownsworth. Ruby ("Cassiopeia"). A pretty hefty fee came my way.

I stop cold. I'm starting to remember. John Brownsworth is a dual citizen of the United States and the British Overseas Territories. Those territories include the Cayman Islands.

Reading the notes and reading between the lines, I piece together the Cassiopeia deal. John needed money fast to get out of debt to the Internal Revenue Service. Sometimes it's best not to know every detail of how a client comes across items they want to sell. But it's always unwise to be completely in the dark. I haven't been caught in a trap by the authorities yet. Didn't plan on it happening either.

I think back to the conversation with John, remember his voice now. Weird that I can't remember the mayor's face, but I remember John. His accent is like the Queen's. Can't judge a criminal by his voice. Although, I'm not exactly sure whether John Brownsworth is a criminal.

"It's not every day that a girl gets to hold a ruby this size in her hand," I'd said to him.

"Maybe some of its luck will rub off on you," he had replied.

"Well, it's nice to know that I'm not touching something cursed."

He laughed. "On the contrary."

"Just wondering if it'll sear a scar onto my palm."

"You'll have to forgive my ignorance, but I'm afraid that I don't quite follow."

"Is it hot?"

He chuckled. "I see. No, no. Nothing like that to worry about. I'm only brokering it through you to avoid the gossip, you know?"

"So tell me about it," I asked. "I understand why you're giving it up. Financial need, which must be difficult."

"Yes, it's been a struggle. But it's like I told my wife, it's only a stone with a peculiar name. We've had a wonderful life, had everything we ever dreamed of, actually. Keeping something locked away in a vault doesn't do much good for anyone. Investments are meant to be used when the time comes. Our time has come—we're in a spot."

"So it's a family heirloom?" I asked.

"Yes, passed down through several generations. Don't ask me who named the rock or where it originally came from. I'm sure the damn thing was picked out of a mountain mine somewhere in Burma or the like. That, I really couldn't say the first about. It's a glitzy sort of thing, I suppose. Shame to see it go. But it's not something you can go prancing around in. It'd be particularly gauche to wear around one's neck—and too heavy. I suppose if one were the Pope, it could be mounted in the zucchetto. Then again, God might have his issues with such self-aggrandizement." He chuckled. "No, it's served its purpose. Time to pass it along. You can get our price for it, can't you?"

"Without a doubt. I'm hoping I can get more." I paused and studied the stone. "Perhaps we'll even see it go to a museum."

He chuckled again. "Yes, let it sit beside the Hope Diamond. Putting good and evil beside one another may balance out the universe."

I laughed. John's humor and insights always amused me. I realize I've had a long association with John Brownsworth.

Of course, we vetted the grade and authenticity of the ruby through my jeweler, Ashem—for a hefty fee. John dropped it off, and Ashem knew I would pick it up. That's why I had the receipt from the jewelry store. All done to legitimize the stone for the upcoming auction on the black market. The sale brought in an extraordinary price.

I turn the page of the journal. The last entry—a transfer of one hundred and fifty million American dollars to my account in the Grand Caymans. From Shane Culbertson. For the Cassiopeia Ruby. So I knew about the stone or, at least, knew its worth. More than that. Meeting with Culbertson set May 22, the day of my fall. Delivery.

Last notation. I backed out of the deal. No reason stated. No money transfers. That means a bare fraction of Culbertson's money is sitting in my account. The bulk of the money had already gone to John Brownsworth. I couldn't refund the money if I wanted to. I don't have it. Anyway, at the restaurant, Culbertson said he didn't want a refund anyway. The ruby was invaluable to him, he said.

I feel dizzy. I grasp the edge of the cabinet and slide down to the floor. I grasp the sides of my head and, bent forward, I begin to rock. I let out a muffled scream. Why would I back out of the deal? What went wrong, so wrong that Culbertson almost killed me and is now threatening my mother? The only reason she and I are still alive is because he believes that I still have possession of that ruby. Which I do.

I have to find my mother.

I pull myself together. I have an old photo with an address on the back of it. I have a starting point. I do a search for Annette and Claude and horse farms. No direct hits. I click on images and find pages of photographs and articles.

I stop on one photograph. The woman in it is the same one wearing my necklace in the photo Culbertson showed me. But it's an old picture, from fifteen years ago, and no names are directly linked. I know why. I advised my mother to put her property into either a trust or a corporate entity—to shield her from liability and to hide her identity, and therefore my own, once I was fully engaged in the illegal trade of buying and selling racehorses to launder funds for criminals.

I do a search of the property owners for the address on the back of the photograph and get a hit. Pierre and Eliza L'Évêque. My father's parents. No phone number.

I pack a small carry-on bag loaded with a change of outfits, the passports, and a wad of money. Then I place the rest of the stuff back in the metal box, lock it, and return it and my journal to the compartment. I replace the boards, then fold and put the clothes back in the drawers.

I have to get out of here before DeLuca returns. He would never let me leave the country. When he discovers I'm gone and haven't returned, he'll know that I'm involved in criminal activities and will think I've gone on the run. Or he'll think I've been abducted. I'm back in that vise. Part of me wants to wait and let DeLuca do his job and find my mother. But every minute matters.

I put on the wig, pop in the contact lenses, and dress in a pair of jeans, a long-sleeve white blouse, a black light-weight raincoat, and a baseball cap. I've learned the craft of deception, all right. In fact, I'm not just a craftsperson, I'm an artist at deception. I grab my bag, turn on the living room lights, and head toward the back of my apartment.

Opening the kitchen window, which leads onto an old-fashioned fire escape, I climb down the ladder. I cross the courtyard, exit the property, walk around the block, and hail a taxi, which takes me to Penn Station. I book an overnight ticket to Québec City, Canada, and pay with cash.

I hate that I'm so good at dissembling. I hate to do this to DeLuca. I should never have let him get under my skin. I should never have let him into my apartment, into my oh-so dark world.

56

Roudebusch walks over to DeLuca's desk and puts a hand on his shoulder.

DeLuca stiffens. "Get your hand off me, Jerry, before I break your arm. I don't need you giving me shit now."

Roudebusch withdraws his arm. "You won't believe me, but that's not what I'm about."

DeLuca glares at him.

"Well, not always," Roudebusch says. He sits down on the corner of the desk.

DeLuca doesn't have the energy to tell his partner to go away.

"About two years after I made detective, I got emotionally attached to a subject, nothing physical," Roudebusch says. "She was a witness, the girlfriend of a wise guy over in Brooklyn who was on trial for RICO violations, extortion, all the usual charges. I was the arresting officer and charged with protecting her. When—"

"Look, Jerry—"

"I'm not here to judge, just telling you a story that not

many people know," Roudebusch continues. "Courtesy of Inspector Taylor, who took mercy on me. Anyway, this woman who I thought was vulnerable, thought had feelings for me, ended up hiring a lawyer, who said I sexually harassed her. Tried to use these trumped-up charges to get her boyfriend off. It wasn't true, and luckily my partner at the time, Jules Beck, she stood up for me. I learned my lesson, and I was trying to teach you that lesson by being a prick. Not the best teaching methods, I guess. But don't worry. You'll come through this. At least Bishop wasn't a key witness or a suspect. Well, not that we knew of, anyway." Roudebusch put his hand on DeLuca's shoulder again. "Hang in there, kid."

DeLuca nods a thanks, but he doesn't feel much better. He let Blue get away—*helped* her get away—and that turned out to be a much bigger deal than he thought.

His phone buzzes. "They're ready for you now," Inspector Taylor's assistant says.

He gets up and goes over to the conference room, ready to hear the lecture about becoming emotionally involved with a crime victim—especially someone who's much more than a crime victim.

Before entering the conference room, the inspector says, "Want to tell me why I shouldn't suspend you, DeLuca?"

DeLuca falters. He expected a reprimand. Not to be thrown off the case. He has to find Blue. He can't let the case go until he solves it. "Inspector, I gotta see this one through."

"Come in, you can tell me all about it. Then we'll see what's what."

57

With my French passport, I get into Canada without a problem and change trains in Saint-Lambert and travel the rest of the way there. That morning after I arrive, I take a taxi from the train station to a small hotel on the outskirts of town.

A quick search of florists in the Quebec City area turns up empty, so in a rented car, I head toward my grandparents' home on Rue de Clermont—the street address on the reverse side of the photograph of my parents. I travel the back roads toward my past, the small rural community where my parents and I must've lived. It's a sunny day, and the simple warm rays of sunshine give me strength.

When I turn onto my street, my heart thumps so hard I wonder if I'll pass out. I pray my grandparents still live at this address, not in a nursing home. I drive, studying the houses scattered amongst the quaint and lush countryside. When I spot the traditional Normandy-style house, with its striped inlaid walls and pitched roof, the air catches in my throat. I've found my home. Of that I am certain, except this isn't a horse ranch. But I'm sure I lived here. I remember it.

Flooded with more and more memories, I mentally trace the hallways inside the house, the one leading to my room. I no longer see the house through the eyes of a child. The home is older now, but it seems smaller. The yard is grassy, and the trees are taller, giving off plenty of shade. On a branch there are remnants of a rope. My father hung a tire swing from that rope. I was young, I think five, at the time. Yes, I remember that.

In the surrounding houses, children are running from their backyards to their front yards and then back around. I park the car, pass through a white-picket gate, and head to the front door. Does my mother or someone from my family still live here? If not, what am I going to say to the person who answers the door? No sounds from inside are audible. I take a deep breath and knock.

When no one comes to the door, I knock again, louder this time. No one appears to be home.

I turn around and study the surrounding homes. I've come too far to give up now. Next door, I see an older woman emerge from her house and walk to her front gate. In French, I call out to her.

When the woman stops and turns in my direction, I wave. I'm heartened when she waves back, although she appears perplexed. She looks at my car.

I walk toward her. "I'm visiting. I used to live here. In this house." I smile, hoping she won't shy away.

She tilts her head as if lost in thought. She must be in her eighties. She could have lived here when I was a child, or so I hope.

"I used to live next door," I say. "Bleue L'Évêque."

She relaxes her stance but clings to the fence for support.

"I lived here with my parents, I think," I continue. "Have you lived here long?"

She studies me with a fixed gaze but still says nothing.

I find the photograph of my parents and hand it to her. She studies it briefly then looks up skeptically.

"I'm Bleue L'Évêque," I repeat. "The two in the photograph are my parents."

The woman nods in recognition. I'm so pleased, I'm bursting inside.

"Annette and Jean Claude L'Évêque lived here many years ago," she says.

"I think my grandparents live here, too?"

At this, she turns pale, and she hands me back the photograph. "You resemble her," she says, as if she's seen a ghost. "Your mother, Annette."

"Do you know what happened to them?" I ask. "Does my mother still live here?"

She's still looking at me weirdly. "Where did you get the photograph?"

"My mother gave it to me a long time ago. I keep it in a music box. With a ballerina inside."

She silently gasps and places a hand on her chest. Her fingers are gnarled. She appears to have aged another ten years.

"Do you know it?" I ask.

"You're Bleue. I haven't seen you since you were a little girl."

I understand what she must be feeling. "I had an accident some weeks ago. A terrible fall, and I lost a lot of my memory. It's coming back, but very slowly. Please, help me remember."

My words seem to alarm her even more. I'm on the verge of falling apart. The first person who might know something about my past doesn't want to talk.

I look at her mailbox for some indication of her name. There is none, but the very act of looking sparks a memory. "You're Madame Dubois. You gave me Madeleine cookies. You baked them yourself. And once, a crepe with chocolate."

Her chest rises and falls as she breathes in and slowly exhales. She glances beyond me as if searching into the past and then says, "You used to run through the backyards. I loved to watch you play. Never had children of my own. You were a very sweet girl."

I take the liberty of grasping one of her hands, which is twisted with arthritis, then give a little curtsy, none of it contrived. "It's so nice to see you again, Madame."

"You say that you had an accident, that you lost your memory?" She's gazing at me with clear eyes, the intensity of the gaze like a polygraph.

"An accident," I lie.

She tilts her head toward my family house. "Then you don't remember her?"

"Who?"

"Your grandmother, Eliza. She still lives here."

Now it's my turn to gasp. Her words are like an incantation that opens a locked door.

"Is she home?" I ask. "I knocked and rang the bell. No one answered."

"No. They wouldn't. She is in the backyard. Come with me. I'll let you pass through my backyard to hers and you can get in that way. But prepare yourself, dear, because this will be a difficult reunion."

58

I breathe deeply, trying to catch my breath as we walk. I've found my grandmother. I hope she'll lead me straight to my mother.

But what does the neighbor mean that I should prepare myself for a difficult reunion?

"Is my grandmother sick?" I ask, afraid of her answer.

"Be gentle with her," Madame Dubois says. "She doesn't like commotion, upsets easily. It's typical of someone with Alzheimer's."

My hearts sinks. Did the sun just set forever? I'm here to recover my past, and I'm about to meet with a woman who's losing hers.

Ms. Dubois stops a moment and presses down on my arm. "Please. Whatever you do, don't mention your father's death. Your grandmother thinks he's still alive."

The memory of him falling over with the hay bale seizes me again, as if it happened yesterday. I'm grieving him a second time. So far, there's not a lot that's good about recovering my memories, except the possibility of saving my mother's life, and my own.

I stand more erect and force myself to set my emotions aside. I nod at Madame Dubois. "Do you know if my other grandparents are alive?"

"Your grandfather—Eliza's husband, Pierre—died when you were very young." Madame Dubois touches her chest. "The heart." She looks at me knowingly, a family condition passed down from my grandfather to my father. "I don't know about your other side."

I smile to show my gratitude.

"There is something else," she says. Her face turns to one of grave concern. "Some men have been here. American."

A rush of adrenaline. "Have you spoken with them?"

"No, I don't open the door to strangers. But I saw them out back speaking with your Grandmother Eliza. The caretaker says they were asking about your parents. Said they went to college with your father."

This explains why she was hesitant at first to speak with me. "Did my grandmother or her caretaker tell them anything? Where my parents live?"

"Eliza can't tell anyone much of anything. She lives in the past. I doubt the caretaker told them anything. She respects your grandmother's privacy."

We walk from the side of the house to the backyard. Madame Dubois is surprisingly spry. The privacy shrubs are fairly high, but I'm able to see the top of two people's heads. When we reach a pass through between the yards, Madame Dubois enters first, and I follow.

"Hello," she calls out. "Fine day for some sunshine. Not too hot yet."

The caretaker, a stout middle-aged woman, and an elderly woman look our way.

"May we join you, Eliza?" Madame Dubois asks. "There's someone here who wants to say hello."

"Yes, of course," Eliza says, smiling. "Did you bring something fresh from the market?"

The caretaker rises and arranges a couple of chairs for us.

"Please," my grandmother says, gesturing with an arm for us to sit.

"I didn't go to the market today," Madame Dubois says. "But I'll bring you strawberries later this week."

I've expected my grandmother to appear like an invalid, but that isn't the case. Her appearance is more youthful than her neighbor's, but the thinning of her body, which comes along with the disease, is beginning to show. Her hair is neatly coiffed; she's dressed in a pleasant-looking dress and wears a strand of pearls and matching pair of pearl studs.

"Do sit down," my grandmother says.

"We only have a few minutes," the caretaker says. I suspect this is her way of telling me not to stay too long. Then she glances up and adds, "The sun is getting too strong."

My grandmother turns to her caretaker. "What time is it?" Then she looks at me and says, "Have we met?"

The words rend my soul, but I force myself to keep my composure. But I don't remember her either. What child doesn't remember her grandparent?

"It's almost ten thirty," I say. "My name is Bleue. I'm your —" I stop myself. I'm not sure how much I should say.

"You look very familiar." My grandmother turns to the caretaker as if seeking emotional support. "Do you know her?" she asks the caretaker. "She's ... Who am I thinking of?"

Before the caretaker speaks, Madame Dubois says, "She wants to ask you about your son and daughter-in-law." She's careful to include my father in the equation.

"That's it," my grandmother says bitterly. "You're playing games with me, Annette. Always the game player."

The caretaker shakes her head at me in warning.

I tread lightly, not sure how to begin.

"Where's Jean Claude today?" Madame Dubois asks. She's a mind reader, too.

"He's working at the bank, in the city, of course," my grandmother says. "Comes and goes all the time. Why aren't you there today?"

"I took the day off to visit you," I say, ill at ease with this ruse.

"Why ever would you think I wanted to see you?" my grandmother asks.

"Jean Claude is such a busy man," the caretaker says to me. "Madame Eliza always says that her son is too busy to visit her."

I note how the caretaker excludes my mother from her last remark, focusing only on my father.

"A son should visit his mother," my grandmother says firmly.

"Where's Bleue?" I ask, looking between my grandmother and the caretaker.

"Ballet school in the city." My grandmother again turns to her caretaker for support. She's showing signs of distress. "Oh, the girl could be such a wonderful little ballerina, if only ..." She swishes a finger at Madame Dubois. "You should not feed her so many cookies. She won't be able to dance. I have told that child not to eat so much, told her over and over. She will get too big and lose her ability to dance on her toes." She pauses. "Is it March? Bleue's at school, no?"

"June," the caretaker says. "Summertime."

"There you have it," my grandmother says, turning back to me. "She's at ballet school for the gifted children in Toronto. Should be studying in Paris, but after ... I took her to Toronto myself. Anything is better than riding around on those farm animals." My grandmother looks at me askance.

I can see the wheels turning inside her head. She's

searching for words. I understand exactly how she feels. "You don't ride horses, do you?" she asks, peering at me.

"Oh, no."

"Good." She shakes her head. "It's Bleue's own fault for not getting into the Paris ballet school. It was that accident. All her fault!" A strong gust of wind suddenly blows past us. My grandmother fluffs her hair, distracted by a few loose strands, becoming more agitated.

The caretaker gets up to help her.

When my grandmother settles back down, she looks back at me. "Have we met?"

I want to ask about the accident. But that would sound too confrontational. I twist my chair, debating what to say, and then decide to answer, "Yes, we have. I'm Bleue. I'm your granddaughter."

My grandmother's pallid complexion turns whiter. The caretaker's expression is one of disapproval.

"It's true, Eliza," Madame Dubois says. "This is your granddaughter, Bleue. She's here now. All grown up."

My grandmother wrestles with the arms of her chair, her hands slipping from the metal slates. She's trying to push the chair back but struggles. "Liar."

"Hold on, Eliza," the caretaker says.

"We need to go inside," my grandmother says.

The caretaker turns to me. "I'm sorry. We must go now. The sun is becoming too intense."

"Wait," I say. "Please."

The caretaker places a tender hand on my grandmother's arm. The touch calms the older woman. "It's okay now, Eliza. Be still. This lady says she's Bleue. Come to visit you after all these years."

This must mean that I don't have much of a relationship with my grandmother—or any at all. My grandmother begins shaking her head again, and her jaw hangs slack. "I don't have a granddaughter. She was taken away. Like my only son."

"You remember your Bleue playing in the yard and dancing for you," Madame Dubois says. "Look at her eyes, how brilliant they are, and so blue, like the sky."

My grandmother places a hand over her mouth but doesn't look at me. "Dear Blue, dear Blue," she says in heavily accented English. She quiets and then continues despondently, "Oh no. What am I saying? This is Annette's fault, they've abandoned me. Evil woman, accusing me of hurting that child. I warned my son about her and those horses. He refused to listen, the pigheaded boy."

From my grandmother's remarks deflecting blame, I realize now that she is the older woman from my fragments of memory. The one who slapped and harshly scolded me. "Where did they go?"

My grandmother looks at her caretaker. "I've said too much. Don't tell them I said Montreal. Will those men come after me?"

"No, no," the caretaker says. "Don't be silly." She glances at me and says, "Claude and Annette left a long time ago. It's unclear to me why. They lost touch."

"Who's the 'them' Eliza is talking about?" I ask the caretaker.

My grandmother's expression turns fearful. "Are they back?" my grandmother asks scanning her surroundings. "Don't let them back here. They weren't invited. Get rid of them. Now!"

"What men?" I ask. "What did they want?"

My grandmother glares at me. "To find Bleue and her mother, of course."

"Did they threaten you?"

My grandmother turns away and looks back at me. "Who are you again?"

It's a good question. Indeed, who am I? Someone not very savvy, from what little I know. Neither was my grandmother. Perhaps the two facts are not a coincidence.

Madame Dubois touches my arm. The signal that we should go.

I'm not ready. "I'm just leaving. One question, Eliza, please," I beg. "Where do Claude and Annette live?"

My grandmother's entire body begins to tremble. "Annette took him back home."

"Where is Annette from?" the caretaker asks.

"Montreal, isn't it?" my grandmother asks in an uncertain tone. "Yes, yes." My grandmother stares at me. "Why are you still here?"

59

After I leave my grandmother's house, I do another internet search for florists in Montreal on my phone, then call the first one I find. I ask to speak with the owner and explain that I'm looking for a business that goes by the name of Marché aux Fleurs. No luck. No hits with a dozen others.

I begin my three-hour journey by car to a country inn just south of Montreal where I've booked a room. I search for any information I can find on both of my parents. No listing for either. Nothing in only Annette L'Évêque's name. I'll call every ranch in the area.

I reach the inn, spent. When I step out of the car, my legs wobble. It feels good to stand, to breathe, to take in the cooler climate. The countryside feels like home to me, with its lush green trees and lawns. There isn't another building in sight. I grab my bag from the back seat and head up the stone walk. I'm met by a Saint Bernard, whom I greet with a friendly hello. He licks my hand and joins me as if he's my personal bellhop. I walk along the pathway, which is surrounded by blooming shrubs, and pass underneath a trellis filled with roses. The flowers' divine fragrance fills the air.

Farther down the path, the inn comes into view. It's an old cottage, much like a farmhouse from yesteryear—so warm and inviting. I open the wooden door, and a bell jingles. The dog follows me inside and plops down on a rug near the fireplace. The rustic inn features exposed rafters and wide-plank floors. The walls are a combination of stone and wood paneling and are adorned with pictures and farming artifacts. A dining-and-bar area is located at the back half of the inn. Visible through the windows are fields and mountains.

No one is at the desk in the lobby or seated in the gathering area to the right of the desk. I wait before calling out. Then I hear the pattering of feet moving along an upstairs corridor.

"Coming," a woman calls.

The innkeeper lumbers down the staircase wearing a broad, welcoming smile. She's a short, round-faced woman who looks to be in her early seventies. She appears as if she's emerged from a storybook.

She greets me and introduces herself as Pavla. "You've missed supper, I'm afraid, but not to worry. If you haven't eaten, there's plenty. I'll fix you a plate. I only have one other guest this evening."

I give her my information, and she checks me in. I use my given name, Bleue L'Évêque, as I've done since I've arrived in Canada.

"While you are here, I recommend that you visit the city's historic district," she says. "The town is so charming, like walking backwards in time. Europe in a North American city. I can help you arrange tours if you like. Just let me know how I can help." She peers over the counter and sees my bag on the floor. "Do you have any more luggage?"

The dog rises when he hears her say "luggage" and walks over to me.

I lift my single bag and say, "Only this."

"You go lie down now, Kaddy," Pavla says to the dog. "Your work is finished for the day." She smiles at him lovingly. "He has a wagon to pull luggage inside. Likes to work. Isn't that right, Kaddy?"

I chuckle and say, "For treats, I guess."

She grins at me with a sparkle in her eyes. "Yes, of course. Don't say that too loud, or I'll be in trouble."

She hands me a key, and I start to my room, but then stop. "This is an odd request," I say. "But is there any way you can loan me a laptop?" The research that I intend to conduct would be difficult using a smartphone.

She laughs. "Of course. This is the twenty-first century. We have a dedicated computer room for guests and free Wi-Fi. But I can also lend you a laptop."

It's too late to begin calling farms, but if I don't hit on a lead tomorrow morning, I'll be forced to call DeLuca for help. I just hope he doesn't try to get me arrested here.

60

Saturday morning, I spread a paper map out on my bed. I prefer a paper map over an electronic depiction as I get a palpable sense of landscape and how the area is situated. I use my phone to search horse stables in the area.

The horse breeding world is small. I reach for a pen to begin circling the points where the farms are situated on the map. As I'm shaking the contents out of my purse to find the pen, someone knocks solidly on my door. I jolt, and some papers, including the business card, slip from my bag and onto the floor.

"Sorry to disturb, last call for breakfast," Pavla says.

"Thank you. Be right there." I lean down to the floor for the business card and, as I'm picking it up, the light shines on the card and I notice some smudges. I bring the card closer and into focus. A portion of the print below the words *Marché aux Fleurs* has worn off. How could I have missed this? Straining to make out the letters, I hold the card directly in front of the light bulb in the bedside lamp: *Marché aux Fleurs de Vigne*. I do a quick internet search and locate the shop in downtown Montreal. Do I call or go in person?

I dial the florist. A young man answers.

"I'm looking for someone who goes by the name Alfie," I say.

"I don't know anyone here by the name," he says. "I'll have to ask the owner."

"I would appreciate that."

"He's not due in for another hour."

I give my name and phone number and ask that Alfie call me back. I throw on yesterday's dress and head down the hall to breakfast. The other lodger, whom I haven't seen, has already checked out, leaving me as the inn's only guest. I prefer the silence and solitude.

Pavla serves me a plate of pancakes with a side of ham for breakfast—more than I usually eat in two days. I ask her to join me, and she takes a seat.

"You appear perplexed," she says. "Can I help?"

I'm reluctant to involve someone who might end up with trouble on her porch but can't resist her offer of help. I've come too far. So, I tell Pavla that I have amnesia and why, and that I'm trying to regain my memory—that I'm trying to find my mother.

My phone rings before Pavla can say anything, so she smiles and leaves.

I answer and wait. It's the clerk from the flower shop. He gives me the number for Alfie, tells me he's expecting my call. I head to my room and dial the number.

When I hear Alfie's voice, another can full of carbonated bubbles pops open. Alfie is my auctioneer, although law enforcement might use another, uglier word—fence. Most recently, he helped transact the sale of the ruby. Suddenly, I see Alfie in my mind. He's wiry, carrot-top, solid muscle, and has retained a hint of an Irish accent. As a boy, he dreamed of being a world-class jockey, but by the time he was thirteen, he was already too big. We hit it off immediately. His humor amused me.

There's no hint of humor in his voice now.

He speaks fast and anxiously. "I'm glad you finally called, Blue. Where have you been? We have a serious problem. It's our buyer, Shane Culbertson. His men are sniffing around all over the place. Looking for me. You too. They roughed up a few maintenance guys out at the track when they got to town. Johnny B. was the first. He called me from the ER. They broke his collarbone and nose. One of his corneas got pretty scratched up. He's lucky he didn't lose his eye. I've been in hiding ever since he called."

"He tried to kill me," I say and give him a recap of what's happened so far.

"Bugger," he says. More than once. He tells me that he never saw anything about my fall in the media. That he's tried to contact me repeatedly. All he got was my voicemail, which was full. He got worried, even surfed the internet news to see if I was dead.

Wait, I think. DeLuca said that he ran my photo in the media. Lorraine's daughter was watching cartoons and recognized me. Did Alfie miss that? That doesn't make sense. None of this makes sense. Unless they never ran the picture at all.

"I've got to find my mother. Culbertson has threatened her, too."

"Look no more," he says. "I know where she lives. I have her phone number."

A river of relief flows through me. I put my mother's details in my contacts. "You're a life saver, Alfie. Just curious, how do *you* happen to have this information?"

There's a shocked silence. "Jesus, Bleue," he says eventually. "We grew up together. Well, sort of. I have a few years on you. We used to hang out at the races. More so after I lost my jockey seat and could only be an exerciser. Don't you remember coming down to visit me at the stalls?"

"No, I don't."

"The mayor of Halifax, remember him?"

"He's in my ledger, buying and selling horses. I remember pieces of him."

"Well, you ought to recall more than a few pieces. He used to show up at the races wearing that white top hat with red roses painted on the brim and horses racing around the side band. The bees followed him around."

As he says it, I can remember it, and more. "Oh, yeah, yeah. Sure. He was a real ladies' man. Or thought he was." He used to impress women with money that no public servant should have. He wore a white double-breasted striped Hopsack suit. Too flashy for a politician, at least any politician since 1960.

"The mayor is how this all started?" I ask. "You introduced him to me. But it was just buy-sell deals." I reflect longer. The guy was the king of bribes. Had his hand in everyone's pocket.

"Bingo. And a whole lot more. You washed his dirty linen."

"What a creep that man was. And a crook, but he saved my family's stable." I remember the day Alfie introduced me to the mayor. He'd just scored a sizable win and was in a grand mood. It wasn't hard to convince him that I could handle his business. It helped that he was smitten with me. First it was just a horseman's account, then it turned to laundering bribes and dirty money he collected outside of the racetrack. The mayor is dead now: massive coronary.

But before he passed, he referred other clients to me. Victimless crimes—or so I convinced myself at the time. He gave me good advice—keep my identity hidden from clients, and work through the dark web. He was a creep and a crook, but not a fool. He never got caught—except by his profligate lifestyle, which resulted in cardiac arrest at age fifty-two. I did the mayor's dirty work all right, pulled Alfie right through that door as my fence. He kept telling me he was done. I kept telling him one more time. Yes, the day I met the mayor was the day I jumped onto the slippery slope I've been sliding down ever since, all the while believing I was climbing greater heights.

"Alfie, I'm doing my best to put my past back in place. The real and very immediate problem is that I don't remember what went wrong with Culbertson."

"Are you sitting down? If not, you better do so." He pauses as if waiting for me to sit.

I feel my scalp tingle, not a good feeling.

"You were representing the seller in the auction," he continues. "Your friend Brownsworth. A legit job, for once."

I like the sound of *legit*. "Go on."

"You were standing by remotely in New York during the auction, like you always do. Intense bidding. Culbertson kept raising the bids, wouldn't back down. You told me you thought the others bid just to see him go higher."

"Who won?"

"Culbertson won the auction, transferred the money to you, and you were supposed to deliver the ruby to him immediately."

"And ...?"

"Right after the auction, one of the disgruntled players contacted me and told me we'd made a grave mistake. That Culbertson has ties to a domestic American terrorist cell, his cousin's group, called The Chancellorsville Militia."

My jaw drops. *What?*

He seems to sense my unspoken shock. "I know. White supremacists with crazy ideas about a conspiracy between the Vatican and Israel to take over America. I immediately called you, and that's when the *merde* hit the fan, as they say in our Quebec province."

So I reneged on the deal. Got a conscience. How could I forget something this big? "So we learned from the disgruntled bidder that Culbertson is a right-wing terrorist. There's got to be more."

"He said he knows of both Culbertson and his cousin. That we'll be sorry."

Now my hair is standing on end. The pieces are finally falling into place. "Go on."

"They're planning an attack. And they seriously believe that the ruby will bring them luck. After the attack, they plan to sell the stone to a real estate magnate in Reno, Nevada, who's foaming at the mouth to have it. Word is, he's going to pay three times what Brownsworth got."

"So it's about funding terrorism."

"The almighty dollar." Alfie paused. "You really don't recall this?"

"Culbertson threw me out of a four-story building. I'm having a hard time remembering what my favorite ice cream is. Much less these details. We must've verified what the disgruntled man told us. People say anything."

"Yes, ma'am. At your behest, I did a little background checking. If you know how far to dig down, the internet is a gold mine. There are only a couple of degrees of separation between Culbertson and his cousin. Lots of chatter about their activities. You know how these guys like to brag to each other. Get everyone riled up."

I drew in a deep breath. No wonder I reversed gears and refused to deliver the goods. "Do we have any idea about the details of this attack?"

"It's supposed to happen this year. Christmas Day. I told you this, and it got us into this mess."

"What a disaster."

"Indeed."

Something begins to niggle at me at the back of my mind. "Let me think a minute, Alfie." I close my eyes, still feeling the tingling on my scalp. I'm now able replay that night in my mind. I went to the hotel. Why? I must've been meeting up with John Brownsworth. No way would I have gone to see Culbertson. He must've played me somehow to get me there. Doesn't matter. I get to the hotel, used the lobby phone and asked for John's room. Whomever I spoke with told me to go up to the suite. I didn't suspect anything, so I went up. When I reached the room, I don't find John Brownsworth, but Shane Culbertson and his goons.

"You okay?" Alfie asks.

"Sorry, I wish I could remember everything that happened that night." Well, part of me does. I try to gather myself. "Who else knows about the plot?" I ask, trying to mask the trembling in my voice.

"No one? Everyone? How the hell would I know?"

I've got to tell DeLuca what I know. If this comes to light, no one in their right mind would believe Alfie and I aren't accessories. More importantly, I have to stop a terrorist on U.S. or any other soil on this earth.

"Do you have the ruby?" Alfie asks.

Everything inside me says to trust Alfie. But do I? "Does it matter?"

His voice turns ragged. "You know what? I don't ever want to see that damned stone again. I just want this over with. I never signed up for this horseshit."

I have no time for his panic. "Where is John Brownsworth? I don't know where he is."

Alfie mock laughs. "You're asking me that? Jesus, Bleue, you really are confused. You don't disclose the clients' personal information. Never have. Keep me at arm's length, you know. Just in case. And right about now, that *just in case* is happening. You've got to have his contact info somewhere. You're the one who vetted him to make sure he wasn't with the Feds."

I had an entry in my ledger for John and others. But I didn't have client contact information in there. In case it was discovered. That means I kept it someplace else. "Alfie, I must've mentioned something to you. How I stored contacts. Think about it."

"Not my part of this gig. I wonder if Brownsworth realized the sale of the stone would bring out the hornets. And man, hasn't it? Why do you need to reach him?"

"Because I transferred Culbertson's money to John, and I have to help get John out of harm's way."

"Oh, fuck. You cut that check a bit too early. Not a good practice."

"Don't tell me how to conduct my business, Alfie." The rebuke is undeserved but reflexive. Maybe somebody should've told me how to run my business, my corrupt business.

I give Alfie my new number and tell him to ring me if he comes up with anything more. I think I trust him. My gut wouldn't lie about him. I hope.

I reflect on what I've just learned. I've spent years piling mistake upon mistake. Each mistake compounds the previous one. However, it gives me a very modest sense of relief to know that even I have an ethical line I will not cross: I won't do business with murderers of any stripe, and I was willing to sacrifice my life to hold that line.

The relief, as I said, is small; it is immediately swamped by the knowledge that my mother's life and the lives of potentially thousands of others are in danger. I must do everything in my power to save them.

61

My mother's horse ranch borders Lac Laurel, northwest of Montreal. From my location, it's less than an hour's drive. The name of the ranch is Lac Laurel Farms. I'll call John later. My instinct tells me that he's sailed home to the Cayman Islands and I may not be able to reach him that easily.

There's only one person I've got to speak with now.

My hands are shaking. I stare at my phone, anticipating the next call. I dial my mother's number. She answers after several rings.

I recognize her voice. "Mom, it's Bleue," I say, trying to mask the fear in my voice.

"Honey, is that you? Oh, thank God. I haven't heard from you in weeks. I've been so worried. You sent me your necklace, said you'd be traveling, to hold on to it."

So Culbertson was keeping her in the dark. Using her to get to me without her knowing. Had my mother known what was happening, she would've called the authorities immediately. That's just who she is. Culbertson wouldn't chance that. It's me he's really after. Not me. The ruby. "Someone took it from me and sent to you, pretending to be me. I'll explain later."

My mother doesn't question me further. "Where are you, Bleue? What's going on?"

"It's a long story, Mom. I'm in Montreal. I'll be home in an hour. Has anyone you don't know been around?"

"No one."

"Nothing's out of the ordinary?"

She hesitates. I can hear it in her breathing.

"Mom, talk to me." I force myself to retain my composure. Culbertson has a photograph of my mother with the necklace—meaning one of the Culbertson's people was or is on the property.

"I don't like how your voice sounds," my mother says.

"Just get your gun," I say. "Keep it close. Have you hired any new people, lately?"

"A new hand, but that was a month ago. He seems—"

"Stay inside and lock the doors. Don't trust anyone, Mother. I'll be there as soon as I can."

"You're not making sense. What kind of trouble are you in?"

"Just get your gun. I'll explain as soon as I get there. Promise. Just don't tell anyone I'm around. Please." I can't say more, not yet. I don't want to scare her any more than I have. My mother is tough, and she's always been a great shot. I just hope she doesn't have to get any target practice today.

I close my bag, find Pavla in the dining room, and tell her I'm ready to check out.

"Good news?" she asks.

I nod, trying to appear relaxed, though I'm frantic. "I found her."

"Let's get you checked out and home to your mother's."

The bell on the front door jingles.

"Hello, anyone here?" a woman calls out.

"Oh my God," I whisper.

"Hello?" the woman repeats.

I hold a finger to my lips and peer around the corner, and there they are. Not a chance those two are here to take me to my next psychiatrist's appointment. My heart jumps into overdrive. I have a burner phone and have only used other people's computers. How did Matteo DeLuca *and* Lorraine Baglietti find me in a remote country inn in Canada?

It comes to me. They must've tracked me to the train, alerted local authorities, who followed me and alerted the Americans. My disguise didn't work. It's the only way.

I think back to the conversation Lorraine and DeLuca were having behind closed doors. Have I misread DeLuca? He kept vouching for Lorraine, even when I argued she was suspicious. Then he told me to keep my distance from her. Lorraine couldn't have been working with DeLuca; she kept giving him a hard time at every turn. Or do I have it backwards? Maybe DeLuca's after the Cassiopeia Ruby for himself and is using Lorraine and her connections to work this. In any case, whether their intentions are good or bad, it's now clear DeLuca and Lorraine are in this together.

Perhaps they've been scamming me the whole time.

"Please, help me," I say to Pavla.

She doesn't question me but points toward the back before calling out, "Be right there."

I hide in Pavla's private apartment. At the front desk, she's chatting up Lorraine and DeLuca, trying to keep them occupied while I decide what to do.

There's only one place I can go—my mother's ranch.

I gather up my belongings from my room, go through Pavla's living room to the back door of the inn, and peer outside. Nobody is there. I make my way around the inn, and take the garden path that leads to the parking lot. There's only one other car, which must belong to Lorraine and DeLuca. I get inside mine and quietly close the door.

My hands are shaking. My entire body is shaking. I press the start button and back out without revving the engine, barely crunching the parking lot gravel. When I reach the paved road, I head north. After a hundred yards, I floor the gas pedal.

62

I've got to reach John Brownsworth before the vise I'm in squeezes me to death. With one hand on the wheel, I use my phone to search for his name and banker and Cayman Islands. First up, his photograph appears. That's him. Silver-haired gentleman in his sixties. I hit the contact button to make the call. A receptionist answers but says I have to leave a message. I give my first name and indicate that it's urgent. How many times has the receptionist heard that one? But it works.

Twenty minutes later, the phone rings and that distinctive British accent says into my ear, "My dear girl, are you all right?"

I skip the formalities and explain the situation.

"I can get you and your mother out of the country," he says. "Help you set up a new life in the islands. Beats the hell out of prison time. Meanwhile, you go find your mother, make sure she's safe, and have her call the cops if she hasn't already. Ring me when you're ready to leave. I've got you covered. Count on it."

"I don't have much time."

"I can have a plane ready in Montreal. Just give me a call and I'll have her ready."

"I tried to find you in Sag Harbor. You left your slip."

"It was time to move on to my second home. Too much heat from the IRS gave me indigestion, if you know what I mean. And thanks to you, that's behind me. Keep me posted, Blue." He gives me his direct number. I don't put it in my contacts. I've already memorized it. Helps when numbers come easy.

Twenty minutes later, I arrive in Lac Laurel. My blood pressure dropped to normal thanks to the dulcet voice of my British friend, but now it's up again. In the distance are the now-familiar grassy knolls of the countryside. When the road splits, I head west-northwest on a narrow lane. I want to fly to the tops of the forest and race across open fields.

I drive on, taking in the sights of the small community. I drive under a patch of low-lying tree limbs; it feels as if my home is welcoming me with open arms. Off to the right by the lake, hundreds of cattails are growing. I remember tearing seed pods apart and watching the fluff sail away in the wind. Finally, an open expanse. I stare into the fields and see horses grazing. The painting above my bed in New York is this very landscape. I'm finally home.

I turn on the long driveway and head toward the barn located on the far side of the pasture. I'm breathing so fast that I'm becoming light-headed. The house itself is now visible in the distance. I reach the front of the barn, park the car, and get out. Horses are whinnying and neighing inside the stables. Outside, I hear the beating of hooves and horses snorting.

I wheel around. At least twenty horses are running my way, curious about the newly arrived stranger. I take a step toward the fence to greet them but stop. That's not what I've come for, not yet.

"Bleue?" my mother calls to me, walking with a graceful but surefooted stride, her firearm secured in a holster at her hip. "Bleue!" My American mom has always pronounced my name closer to my bogus American name *Blue*.

She didn't heed my warning and go hide from the others. I should've known. My mother is stubborn.

I stand frozen. She hastens her pace. I watch her. Her face, her stride, her quiet demeanor. But I'm also beginning to see my mother anew. She's a confident, proud woman. Strong. In her late sixties now, she could pass for fifty. She's taller than me, but we're both thin with high cheekbones and wide, blue eyes. Her hair is graying, her face tanner and slightly lined from sun exposure, but her beauty outshines any imperfections. She wears my necklace around her neck.

As she comes closer, more and more memories of my past near and far begin to rain down on me, propelled by the force of gravity that is my life. My cup of recollections isn't yet full, but it's close. I break down in sobs and run to my mother. "Oh, Mama!"

A couple of workers emerge from the stables. One asks, "Is there a problem?"

She shakes her head and looks over her shoulder. "No problem. Johann, you, Hank, and the rest of the men can leave us."

Johann lingers longer than the rest, looking at me through squinted eyes. I remember him. It's been a while since I've seen him. He's aged. I smile. His response is a slight nod. Then he returns inside. I don't recognize the other man, Hank. Is he Culbertson's plant?

My mother hugs me and, when she pulls back, she struggles to speak.

Tears are streaming down both our faces. How could I have brought danger to my mother? All she ever wanted was peace and harmony.

I, too, am at a loss for words. She thinks I'm her savior, a savvy businesswoman who knows horses. She has no idea what I've done.

"What happened to you?" she asks.

"I had a terrible fall. I wasn't hurt badly, a miracle, but I suffered amnesia. I couldn't remember *me*, my past. I couldn't find you or this, my home. It was just gone. Little by little, memories are surfacing. Sounds, images, smells. I'm still confused about a lot. A man took my necklace and sent it to you. He's after me. He'll stop at nothing." I pause. "Mom, I've done some bad things. I ... I'm so, so sorry. You don't deserve any of this."

My mother holds her hands to her mouth. "We have to call the police."

I don't tell her that after a call like that, I'll be a fugitive from justice. And if she doesn't come with me, I don't know when I'll see her again. I've already hurt her enough. I just want it all to stop. "There's another way," I say.

My mother's eyes widen. I see fear in them, then stony resolution. "Quickly. Let's go to the house. Don't call anyone yet."

"Mom, I—"

"Listen to me, Bleue!"

I follow my mother up to the house. Neither of us speaks. I have to convince her that we need to get out of there.

She puts the plug-in kettle on to make tea. *We don't have time for this.*

"I've done some bad things, and people are after me," I begin. "I'll explain later. We have to go now. I have a way to get us out of the country. To start over. It'll be like heaven. The beach. Blue waters. We can buy a new farm. Raise horses there."

She stares at me, her expression growing harder by the moment.

"Please, Mom. I know that look. Listen to me."

Her face turns so stern that I feel the cold in my bones. "No one is going to turn me out of my home. No one. Do you understand that, Bleue? Not even you. I'm not running away, flying off to some island to live like a fugitive. Don't you know what kind of person I am? The question is, what kind of person are you—or will you be in the end? If what you're saying about your memory is true, you've been given another chance. Take it."

"But you don't understand these people. They will kill us after they force me to give them what they want. Or even if I don't give it to them. I have money, resources. I can find us a new life."

"Are you listening to yourself, Bleue? You took a wrong turn, okay? We can live through that, work it out. Whatever the consequences." She frowns, her disappointment slicing through the air and cutting me to the core. "When did you ever become a coward?"

Tears of shame stream down my cheeks, and I reach for her hand without making contact. "I just want you to be safe. I'm sorry I did this to you."

She grasps my hand and squeezes it. "And running from these people or the police won't change anything. We need the police's help."

I hang my head. The only way to protect my mother is to get her out of here. Fast. She's too proud. Won't listen. I'll never forgive myself if anything happens to her.

"Listen to me, Bleue, I don't have anything to run from. You're a grown woman now. You have to decide what's best for you."

"I want to do what's right, but I also know ..." If I turn myself in, I won't be around to protect her.

She clears her throat, and stares at me long and hard, then takes my necklace from around her neck and gives it to me. "It's a family heirloom. Do you recall? I'm giving it back to you to remind you of who you are, who I am, what my side of the family stands for."

I accept the necklace and look down at its circular design. The pendant is covered in rubies and diamonds.

"Put it on," she says.

I do.

"Do you remember what this necklace stands for?"

"No. Please tell me."

"It came from my grandmother, and her mother before that. I gave it to you when you graduated from college. I thought it was the right time. It's always gone to the oldest girl through the generations. The women of my family say the rubies are like the blood that runs in our veins, the hardships we overcome, the children we bear. The diamonds represent the promise of a bright future, not simply an object of wealth or fortune, but a reminder of strength, courage, and blessings." She sets her jaw. "I worried that when the necklace came, you were rejecting our family. I'd never known you to take it off. I wouldn't let myself believe you had had a change of heart."

I swallow hard and lift the pendant to look at it again. Although I don't say it, I feel that there's some higher power in this necklace that will keep me safe.

The back door opens. It's Johann, our longtime ranch hand.

"We're having a private conversation, Johann," my mother says. "Can you give me a few minutes?"

But he ignores her and advances on us. It's only when he's five feet away that I see the knife in his right hand. As my mother rises, he wraps his arm around her neck and holds the knife to her artery.

63

My mother doesn't scream, but her eyes are filled with fear. *How did Culbertson get to Johann?* He's been part of the family for years. Could he really have turned on my mother for money?

I take a deep breath, don't move. "Please, Johann, don't hurt her."

He reaches inside his pants pocket with his left hand and tosses a phone onto the table. "Press 3," he says.

I pick up the phone, not taking my eyes from him. One wrong move from me and my mother dies. "Johann, please. I'll give you whatever you want. I have money, lots of it. Just name your price."

He shakes his head. "Press 3," he says again.

"Culbertson will kill you when this is over," I say. "He won't leave a witness. He's using you. He uses people and then disposes of them."

His face doesn't change. "Call."

I don't move but keep looking directly at him. "There's time to change your mind. You don't have to be a part of this. My mother never did anything to you to deserve this. Please."

"Bleue, do what he asks," my mother says, gasping. She's gripping his wrist at her throat.

I feel helpless. I hold the phone up but don't press 3. He can't see that. I lift the phone to my ear.

My mother's shotgun is lying against the counter. Not nearly enough time to grab it and take a shot. Then I realize that I'm holding the answer in my hand—my phone is a weapon, a blunt object.

When I look at my mother, she subtly shakes her head, as if reading my mind and rejecting my plan.

In one fluid motion, using both hands, she grasps the wrist and hand around her neck. She twists and ducks below Johann's armpit without releasing his wrist. She doesn't let go, but deftly twists his wrist backwards and pulls down so that his forearm turns vertical. Using her chest and his body weight, she forces his bent arm and hand down. He's still holding the knife. The blade is poised and ready to penetrate the soft flesh beneath his ribs. The rapid-fire maneuver happens so fast that barely a second passes. How quickly the tides can change.

In a flash, I remember—my mother and I took self-defense classes together after my father died. Of course. That explains my skills back in Central Park. The classes weren't the usual mother-and-daughter bonding experience, but she insisted. Turns out we were good, really good. Growing up on a ranch taught me a lot. Such as: always be ready to protect yourself.

I want my mother to plunge the blade into Johann. But he punches her in the face with his left hand. My mother falls to the floor. I make a move toward him. He comes at me wielding the knife.

I sidestep him.

Hank appears at the back door with a gun trained on Johann. "Drop it, Johann," he commands.

Johann ignores him and comes at me. Hank fires multiple times. Three bullets strike Johann in the chest. He continues toward me. When he reaches me, I duck and lunge to the side, punching him as hard as I can in his knife arm. He doesn't drop the knife.

Hank fires again.

The bullet strikes Johann in the face. He drops to the floor, convulses horribly, and then goes still.

Hank and I stare at the dead man for a second. It all happened so fast that I struggle to comprehend what I'm seeing.

The sound of a car racing down the driveway, gravel crunching and spitting, rouses us.

"Someone is outside," I shout and race to the window.

"The police?" my mother asks.

"No." The car stops just outside the barn. Men get out. They're armed. No sign of Culbertson. Are they Culbertson's people or the terrorists?

"We should call the police," my mother says.

"They'll never get here in time," Hank says.

"They're after me," I say. "I can put a stop to this."

"No, Bleue," she says. "Don't go with them."

"Both of you need to get out of here," Hank says.

My mother walks to her shotgun. "I'm not going anywhere."

We might not have a choice anyway. There's no way we can make it to my car.

"We need a diversion," I say.

I hurry over to the security system's wall panel and press the button that calls the police and sets off an alarm. The alarm system whines and blares in both the house and down at the barn. The siren doesn't deter the gunmen. Just the opposite. They're now sprinting toward the house.

"Follow me," my mother says.

We follow her toward a side door and leave the house, racing toward a pasture. Horses are grazing. My mother whistles, and five horses come cantering toward us.

"Get on," she says and mounts one of the horses. Remarkable that she can still perform such a feat after being punched in the face.

I hesitate for a moment, not sure I can do it. It's been a long time since I rode bareback.

"*Move*, Bleue," she says.

"I'll give you a hand," Hank says, hurrying my way.

The hell with that. I grab the horse's mane and thrust my body upward and onto the horse.

Hank jumps on the horse closest to him.

"Good job," my mother says and takes the lead, racing toward the end of the pasture. I know my mother's plan. She wants to hide in the woods.

Shots ring out in the distance behind us.

I look back. The jeep is heading our way. A man on horseback is riding alongside the vehicle. We'll never outrun them.

64

"Keep going," my mother shouts. She's heading toward the trail into the woods. We race down a slope toward the end of the pasture, where there is a four-and-a-half-foot fence separating the ranch from the trail. Just when I think my mother is about to stop, she lays in hard on the horse. She can't be serious. She secures her seat and shouts, "Lope!" and nudges the horse with her legs, controlling the horse by the mane. The horse digs in its hooves and takes those first steps forward. Moments later, she and the horse are over the fence. I don't think, just follow. Hank is right behind me.

We clear the fence and reach the trail that leads into the woods.

"You two head up the hill and I'll hang back," Hank says. "If they come this way, I'll steer them away from you and around the lake."

"It isn't happening, Hank," my mother says, shaking her head. She can be a stubborn woman. "Too dangerous for you."

"Ms. Bishop, if you want me to move, you'll have to carry

me and my horse. Go. I'll be fine." Hank can obviously be stubborn, too.

They stare at each other.

"There's no time to debate this," I say.

She sighs, nods at me, and then Hank. "Watch yourself, Hank. Thank you."

He gives a slight nod. "Go!"

We proceed down the rocky path. I can no longer hear the jeep. We reach a large foothill at the base of the Laurentian Mountains. We ascend. Midway up, a horse snorts, and it isn't one of ours. My mother hears it too, because she urges her horse forwards. We ride as fast as we can, until we reach a precipice hidden by tree branches and manage to get a look back through a gap in the foliage.

My mother reaches for her gun.

I put a hand on her arm. "Don't. Chances are, you'll miss. Don't give our position away."

She doesn't argue.

"You think Hank is on the up-and-up?" I ask. "You say he hasn't been here long. Why would he help us? He might be making sure they know the way we've gone, setting a trap."

She shrugs. "Then why would he kill Johann to save us?"

"Let's hope he really is a friend. We have to move."

I look out toward the lake. The jeep is inside the fence and heading north toward the other side of the hill. It looks like Hank has led them across the field and away from us.

"We need to take the back trail down the mountain," my mother says. "The person following us probably won't know to go that way."

I remember the back trail vividly. That trail lies just beyond a grove of pine trees, and it's treacherous. "I don't know if I can do that anymore," I say.

"No choice. They can't drive the jeep up here. They'll circle around the lake to intercept us if we head down the main path and come off the mountain that way. That leaves the person on horseback. He or she is moving fast, faster than we can." She means faster than *I* can. I've been the one living a different life.

"We've got to get you back to your car and hope we can get you out of here before the police arrive," she adds. "The only way is taking the back trails."

Her words surprise me. "You think I should run from the authorities?"

"For now, yes. To give you time to sort this out. Let's go, now." She turns her horse and heads farther up the steep hill to the fork in the main trail.

We duck down as we ride under tree limbs, the branches whipping against our faces and shoulders. We get high enough to emerge above the tree line, and turn off onto the back trail, which narrows to only a few feet wide. We're riding only inches away from the mountain's ledge. My stomach drops. The ground is rough, pitted with loose rocks. A drop off the hillside means instant death.

"Don't look down," my mother calls to me. "Take it slow. Keep low in the seat. You did this many times when you were a kid."

We come to a bend in the path. A tree limb has fallen and is blocking the trail. My mother's mare stumbles on a rock and spooks. One of the horse's hooves slips from the trail. My mother's body slips in the direction of the drop off, but she manages to grab the mare's mane and right herself as the horse struggles to find solid ground, dancing in place.

I grip my horse's mane hard as I watch in horror. My horse snorts, and I pray the animal doesn't spook.

My mother's horse whinnies, jerks its head, and scrambles for surer footing on the path. One thrust or jolt and the horse will throw my mother off the ledge.

My mother, sliding erratically across the horse's back, speaks calmly to the mare. Finally, the mare settles down.

I breathe a sigh of relief. How my mother stayed on that horse is a wonder.

We continue downward, the path so narrow that I have to hold my legs in close to the horse. Regardless, my legs brush against the hillside. But I'm able to hold them up to avoid the sharp rocks. I feel for the horses as their rib cages rub against the jagged rocks. Though their hooves continue to slip, my mother and I manage to stay low in our seats and hold on.

We round a bend in the trail and come to a chasm. The hillside has eroded and crumbled, creating a four-foot gap that plunges downward. Too wide to walk across. The path is wider on the opposite side. But we're stuck. I meet my mother's eyes.

"We have to jump," she says.

"We can't get much of a running start, Mother."

"There's not enough room to turn the horses around. We'll have to get them to walk backwards a few steps and go for it."

I haven't jumped like this in years. But there's no other choice. It's this or Culbertson's men. I engage my seat and urge my horse back. "Come on, girl," I murmur. "Move your feet with me. Come on." The horse cautiously begins moving her feet in rhythm with my seat and legs as I shift my weight back and apply a gentle pulsating pressure with my legs. "Atta girl."

My mother does the same, then secures her seat on the horse and shouts, "Lope!" as she simultaneously nudges the horse with her legs. The horse digs in its hooves and takes those first galloping steps forward.

My stomach roils as I wait for my mother's horse to leap from the edge. I hold my breath as the horse springs into the air and crosses the gap with its body open and extended. I both tremble and thrill at seeing my mother in action. She still has it after all these years. The horse lands, takes three steadying steps, and stops on my mother's command.

She looks over her shoulder and signals for me to go. There's determination in her eyes. She believes in me, and that boosts my confidence.

I cry, "Lope!" just as she did, and in an instant my horse is digging in its hooves. The horse makes one giant thrust at the ledge, and we're flying through air. I close my eyes for a split second. I put my trust, my life in this horse. Then I land with a hard jolt and open my eyes. My horse stops, but my mother's horse spooks again. She struggles to hold the horse steady, but the mare is out of control, slipping and struggling.

"Whoa, whoa," she cries.

The horse bucks. My mother is thrown from the horse and down on the path. Her body slips toward the edge.

"Mom!"

65

As I watch helplessly, my mother slides toward the precipice. She gropes for anything that might save her from slipping over the sheer ledge. Her nails scrape the dirt, but her body keeps sliding. At the last second, she grabs a tree root extending above the ground, and her body jerks to a stop. She's hanging precariously over the cliff, her legs dangling in the air.

I dismount, dash to her side, and take hold of her arms. I brace my foot against the exposed root and pull with all my strength. My left foot slips in the dirt, but my right foot holds firm.

"I need a foothold!" my mother cries. "Hold me steady."

I stop trying to pull her up and hold her in place.

Then she says, "Okay, pull."

Together we work until she's back on the path, face down in dirt. She lifts her head and brushes some of the dirt from her eyelids. She's breathing hard.

"Are you all right?"

She brushes it off. "We have to get going."

"Your horse is gone. Bolted down the path."

"I know, I saw." Using her shirtsleeve, she wipes what dirt she can from her face, continuing to blink hard. "We're only halfway down. Let's walk until the path widens, and then we'll ride together."

In the distance behind us, a horse whinnies.

"The asshole is daring," she says.

I'm startled at my mother's use of profane language. It's unusual for her.

As soon as we reach the wider part of the path, we both mount my horse and ride until we reach the base of the hillside, where I take the horse into a full gallop back to our deserted ranch. The authorities haven't arrived. Way out here in the country, it might be another half hour. So much for an alarm system.

"Leave, Bleue," my mother says.

A couple of hands come racing out from the barn, weapons at their sides. There's an eruption of confused explanations. From the bits and pieces I'm able to discern, all the workers are unharmed—except, of course, Johann. After the gunmen left, one of the workers went up to the house and found Johann's body. They didn't know if we were dead, kidnapped, or on the run.

Then several of our workers armed themselves and set out after the men and to search for us. They found our pursuer's horse, riderless. He or she must've turned back before the trail narrowed. Our pursuer must've gotten away in the jeep, fled when they heard the security alarm go off at the house.

"Come with me," I say to my mother. One last try.

"I won't, Bleue. This is my home. The police will be here soon. Go."

I'm still surprised that my mother didn't encourage me to stay, to turn myself in and let the authorities work out the mess. I suppose, in the end, she doesn't want to risk seeing me spend the rest of my life behind bars. How low and dirty I feel.

One of the workers, a grizzled man with rheumy eyes and chipped teeth, steps forward. *Maurice*, I now recall. When I was a little girl, he frightened me at first, but then we became friends. His nature is as gentle as his demeanor is gruff. He helped teach me to ride. I think we can trust him. But, then again, we trusted Johann.

"Mademoiselle Bleue," he says, touching the bill of his cap. "Long time."

"Bleue is leaving," my mother says in her accented French. "No one needs to know she was here. Agreed?"

Maurice turns and spits chewing tobacco. "I'm not a turncoat like Johann. None of us are."

"Why did Johann turn on us?" I ask.

"No doubt, his gambling debts," Maurice said. "He bet on sports, he bet on cards, and he bet on the horses when he shouldn't have. And, Madame, he was caught doping."

"My God," my mother says. "Why didn't one of you come to me?"

"You have enough on your plate," Maurice said. "We thought we could take care of Johann. Didn't know how bad it was until recently."

I can guess—blackmail and extortion. People like Culbertson can find the soft underbelly of any business. Johann was an easy mark.

I stare into my mother's eyes. There are a thousand things I could say, but I say the most important words in the world: "I love you."

66

I run to my car, start the engine, and pray that my mother and her ranch hands will remain safe. Culbertson's goons are gone now, but I'm sure they'll come after me again. I hope they don't come back to the ranch, hope that my mother is right, that her workers can and will protect her. Meanwhile, I must act fast if I want to have the chance to bring an end to all of this.

I start down the driveway, rocks kicking up and spitting wide. I reach inside my purse, find my burner phone, and dial the inn. Pavla answers.

"It's me, Bleue," I say. "Are those two still there?"

"No, they left. I told them we were fully booked. They asked about a Blue Bishop, described you. I told them I had no record of the name or anyone fitting that description."

I thank her, tell her I need a room for the night, and end the call. Going back to a place where Lorraine and DeLuca found me seems risky, but because I was there before, it's probably the last place they'll look. Besides, Pavla has helped me, and I need a friend.

It's time to make the call. I dig out my cell phone and dial

John. "It's me. Don't say my name or yours. Someone may be listening in. I don't have much time to talk. I need help getting out of the country. I'll call you back as soon as I can. If you don't hear from me in twenty-four hours, assume the worst." I disconnect the call.

Before I'm anywhere near the end of the drive, I see in the distance two cars driving in my direction. The vehicles don't appear to be police cars, but I'm sure they are. Damn. I should never have left my mother only to protect myself. I turn my car around. I've come this far, survived Culbertson's people, and will not let these cops stop me.

I speed back to the house, reach the barn, park the car, and get out, not even bothering to close the car door. My mother and five of her workers, including Hank, meet me at the barn door.

"Bleue! What's wrong?" she asks.

"Someone's coming," I say. "Get your weapons. We have to take cover. Now."

The cars are heading down the drive, picking up speed.

"Get the horses out," my mother tells the workers as we run into the barn.

The men open the stable doors, and the horses trot outside.

"We've got to split up," I say. "Let's leave the barn doors open, lure them in. I'll stay close to the entrance doors. I need to get the first look at these people. I'll know who they are. At least, I hope I do."

"I'll take the other side," her mother says. "Hank, you and the men split up. Some of you take the loft."

We all get into position. "Wait for my signal," I say. "Let's make sure they're truly hostile."

The cars swing toward the barn entrance and come to a hard stop. Back doors open. Four passengers—all men—start out. The drivers remain inside but open their car doors.

I don't recognize any of the men on the move. They've got to be with Culbertson. They're brandishing weapons.

Someone inside the barn fires a shot.

The men split and scramble for cover.

I duck behind metal to avoid a barrage of bullets and try to get a read on who's where.

Shots fire from the loft—our guys. A man approaching the barn entrance is hit in the leg. He cries out in pain and goes down.

I peer around the edge of the barn door.

The wounded man aims toward the loft and fires. Someone in the loft groans and falls hard to the ground. Culbertson's guy tries to get up, but someone from the loft shoots him in the chest.

I lean forward with my gun raised. One of the assailants is scrambling toward the side of the barn where my mother is. With shaky hands, I shoot, and he goes down. Right—my father taught me to shoot when I was a girl. *But not to shoot human beings*. A wave of nausea overcomes me. Is this the first time I've killed someone, I wonder?

Four gunmen remain, two of them still in the vehicles. Doors open. The gunmen use the doors as shields.

My mother peers out from a window and shoots but misses. I motion for her to get back.

Then Culbertson's people all start shooting at once. The sound of gunfire is deafening and coming at us from all sides.

Someone inside the barn shouts in agony. Across the center aisle, one of our men stumbles and hits the ground. That leaves Hank and two more hands, along with my mother and myself. I shake with fear. The people outside seem like trained assassins, and we're just a bunch of ranchers. They're far better armed and skilled.

But we can't just stay here picking each other off. I created this mess and brought trouble down on innocent people. It's my duty to try to clean the mess up. If I can't, maybe they'll go away if they have me.

I signal for my mother to remain down and crawl toward the back of the barn, avoiding gunfire aimed in my direction. I hug the walls to get out of sight. Then I pass the two bodies of my mother's men. Blood is spattered everywhere. Their deaths are on me. What will their families do?

Trying to ignore the feelings of guilt and despair, I reach Hank and join him in his stall for cover. There's more shooting from inside the barn, and someone outside screams in pain.

Then the gunfire suddenly ceases.

I whisper to Hank, "Get my mother out of here somehow. Don't come back." Then I notice blood on his shoulder. He's been hit.

Before I can stop him, he starts across the center aisle, leaving a trail of blood.

Someone begins firing from the vehicles. One of our men falls from the rafters. More blood.

Hank somehow makes it to my mother and guides her toward a storage room. She's safe for the moment.

I creep toward the rear of the barn. Just as I round the door to the outside, I'm face to face with a gunman. He slaps my shotgun down. I lose my grasp on the weapon. He kicks me in the stomach. I fall to the ground hugging myself, only to look up at the barrel of his gun aimed straight between my eyes.

A hard cold object strikes the back of my head. All goes black.

67

I wake, disoriented, unsure where I am or how much time has passed. The lights are bright. For a moment, I wonder if I've dreamed everything, if I'm back in the hospital in New York. I blink hard and try to stand, but I'm restrained in a chair. Inside my mother's kitchen. Not a dream, not a nightmare—reality. I shout for help, but no one comes. Where's my mother? What have they done to her?

Even in my panic, I realize how much I missed this place: the worn floorboards, the large work island with a hardwood surface and the back-slated wooden chairs with seat cushions that surround it, the light-yellow-and-white striped curtains that hang above the double windows over a farm sink with a faucet that starts dripping randomly and whistles when the weather is changing. My father used to say that we had haunted pipes. Rustic cabinets with windowpane glass doors —all filled to the brim with sundry dishes, pans, food, medications. Canisters of flour, sugar, oats, shoved to the back of countertops. Old juice cans and jars filled with pens and pencils, cooking implements, or small tools. The refrigerator's light-gold porcelain door nearly invisible for all the magnets holding notes and lists. I made most of the magnets; the others my parents bought from the school because they have my yearbook pictures on them. The memories of my childhood could be written from the contents of this room alone. I hang my head.

"Look at me, bitch," a man says from behind me, jerking me up. I know the voice—Culbertson. I shiver.

"Where's my mother?" I ask.

Someone grabs my hair and yanks my head up.

Culbertson appears in front of me. I want to ask about my mother again, but he won't play that game. I'll try to play his.

"How did you feel when I refused to give you the Cassiopeia?" I ask. "Because I enjoyed it. You must've felt the way I did when you dropped me out that window."

He smirks. "If you hadn't struggled, my late associate, Nelson, wouldn't have dropped you. Your own doing. Of course, I'm sure you've forgotten that."

I shiver at the mention of Nelson's name—the man who attacked me at Lorraine's house in the Hamptons. I remember the feeling of slipping from someone's grasp. I feel a rush of panic but tuck it deep inside. I have to stay calm.

"Let's talk about the future, not the past. If you don't deliver the ruby to your buyer, you're a dead man."

He scowls. "Give me my property." He nods at the man behind me, who yanks my hair again. It takes everything in my power not to squeal in pain.

"It's not that easy, Culbertson," I say. "You're falling to your death as we speak. But you know what? I'm your awning. Only I can break your fall."

He looks at me coldly. "Nice necklace," he says and then jerks the chain tight around my neck.

I force myself to chortle. "You're falling, Culbertson," I say again, "and the cold, hard ground is getting closer. Where's my mother?"

"Where's the Cassiopeia?"

"Shane, I know about your cousin's group, the Chancellorsville Militia. And I have to say, I'm really glad I won't be in D.C. on Christmas Day. Or anywhere near it. Of course, you probably won't be anywhere unless you do as I say."

"Stop playing games," he growls.

"Or you'll kill me?"

Culbertson slaps my face, hard.

My head jars to the side and rolls round my neck. I taste blood, which I spit in his face. "You kill me, you'll never get what you want. So fuck you."

He strikes me again.

The lights in the room flicker. That white-walled room. But I'm not falling yet.

"Get the mother," Culbertson says to his partner.

The man leaves and comes back dragging my mother. He forces her to sit down in one of the chairs. She's shaking uncontrollably. What have I done for greed and power? The goon walks behind my mother and puts a knife to her throat.

"Where's the Cassiopeia?" Culbertson asks.

I burst out laughing.

Now, for the first time, Culbertson appears rattled. He probably thinks I hate my mother.

"You're a fool, Shane," I say. "You're the kind of person who makes the same mistake twice. If you murder my mother, you'll be signing your death warrant, because you'll never get what you want. The only way you get the Cassiopeia is if you let her go." I look into his eyes. "Now."

He considers this, looks at his henchman, and my heart almost stops, but then tells the guy to back off. The goon retreats.

"Hank?" I ask my mother, buying more time.

"He's wounded," my mother says.

"The man gets help," I say to Culbertson.

Culbertson's lips turn up in a malevolent smile, and I realize I've overplayed my hand, and he turns to his man and says, "Do it."

I scream, "No!" Then the henchman falls to the ground. There's a hole in his chest, blood oozing. Who shot him?

Culbertson covers his head as he turns around. His mistake. I kick him in the groin, and my chair falls backwards to the floor. Startled, he lifts his gun and points it at me, ready to fire, but he falls back in a barrage of bullets.

I look around for my mother, who's also on the floor, and I want to scream again, but she looks up at me, relief in her eyes. I burst into tears.

68

Lorraine Baglietti and Matteo DeLuca run into the room, accompanied by a phalanx of uniformed police officers. DeLuca goes over and checks on Culbertson, putting a hand to the man's carotid artery. He shakes his head.

To her credit, Lorraine goes to my mother first. "There's an ambulance on its way, ma'am," she says. Lorraine sounds sophisticated. No sign of the brassy accent.

"I'm fine," my mother says. "But some of my ranch hands were shot. They're in the barn."

Two of the uniforms hurry out.

"Will someone untie me?" I ask, through my tears.

"It's more than you deserve," Lorraine says, but DeLuca, a sheepish half-grin on his face, comes over and unties my restraints. I stagger over and embrace my mother.

Lorraine joins us. There's no more prance in her step, no high heels click-clacking against the ground. Her gait is strong and determined, a product of the flat shoes she's wearing, or the fact that she's on the warpath—and I'm the enemy.

"Ma'am, will you excuse us?" Lorraine says. "I need to speak with your daughter alone."

My mother shakes her head, but I say, "Give us some time, Mom."

She nods and reluctantly leaves the room, along with DeLuca and the uniformed cops. Lorraine is clearly the boss.

"Let me guess, FBI?" I say.

She pulls her badge out. "Good guess."

"You're out of your jurisdiction."

"We work with the Canadians when federal crimes are committed in both countries." My stomach drops when she reads me my Miranda rights. "We need to know what you remember."

"I haven't violated any laws. Is it Agent Baglietti?"

She nods. "Officially."

"DeLuca, too?"

"He's a New York police detective. I was undercover. He didn't know anything about my investigation of you until he let you slip away. He insisted that he tag along up here, because he says I let you slip away, and I knew who you were. He didn't."

"Seriously? The FBI keeps its operations secret from local law enforcement?"

"Not from the top brass in this case, but from working detectives like DeLuca and Roudebusch, yes."

I'm glad DeLuca isn't in the room. I couldn't bear to look him in the eye. Then anger rises in my chest at what Lorraine has just said.

"What you're saying is bullshit, Lorraine. He must've known."

"Not bullshit. Locals are left out of the loop all the time. A few years ago, local police in a small town in Colorado arrested an undercover agent posing as a journalist. Look it up. My point is, Matteo DeLuca and his partner had no clue."

"You're not such a great agent. Forget about letting me escape. You let Shane Culbertson get away when he was sitting at a restaurant in Southampton, right under your nose."

She glowers at me, a replacement for the horsey laugh she would've let out a week ago. "Just so you know, we picked up your pal, Alfie, a little while ago."

"He's a respectable businessman."

She scoffs at that. "We've been investigating your activities for months. When a certain ruby went on the black market, your name matched up as the auctioneer. We had an undercover agent at your ruby auction. Culbertson has been a person of interest for some time now. You two sure looked like a match made in … I was about to say *heaven,* but that's the wrong geography."

"Culbertson and I are no match." I twist toward her. "With all your intel, you must know that once I found out who he was involved with, I refused to do business with him. Which is why he dropped me out of that window."

She ignores this. "Where did you get the ruby?"

"I bought it at a gem show. Sorry, no receipt."

She rolls her eyes at my sarcasm, then slowly places a hand on the table and leans into it. She just stares at me, trying to use the silence to get me to talk. Or beg.

"Hey, Lorraine, since we're being honest here, are those kids I met really yours? If the FBI is using children as decoys, that kind of sucks."

"The kids are mine. Gaby did see you at the dance studio through the window. You weren't supposed to meet any of my kids, including Gaby. But I did enroll her in your dance study, just so I could surveil you. The day you met them all at my place, they should've been gone."

"And that's why you used your real name? Because I met the real you at the dance studio?"

Lorraine shrugs. “It got complicated when my daughter recognized you at the dance studio.”

“I can’t believe you people. Holier than thou, but you jeopardize innocent children. How does George feel about that? If he’s really your husband.”

She looks away and down. That one stung her.

“What about your houses? Are they just props? Ten million-plus-dollar stage sets for an FBI agent? So much for our tax dollars going to good use.”

“*Your* tax dollars? That’s a laugh. You’ve helped a lot of people evade taxes. That home is mine. I’m what you call a trust fund baby. I’m not ashamed of it, although many of my colleagues think I should be ashamed. I’m also a workaholic. And an honest federal officer. I take my job seriously.”

I feel a grudging admiration for this self-description. “And Gino? He’s not your uncle, is he?”

“He is, and he’s exactly who you read about online. Let’s say he and his brother—my father—took different paths in life. Uncle Gino is cooperating with the authorities these days —as well as helping out his niece.”

“And Stallworth?”

“Stallworth is who she says she is. She’s called in from time to time to assist. That doesn’t make her records open to us.”

“And the park—a set-up to get me to the Hamptons, where I’d open up and start talking, to my quote my chummy girlfriend?”

“No, that was all Culbertson. Good thing you knew how to defend yourself, or we wouldn’t be having this conversation right now.”

I look away again to clear my head, because I would really like to curse at the woman. “Glad to know you have my back,” I say, a little bitterly.

“I never let you out of my sight.”

"Oh sure. You kept tabs on me. You browsed through my journal and traced my every movement on the computer I used at the guesthouse. I wonder why you didn't become a stage actress. I liked the old Lorraine Baglietti better. Up until the moment you stole my journal and I discovered you were a common thief, that is. I still don't see why this charade was necessary. You could've just asked me to cooperate. I would have. You could've saved a lot of time and expense—and saved lives, including the innocent ranch workers who've been killed."

She exhales. "You were very good at hiding your activities. We needed proof. You couldn't remember anything except your first name. That threw a wrench in the plan. So we reset, thought we could learn more about Culbertson through you, then corner him. Two birds with one stone. We needed you to get the confession straight from the horse's mouth, if you'll excuse the pun." She stares at me hard, a cop's stare.

"So you bugged my mother's house, just waltzed in and invaded her privacy."

"Judges issue subpoenas that allow us to listen in."

"What took you so long to get to us?"

"We got here as soon as we could."

"Yeah, right. And a lot of innocent people are dead because you can't do your job."

"Where's the ruby? You might be able to cut down some prison time if you cooperate."

"I've done nothing wrong. I made a legitimate purchase."

"That ruby is stolen property. From none other than the Vatican."

My jaw drops. "I don't believe that kind of horseshit."

"In Italian history, which interests me for obvious reasons, the ruby appears in a painting of Camillo Borghese when he reigned as Pope Paul V from 1605 to 1621. It was stolen from the Vatican in the eighteenth century. I admit the rest of the story is probably garbage. But the folklore doesn't diminish the Vatican's claim to ownership."

"Even if it's true that the stone belongs to the Vatican, you can't prove I had knowledge of that. So, no crime. Hell, I was a victim. Next thing you'll be telling me is that the American government actually believes that the ruby has magic powers. So let's get down to business. Like I said, if you'd leveled with me, you would already have had him—once I regained my memory. I was going to go to the authorities before my fall."

"Hard to believe, given your criminal history."

"I may be a crook, but I'm not a terrorist."

"How do I know you would've cooperated?"

"Why do you think I went out that window? I was going to provide this information for free and wouldn't give Culbertson the jewel. So he used the window to persuade me. His goon, Nelson, had butterfingers, or so Culbertson claimed, and down I went. Now, you'll have to make a deal with me, and I'll tell you the information you need to know. About a terrorist attack."

"You're telling me that you were going to come forward with this information voluntarily?"

I smirk. "Must be hard for you to believe, given my criminal history? But it's true. And now things have changed."

She lets out a loud sigh. "We can bargain, but that doesn't mean you won't serve time for what you've done in the past. You push it, and a jury gets to decide. I don't have to tell you that the ordinary citizens don't like people who associate with terrorists." She stuffs a hand in her pocket. Metal clinks. Her not-so-subtle threat of handcuffing me isn't cutting it.

"Well, then, Lorraine, sure seems like I'd better get a lawyer. Because if I don't have a deal on the table, I'm done talking."

"Let's back up. The deal is five years in prison. You behave, and you'll get parole months before that. You'll forfeit all assets, including the Cassiopeia. Because we know you have it. We just don't know where you've stashed it."

"Doesn't belong to me, never has, but if it's truly stolen property, it belongs back in Vatican City. We're both virtuous Catholic girls. Well, I guess *you* are at least."

"We have a deal?"

"My mother, Annette L'Évêque, won't be arrested or harmed in any way. She's innocent. No exceptions."

"I'll make it happen. So, what do you know?"

"And Alfie walks. Otherwise no deal."

"Can't do that."

Our eyes meet. Let her sweat it out.

69

A day later, I've signed the agreement with Lorraine. She agreed to let Alfie walk and to leave my mother alone. I thought handing over my property and assets would hurt, but the truth is, it's painless. More than that, it's a relief. Living in hiding and watching my back all the time, now *that* sucked the life out of me. That way of living hurts. My home is in Canada with my mother; that's all I need. I tell Lorraine about the impending attack. The U.S., Christmas Day, Washington, D.C. And it's a good thing I do. The Feds were behind on that one.

I don't call John back. He's smart enough to figure out what happened. Besides, he did nothing wrong. The Feds can't get anything on him.

I take off my necklace and unfasten a catch on the pendant. I slide open a very small compartment, which holds a key to my safety deposit box back at the Beacon Hotel. No wonder I reached for my necklace when I woke from the coma. I keep my important possessions in that security deposit box. I look at the key.

"I want a night with my mother before I leave Canada," I say.

"No can do," Lorraine says. "She's waiting outside. You can say your goodbyes now."

"You're a real pal, Lorraine."

She shrugs.

I write down the address of the Beacon Hotel and the number for the security box.

Without a word, Lorraine leaves the room. In a minute, my mother comes in. We embrace for a long time.

"I'll be back," I say.

"I know."

"Just stay safe."

She nods. "Hank will help when he recovers from surgery. We'll hire new hands. It'll be tough for a while. But we'll get through it."

"You're the toughest woman I know. You'll manage fine, Mom. And then, before you know it, I'll be home to help out."

We say our goodbyes, and she leaves the room. I don't want her to see me escorted out in handcuffs.

I sit in silence, waiting for Lorraine to come get me. An hour passes. I'll have to get used to time passing without anything to do.

The door opens. It's DeLuca. He's decked out in a suit that fits him to a T. He cleans up well. Exceptionally well. He must've dressed like a beaten-down street detective to play a role in the deception of Blue.

Something tugs at me hard, and I'm not sure I understand it. Once again, I see DeLuca half-asleep in that miserable metal chair when I woke up from the coma. Had he really spoken to me, encouraged me to wake up? I don't ask. I want to believe he did that for me.

"Are you going to be all right?" he asks.

"Yeah. I'm tough. I take after my mother that way."

He sits down across from me and adjusts his tie. So, the habit is genuine.

"Your kid brother, Mackey, did he ever exist?" I ask. "Did he and your mother die in that fire?"

He nods slowly. "Yeah. I didn't lie to you. That was Baglietti. Wish the part about my family was a lie."

"I'm sorry I doubted you."

"I was as surprised as you when I found out who Lorraine was. Walked into a conference room at the precinct with the inspector, thinking I'm about to get chewed out, and who's sitting there but none other than Special Agent Lorraine Baglietti." He looks sad.

"You never ran my picture in the media, did you?" I ask.

He shakes his head.

"All part of Lorraine's ruse."

He shrugs. "Sometimes we just do what we're told."

"And the restaurant, did Lorraine cover that shooting up?"

He nods. "You'd be surprised what people will believe. Redress a story, people buy it. Eyewitness testimony is the least reliable. Thankfully, no one was hurt."

I half smile. "I liked you, Matteo. A lot. I guess another time, another life."

"I liked you, too. A lot. I've wondered if you were using me that night."

I chortle at this. "Given the circumstances, logic would say it's the other way around. Who's the con man and who's the mark?"

He exhales as he turns away. He scratches the side of his head and looks back at me. "It was real."

It's not the time to talk. There probably won't ever be a time for us to talk. His sad, longing eyes remind me of how he stayed by my side in the hospital. He's the good guy. I'm the bad guy.

There's a rap on the door, and Lorraine walks in. Time to go.

I rise and take a step, my first real step forward for as long as I can remember.

ACKNOWLEDGMENTS

My thanks and appreciation to Brian Lynch, Garret Ryan, Lori Jones, Matthew Sharpe, Jessica Verdi, Danielle Poiesz-Luby, Nancy Nollmann Waldron, Isabella Auffenorde, Andrew Auffenorde, Robert Rotstein, Katherine F. Smalley, and the late Dr. Larry Lee Smalley, Sr.

ABOUT THE AUTHOR

Daco S. Auffenorde is an award-winning author of thriller and suspense stories. She's discussed her books in multiple interviews, including Bob Kustra's National Public Radio show *Reader's Corner* and George R.R. Martin's *Jean Cocteau Cinema*. The daughter of a physicist, Daco is a southern girl from Huntsville, Alabama (known as Rocket City for its role in building the rocket that took astronauts into space), who pens fast-paced, edge-of-your seat tales that keep the reader guessing.

Daco holds a B.A. and M.A.S. from The University of Alabama in Huntsville and a J.D. from the Cumberland School of Law. She is a member of the International Thriller Writers, Mystery Writers of America, Alabama Writers' Forum, Authors Guild, and Alabama State Bar. When she's not writing or reading, she enjoys long hikes, painting with watercolors, and hacking away at golf balls.

Did you enjoy *The Forgotten Girl*? Please consider leaving a review on Amazon to help other readers discover the book.

www.authordaco.com

Made in the USA
Columbia, SC
25 August 2022

66062796R00205